Wait for Me

Wait for Me

Eleanor Green

Contact information: contact@authoreleanorgreen.com

Cover Art by: Kiley Murphy

www.authoreleanorgreen.com

Eleanor Green

For all those who found love in

unexpected place

Wait for Me

The chords of love must be strong as death. Which hold and keep a heart, not daisy-chains, that snap in the breeze, or break with their weight apart.

Phoebe Cary

Wait for Me

One

Briley

Standing tall, I filled my lungs with air before exiting the bathroom. I needed to gather my wits, or I was going to lose it. This was the last time he was doing this to me. When I came out, I stared into Blake's puffy, I've-had-too-much-to-drink, blue eyes.

He opened his mouth to speak, but I held up a hand, cutting him off. The wall behind him tried to distract me—framed memories of the two of us together, happy as we tried to build a life and home—but I clenched my fists and refocused.

"I'm going out. I'll be gone for an hour." My voice was shaky which only made me angrier. "When I return, I expect you and whatever you can pack in that amount of time to be gone." Turning on my heels, I stormed toward the front door.

"Don't you walk away from me." Blake grabbed my arm and stood in front of me, blocking my path. "Let's talk about this." He scrubbed his hands over his face, then let them fall to his sides. He was putting on a show, trying to show me his vulnerability.

I wanted to laugh. Instead I just shook my head at the man before me. My shoulders slumped with disappointment, disgust. It was hard to determine which was worse: his actions or the fact that I allowed him to do this to me . . . again.

Twenty-five was too young for bags under the eyes, but no matter how many times I replayed these last two years, I couldn't find the unpredictable fault line. Our relationship had been as close to the fairy tale I had ever dreamed possible, or so I thought. Sure, like every couple, we'd had moments, arguing over the silly stuff. I took a moment now to let a few of the memories skip through my brain.

"Do you have to paint your fingernails in here? That stuff smells." He scrunched his nose, the few freckles that dotted it, disappearing between the creases.

"I was here first and I'm all set up." I waved a hand over my display.

"Well, the game's on and this is the only room with cable." The whoosh of air escaping a can of beer let me know he wasn't moving.

"Fine," I muttered, instantly pissed off. I had every intention of raking the entire contents onto the floor, but I knew who'd be cleaning it up . . . moi. Blake didn't care if the mess stayed there until Christmas.

We got on each other's nerves on occasion, but always laughed and apologized before things got too heated. Now the question that loomed over me like a black cloud was . . . how could the man who couldn't keep his hands off me on Tuesday, cheat on me by Friday? I'd been so sure our relationship was solid.

I'd thought that's where Blake and I were.

Heartbroken over the last few months and on the verge of crumbling, I stood strong while he overcame his demons. I had everything lined up. Our wedding was scheduled for June, then I had planned to conceive the following March.

Thankfully I found out about Blake's infidelities *before* we were married, and thank God I was faithful about taking my pill. I wasn't keen on sharing the father of my children with half the women over at Charlie's Pool & Bar.

"Bee—" Blake looked miserable. I couldn't tell if it was heartache or desperation darkening his usually clear blue eyes.

"Don't!" I pointed a warning finger close to his face. "Don't ever call me that." My mom was the only one who would ever call me "Bee" now. She'd started it in middle school when I became obsessed with honey bees.

Hers were the arms I needed to crumble into. Part of me hoped she didn't kill him when she learned how he had hurt me, but another part of me hoped she didn't look at me with pity. And finally, the strongest part of me prayed she didn't say those four dreaded words that I deserved—"I told you so." Of course my mom wouldn't say it, but if my bleary eyes ever cleared, I'd see it in her expression.

Blake took me by the shoulders, leaning down to make eye contact. "Please don't do this."

"YOU did this, Blake!" I wiggled out of his grip and turned for the kitchen. Pulling a glass from the cabinet, I filled it with ice and poured in a healthy amount of Glenfiddich that Blake bought on a recent business trip. It was expensive, something we only pulled out on special occasions, but I didn't care. The liquid was smooth as it traveled down my throat and warmed every inch of my body. I winced from the bitter aftertaste and strong resemblance to liquid fire before gulping the rest down.

"Yes, I did this." His shoulders slumped with what I could only imagine was deep regret. "Give me a chance to make things right again."

"You're out of chances, Blake. No more nice girl." Unlike the past, I was serious this time.

He held out a hand, but instantly withdrew it when he saw me wince. "You *are* a nice girl. Kind, giving . . . the peacemaker. So damn sweet, it's one of the reasons I fell in love with you."

"Bullshit!" I spun around, my long dark hair swishing against my back. "You've never fallen in love with anyone but yourself. I was a sucker and you're a thief!" My blood boiled in my veins, my stomach churning. I swallowed hard before continuing. "You took what you wanted and trampled it." I squared my shoulders, trying hard to look tougher than I felt. "But don't you worry about me. I've studied you and all the ways a snake can disguise himself. I'll benefit from this."

Somehow, one day.

"I'm begging you . . . I love you." Pain flickered in his eyes. "Together—"

I shook my head. This was over and I was done listening. "Save your blubbering for someone who actually gives a crap, honey. I've heard Andi prefers leftovers—she can comfort you now." My words spewed like venom, the poison visibly affecting his mood.

His eyebrows narrowed, finally revealing his true nature. He had lost and knew it. Like a little boy that didn't get the toy he saw on the store shelf, I wondered if he'd throw himself on the floor, or worse. He'd never hit me before, but I'd never seen his eyes darken this much. His pupils were so large, the only visible blue was a fine navy circle around deep pools of wrath. With clenched fists, he leaned toward me. I flinched, my body tense and ready to take a blow. It didn't come, but the threat had done its job in shaking me.

Scotch on an empty stomach was never a good idea and the buzz hit me hard. Trying to keep my shoulders back in confidence as I walked away was more challenging than I had anticipated. I gripped the counter, regaining my balance and strutted out of the house like a drunken goose.

Blake was right behind me, but I kept moving forward, refusing to acknowledge his presence.

"You can't drive, Bee—Briley." He clutched my arm, digging into the flesh until I grimaced. "You've been drinking."

"I know that," I hissed. Jerking my arm loose, I turned and glared at him through narrowed, furious eyes. "Drinking makes you do stupid things. Like throwing your life away for a ten-minute roll in the sheets."

With impeccable timing, my mother pulled into the driveway. I'd texted her three pound signs—my get out of jail free code from high school—and prayed she'd remember what it meant.

Blake huffed and ran an angry hand through his thick, blond hair. "You called Nina?"

Without answering, or looking at him, I stepped into the car and managed not to slam the door. Cool as a cucumber, I buckled my seatbelt and pretended to fish through my purse for a piece of gum. I could sense my mom's anger penetrating Blake through the window even though I hadn't told her anything. She could always read me like a book and knew everything that was going on in my life without either of us speaking a word. I waited until she was out of the driveway and around the corner before I released the sob that played at my throat.

Sucking in high-pitched breaths between words, I tried to explain. I was sure none of it was intelligible, but knowing my mom, she got it.

"I need . . . to see . . . Cooper." My words came out choppy and sounded like I had a nose full of cotton.

"You know it's not possible, honey." My mother white-knuckled the steering wheel, revealing the depth of her anger. It must've been difficult to watch your child go through something so traumatic and feel completely helpless.

"It *is* possible," I argued. "He doesn't want me there, but I *need* him. Surely he can understand that."

Two

Cooper

I'd never get used to this place. Surrounded by dingy gray cinderblock walls, it was hard to understand how some of the guys had served more than one sentence. Lying on this plastic mattress—a generous word; it felt more like my kindergarten nap mat—I was boxed in like an animal.

I would've gone insane if it hadn't been for Briley's care packages and letters. This last one didn't feel right though. Something was going on with her. I could sense it in her words. She hadn't mentioned her writing, her work, or *him*. I admit, it was a nice change to not hear how in love she was with him. I wished she could see what an ass he was, but someone else would have to convince her this time. It wasn't worth losing her friendship again. I never wanted to see that look in her eyes, the look she gave me the last time I tried to point out one of his many flaws. Maybe I could live with the hate, but not the hurt. That look still haunted me.

I only had a few more minutes before the guard called lights out, so I read the letter again.

> *Cooper,*
> *Hang in there. Only a few more months until you're home.*
> *I wish I could come see you. Please change your mind and tell me I can visit.*
> *Just once. I don't understand why you don't want me there.*

*I'm stronger than you think. Nothing I see or hear
will affect me.*
I need to see you.
I miss you.
Be strong. I believe in you.
Love,
Briley

First of all, she never called me Cooper. *Why so formal, B?
Is he looking over your shoulder?* And she knew why she
couldn't come here. I'd managed good behavior my entire
sentence. I couldn't risk a fight now, which is exactly what
would happen if she came here. All the whistles and crude
comments from the guys—how would I be able to ignore that?
If she were my sister, then maybe they'd have some respect. But
what kind of pussy had a girl like Briley for a best friend?

 She was gorgeous: fantastic legs, tight body, and long dark
hair. She's every man's dream. And those big, innocent doe
eyes—I'd have to fight every guy in this place for countless
reasons.

Damn, did I know how to pick a best friend. Why couldn't
she have been a dude? Instead, my parents had to be best friends
with the Sheffields. Parents of a tomboy who liked all the things
I did. Until she hit puberty. Something snapped inside of me the
day I'd noticed her. I mean *really* noticed her. She'd worn a
fitted pink T-shirt, ribbons tied around the shoulders to cinch in
the material like a tank top. I couldn't keep my eyes off her
boobs and she knew it. Got really mad about it actually and
wouldn't speak to me for days.

We remained friends—good friends—fooling around a few
times in high school and college. The farthest I got with her was

third base at a party. It took all the control I had ever collected in my life to not go all the way. She was all over me, begging me to be her first. Said I was the only one she trusted with her first experience. Of course I couldn't go through with it, drunk off her ass from some purple concoction. I wanted her first time to be special, memorable.

Later I'd regret that decision. Turned out, she was wasted when she lost it anyway, to some fraternity boy in the woods. She cried for days, refusing to tell me why, but I finally got it out of her.

I made sure when I found him, in front of all his frat brothers, he wouldn't want to take advantage of another girl again. Only a handful of the guys tried to stop me from beating the shit out of the dude. I came away with a bloody lip; he was far worse off. It was my job to protect her. There was just something inside me that wanted to, needed to.

My jaw tightened and I shook my head at the ceiling.

Yeah, no way in hell she was coming here. Just a few more months . . . surely I could keep her away until my release date.

"Lights out!" one of the guards shouted, dragging his baton against the bars. "Get your beauty sleep, ladies."

Stuffing the letter beneath my pillow, I shut my eyes, trying to get the rest I needed. After flipping my pillow over and changing positions, I knew it was useless. I wouldn't sleep tonight.

What was going on with Briley? I'd make a call tomorrow.

I needed answers.

Three

Briley

I had to find a way to see Cooper. I needed someone to talk to besides my mother. Honestly, the real truth was I missed him. Terribly.

Writing my article on sea salt normally would've excited me. The different types of salt: pink, gray, white, and brown. Where they came from and why their distinct flavors were important for different dishes. I'd finally landed my dream job with *World Cuisine* magazine, but couldn't focus.

Fleur de sel, or "Flower of Salt" in French, is a finishing salt for subtle foods, adding a mild, delicate crunch. Sel Gris, also known as gray salt, is preferred for heartier dishes such as steak, chops, hearty vegetable dishes, and roasts. If you prefer—

"Dammit!" I hissed into the empty home office. My head wasn't in it. Instead it was on Cooper.

After pouring my second cup of coffee, I curled up on the couch and let my mind do what it craved . . . think about my best friend. Trying to rid my brain of every bad thing that could happen to a man in prison, I focused on Coop's smile—the one that made the dimple in his left cheek sink so deep you could hide candy in it.

A late morning thunderstorm darkened the room, rumbles of thunder shaking the house and sending chills down my spine. Wrapped in a blanket, I snuggled into the cushions and enjoyed another memory. Prom.

Cooper had taken me to his senior prom when his date broke her leg in a bicycling accident. It was treated like a wedding as the Sterlings filled two SD cards from their camera. Everyone knew we were only friends, but Cooper's dad beamed as he positioned my corsage-laden hand on his son's lapel. *"Scoot in closer,"* he'd said, readying the camera.

Cooper and I were as close as two people could get by friendship standards. I trusted him and looked up to him like an older brother. He fought anyone that picked on me. He lost some, won most.

The last fight landed him in prison. Just when I needed him most, he was completely out of reach. I wasn't sure why he wouldn't let me visit, but he was adamant. Made me promise through my uncontrolled sobs as they took him away.

***

Fourteen months earlier…

It was Matt Lasko's fault, but sometimes—more than some—in the middle of the night when sleep evaded me, I'd recall that night and decide it was *my* fault.

We were playing darts at Charlie's, a local bar and hangout. The place was packed, even for a Saturday night. Beer, cigarette smoke, and testosterone filled the space, riling the rooster-chested guys and causing the ladies to heave their cleavage so high it made their backs arch and walk with an extra sway in their hips. I can't boast that I was too mature for those antics, I swayed and flaunted with the best of them, hoping to make Blake jealous.

Blake and I were engaged but it didn't keep the girls from flirting and everyone knew my fiancé was a sucker for the attention. It started out harmless enough but hurt my feelings all the same.

In a fun-turned-competitive game of darts, it was my turn to throw. I might've brushed up against Matt as I passed. I most likely took a provocative stance as I lined up my throw. I missed my mark on the board, but got the attention I sought, so the game began. Throughout the night, the more Blake flirted with the ladies, the more pissed I became and I ended up throwing myself at Matt Lasko.

Choosing the guy with the worst reputation was a huge mistake. Matt had been our high school football captain. He was cute, in that jock sort-of-way, light brown hair and a stocky build. He was our high school homecoming king and all around Mr. Popularity. Until graduation. Something happened after that. Lack of admiration maybe, when we all moved on to become adults? Whatever the cause, Matt Lasko became a drunken man-whore. I shouldn't have played with him that particular night—or any night for that matter—but I was insane with jealousy and anger. I needed to get Blake's attention, and Matt was the smoothly paved road to take me there.

The next dart game was Cricket. Cooper explained the rules.

"You have to hit each of your numbers, fifteen through twenty, and the bull's-eye." He shoved his hands in his pockets before continuing, a grin playing at his lips. "But if you hit anything below fifteen, you have to drink."

"What's the poison, Coop?" I asked, rolling a set of steel-tipped darts in my hand.

He eyed me cautiously. Always the overprotective brother type. "Let's stick with beer, B. It's a long game."

I was up first, concentrating on hitting my mark while making sure Matt's eyes had a reason to linger on my denim-clad ass. The triple twenty was easy, so I knocked that out first. Next I tried for nineteen and scored. On my third throw, I missed and hit the seven.

"Damn it!"

Cooper filled a shot glass with beer, but I swigged my Rolling Rock longneck before he could hand it to me.

"Slow down, B," he cautioned.

"I don't miss often enough for your concern, Coop." The words came out too harsh, but I wasn't taking them back. I winked, hoping to soften the situation. Still, I wasn't in the mood to be babied. With my fiancé across the room, soaking up unwarranted attention and Cooper treating me like his little sister, it was either going to be a long night or I was going to need to miss a few more darts.

Cooper, Matt, and a girl we'd just met in the bar, Delia, took turns while I nursed my beer. Cooper didn't miss. Matt and Delia were mediocre throwers at best. Set up for my turn, I aimed and let a dart fly.

"Yes! Triple seventeen." The booty shake that happened after that couldn't have been helped. I was on a roll.

As I lined up for the next shot, Blake was at my side. "Wanna play?" I asked.

"Nah. I'm gonna go on home. My head is killing me." He rubbed at his temples.

"I'm sorry." My lips puckered into a phony pout. *Go home and sober up!* "Want me to drive you?" I looked around for the blonde he'd been flirting with earlier. She was nowhere in sight. Boredom seemed most likely the cause of his retreat. I hated that he felt the need to lie about a headache.

"No, no. I'm okay to drive. I'll call you later, babe." He gave me a chaste kiss on the cheek and then looked at Cooper. "You'll make sure she gets home?"

Cooper nodded once, all emotion absent from his expression. But I could read his eyes. Cooper loathed Blake and didn't approve of our relationship at all. It almost wrecked our friendship and I finally had to do the bitchiest thing—make him choose.

"Our friendship or your hatred for Blake?" Cooper didn't say a word, so I guess he didn't really choose, but the comments and threats ceased; his way of a compromise, I suppose.

With Blake gone, along with the threat of rejection, I was over the game I'd cruelly started with Matt. I tried to blow him off by not glancing in his direction and returning to my normally quirky self who lacked any kind of seductive skill.

During our second round of Cricket, Matt went to the bar and came back with a round of shots. The guys got tequila. Delia and I got some girly shit that tasted like blueberry Kool-Aid, but I shot it down and slammed the shot glass upside down onto the table.

"My turn." I grinned and walked to the line, readying my shot.

I shouldn't have smiled, I shouldn't have accepted the drink, and I never should've gone to the bathroom.

"Excuse me," I gave my best British accent, bowing before I turned to leave. "The loo calls to me." One beer and a girly shot and suddenly I had a British accent?

I made it just inside the bathroom door when everything became foggy and dreamlike. My legs felt unsteady and my insides fluttery. I had to lean against the wall for a minute before I could walk to the stall. One Rolling Rock and a shot was usually enough for a buzz but nothing more. I just needed a moment to find my balance. When I opened my eyes, someone's lips collided with mine.

I'd never kissed a girl. Sure, I'd thought about it in college, but who hadn't, right? But I wasn't into girls; it was more of a curiosity. Were girl's lips softer, making them deliciously sexy, or too soft, making the kiss gross? What did sticky, glossed lips taste like? Was a girl's tongue so different from a guy's that I could tell the difference if my eyes were closed? None of those questions needed answering so desperately that I dared do it. I also wanted to know what it felt like to skydive, but I wouldn't try it for any amount of money.

But there I was, pinned against the bathroom wall, between the hand dryers. She was taller than me, with short hair and dark eyes. Time passed in chunks rather than a normally level timeline. I knew I was in the bathroom, but hadn't used it yet. I wasn't sure how I'd gotten pinned against the wall or what kind of invitation was given to the one pinning me.

Instead of fighting for the strength to ask questions, I closed my eyes and tried to savor the experience. Her lips weren't as soft as I thought they'd be and they didn't taste like strawberries. I can't say I enjoyed the kiss, but I did enjoy taking part in something so taboo. When I wanted to open my eyes and look at the person I was sharing my first taste of forbidden fruit with, they wouldn't budge. In fact, I was having trouble holding myself up.

She backed away as I started to slump, my body slithering down the wall. It seemed like I'd never find the floor, the place that offered rest for my too-weary body. I needed to sleep. Before I found the ground, my body was lifted, being supported against the wall with a knee between my thighs. My muscles were useless in helping the cause, so I relaxed, letting the stranger hold me up while her lips found mine again.

Her mouth was urgent and rough, all traces of femininity and softness gone. When her hand traveled over my breast and squeezed too hard, my eyes fluttered open. Blurry and unfocused, I stared at the person in front of me.

Matt.

My head was spinning. Hell, everything was spinning.

"What the—" Before I could finish, he claimed my mouth again. The taste of beer, liquor, and vulgarity robbed me of breath. Using both hands, I tried to create a barrier between us, pushing him back with arms that felt like noodles. He was too strong and kept me pinned. With my hands trapped, I had no leverage.

I tried to speak through his mouth that was crushing mine, my slurred words vibrating off of the tongue that violated my mouth. "Stoppp!" I managed to get out.

"I want you, Briley. I'm gonna have you." One of his hands traveled up my shirt, gripping and squeezing my breast so tight it was painful. "The way you were looking at me, and then to blow me off like that . . ." He continued to grope, trying to cover each surface of my body in haste.

The last thing I remember was sliding down the wall until I met the cold, tiled bathroom floor.

Four

Cooper

I should've killed that bastard. And I might have if I hadn't noticed Briley choking on her own vomit. No matter how hard I tried, I couldn't get the image of her out of my head. Slumped against the wall, her mascara smeared down both sides of her face like Alice Cooper. Nothing but an unclasped bra covering one of her breasts and her body trying to rid itself of the poison Matt put in her drink. Thank God my mom was addicted to those medical shows so I knew to turn her on her side.

A crowd was gathering around us, watching like it was a true life episode of *NCIS*. Someone, a female, offered to help but I waved her off.

"I've got it. Just get out. Everyone get out!"

Once Briley began dry heaving, I scooped her up and took her to my truck. She was semi-conscious and able to sit up while I buckled her in.

"Hang on, B, I'm taking you to the hospital."

"No!" she urged, snapping her head around to face me in the driver's seat. "I'm fine. My mom will freak . . . don't you dare wake . . ."

Her voice trailed off as she passed out again. I sped down the road, not sure where I was taking her if it wasn't the hospital. It crossed my mind to take her home but there were two scenarios to that situation and neither of them was good. If Blake was home, I wasn't sure he could be trusted to watch her all night. Narcissistic bastard probably couldn't be bothered and would let her sleep it off. If he wasn't home—which I assumed was true by the way he was flirting and leaving within minutes of his plaything—she'd be alone.

After making a U-turn, I drove toward my house. My roommate was probably staying at his girlfriend's house for the night. We pulled into the driveway, Briley drifting in and out of consciousness the entire drive. I scooped her out of the passenger seat, carrying her toward the house when her body started convulsing again.

"Ungh," she moaned, trying to wiggle out of my arms. Having held her hair many times in the past while she puked, I knew the sound too well.

Moving toward the lawn, I set her down, holding her hair back as she wretched again. The entire night played out the same way. She'd sleep for about an hour between spells of sickness. Worried about hydration, I'd give her sips of water, but she'd heave it up almost immediately. We slept on the bathroom floor, wrapped in a large blanket. Or rather, I held her while she dozed. I stroked her hair while she slept, rubbed her back and arms. When I knew she was out for the count, all the poison emptied from her fragile body, I plotted my next encounter with Matt. I'd kill him for what he'd done to her.

Five

Briley

Waking up in Cooper's arms didn't feel right. Something was wrong, different. I tried to lift my head and look around but it refused to move and felt like it was filled with concrete. My only view was the waistband of his unbuttoned jeans, revealing gray boxer briefs with a black band sporting the Ralph Lauren logo. My head was cradled in his lap, one of his hands supporting my head, the other resting on my back. Why was I here, in this position? Had we spent the night together? The first thought that crossed my mind was the obvious reason one would be in this position.

A feeling of disgust washed over me. I wasn't a cheater. Yet here I was, on the floor of Cooper's bathroom, head in his lap like a cheap slut. I couldn't imagine a woman who wouldn't love to be in my place. Cooper had the body of a god and enough charm to make your clothes peel themselves off, but we were only friends. Good friends. Never meant to be lovers. And I was in a monogamous relationship. All I could think about was Blake and his rage. I had to move. Had to make this right.

Again, I tried to lift my head, using my hands to push up. It ached with such intensity I would've sworn I'd been hit by a Mack truck. I groaned, lifting myself to a sitting position. Cooper opened his eyes and looked down at me. His brows furrowed with what appeared to be worry—or was it regret? Of course, it must've been a look of regret. We'd finally been intimate after all of these years and I was too wasted to remember it. It wasn't like Cooper to take advantage of a situation. He had an opportunity in college but refused me when I was intoxicated. What changed? Why this time? My guess was that he'd been too drunk to remember. Rubbing my temples, I thought about the night's events. The last thing I remembered was playing darts. We had a drinking game going, but I didn't remember finishing even one beer.

"You," He cleared his throat. "You all right?" He rubbed his fingers across his forehead, kneading the skin. His pained gaze made me wonder if we could save our friendship after this.

"How much did we drink?" I wrapped my arms around my stomach, feeling sick. "I'm sorry Coop . . . this . . . I can't even. What we . . ." I couldn't get the words out. The thought of it was too much. The thing that sucked the most though, wasn't just the fact that we'd slept together—even if we were buddies, I appreciated his beauty—but that I wasn't lucid enough to experience it or remember even one detail.

"No, no, B." He shook his head as he spoke. "Nothing happened between us." His lips curled apologetically. "Nothing happened to you at all." He shifted his weight and focused on a loose thread in the hem of his jeans. "You were drugged but I got to you before anything happened." He glanced up, watching my face as I processed the information.

"Oh, God," I whispered. "How? We were playing darts." I racked my brain trying to remember the night. "I can't remember anything." Tears welled in my eyes as anger and fear washed over me. I couldn't think of anyone with that much hate in their heart to want to hurt me, or take advantage of me. "Who?" I managed to choke out on a whisper.

"Matt Lasko."

"Matt?" I asked, incredulous. "No way. He couldn't have, right?" I looked at Cooper. His face morphed from kind and worrisome, to rage. "Tell me, Cooper. What did he do?" I cupped my hand over my mouth, certain I'd vomit again if he told me what I'd feared.

He pulled me into his lap, stroking my hair. "I told you, I got to you in time."

"What did you do to him, Coop?" I knew it was going to be bad. He was a big guy—Matt wasn't tiny by any means—but Cooper was strong and he'd rarely lost a fight.

He hung his head and kissed the top of mine. "I only had time to worry about you."

I looked around the bathroom then, taking in the scene. A blanket was the only source of comfort in the small space. Cooper leaned against the bathroom wall, his legs crossed, forming a lap for me to sit on. He looked miserable. His eyes, heavy with lack of sleep, haunted me.

"We need to get some food into you; all you've had is a little water." He started to lift me off his lap to stand.

"Please," I gripped him around the waist, snuggling into his chest. "My stomach feels like death and my head is trying to kill whatever life is left in me."

"You've got to get something in your stomach. You were sick all night. You could be dehydrated."

"Sick as in sick-sick?" I asked in horror. Had he seen me puke all night? He nodded and I imagined how it played out. Him holding my hair while I wretched God only knew what into his toilet. Snuggling into his chest, I thanked him for taking care of me all night. Cooper was always there for me, but this was a big deal. He was the most sacrificial man I knew. He wrapped his arms around me—arms powerful enough to crush me with his hands alone, but he was kind and gentle.

Even after holding me all night while I vomited, he smelled divine. His scent was fresh and clean, but all male with a crisp punch that made me want to inhale him until my lungs were at capacity. It reminded me of fall and I could've stayed in his arms forever. For those few moments, I let my mind wander to something more than friendship. We understood each other, had been through everything together. We just fit. There was no doubt I was sexually attracted to him but relationships were more than sex, and in my experience sex wasn't all that. A relationship needed work, fight, and a future goal. Cooper and I were amazing together, always having fun. I'd never screw that up with a relationship.

Panic washed over me as I thought of my current, actual relationship. "Does Blake know where I am?"

"I texted him. He doesn't know what happened. I told him you drank too much and passed out. He thinks you're asleep on my couch."

"Oh, good." I exhaled the breath I'd been holding, relieved but surprised Blake went for that. He hated Cooper.

"Now, let's get you some food."

"Ugh," I groaned. "No food."

Cooper handed me a cup of coffee and I sipped on it as he made French toast and bacon. The smell of bacon had the opposite effect than I thought it would, making my stomach growl and my mouth salivate.

"It smells so good. I hope I can keep it down."

"I'm sure you can. You were able to keep some water down last night—or earlier this morning rather." He looked at the clock on the microwave. "You haven't been sick in three and a half hours."

We sat at the bar to eat and the food was delicious. I couldn't have slowed down if I'd tried, and I scarfed down half of what was on my plate. He had two tools in his culinary repertoire, grilling and making the best damn French toast in the country.

By noon I was home, readying the key in the door. Blake swung it open, anger in his eyes. He faked a smile for Cooper and pulled me in for a hug until Cooper was out of the driveway and around the corner. As soon as the show was over, the fun began. I could've told Blake the truth about that night, but he was pissy all day and I tried to stay away from him. An argument with him while he was in one of his moods was the equivalent to arguing with a stop sign. No, Blake would never know the truth about that night, which was too bad because I'd never know what he would've done. I found myself questioning whether or not he would've been as sweet as Cooper. It wasn't the first time I'd compared the two and I felt sure it wouldn't be the last.

Six

Cooper

It was time for him to pay.

After dropping Briley off, I drove across town. In the twenty minutes it took to get to Matt Lasko's house, I thought about what that asshole could've done to her, what he'd planned to do to her. Visions of her, barely able to hold herself up while his hands gripped and fondled her, trying to get inside her. My fist slammed against the steering wheel as I tried but failed to get the images out of my head.

How could anyone do that to Briley? Dammit, I was supposed to take care of her! One minute she was fine, the next she was drugged and nearly raped. In a matter of minutes her life could've been turned upside down.

I didn't even slow down as I pulled my truck into his front yard and slammed on the brakes, tearing up his lawn. Leaving the truck running, I swung open the door and stalked toward his porch. My fist pounded his front door continuously until he opened it, clearly stunned to find me standing there.

He might have tried to say something, but I gripped him by the shirt and tossed him onto the front lawn with ease. He stumbled to his feet and put his hands up, trying without success to protect his face from my blows. The first punch knocked him to the ground. It was a good place for him to be as I planned on punching him straight into a self-made grave.

Immediately I saw a red haze; bones crunched beneath my fist. I couldn't have stopped hitting him if I wanted to, especially with the images of him on Briley flashing through my mind, egging me on to kill him. He didn't deserve to live.

Strong arms on each side of me wrestled me to a standing position. I shrugged them off long enough to get a few kicks in before a painful electric current jolted through me, seizing every muscle in my body until I dropped to the ground. It took a good five minutes before my muscles finally relaxed. My anger didn't follow. Looking at Matt's mangled body, I still wanted to finish the job. I was cuffed and being escorted toward the police cruiser when I tensed, eager to get back to the task at hand. Both cops reached for their Tasers, promising to load me up again if I tried anything.

***

Matt was alive but I'm sure he wished he was dead. His face was shattered, jaw had to be wired. Four broken ribs, a broken femur in his left leg, and a lacerated liver from one of the ribs earned him an extensive stay at Brandon Regional Hospital.

So Matt was in the hospital and I was in jail . . . again. I'd been locked up before from fighting. Messed the guy up pretty bad in a bar, but he was a punk and had started it. A felony battery charge landed me in jail for that fight.

My lawyer, Richard Ellington, had a stellar reputation. He cost a pretty penny but was supposed to be worth every dime. He seemed to know what he was talking about and although I disagreed with his plan, I figured he knew more about the process than I did.

"Here's what's going to happen," he began. "You'll be released on your own recognizance. That means there's no bail but you have to stay in town and show up for your arraignment." He was patient as he explained the details, but hardly made eye contact as he thumbed through a file on the table between us.

"Is the date for my arraignment set?"

"No, but it'll be within the next seventy-two hours. That works for you?" he asked. I knew it wasn't a question. I was at the mercy of the court and would do what I was told or suffer the consequences. I knew in my gut that things could go badly. "After the arraignment the DA and I will work on a deal. He'll want to go for attempted murder—"

"Attempted murder? What about defense of necessity or heat of passion?"

"We can't use either of those because you had a cooling off period. Now it's premeditated. The best I can do for you is work a deal with the DA. Because this is your second battery charge in less than three years, you face a third degree felony battery charge." He closed his folder and glanced up at me from across the table. "This is the best we can do, Cooper. The judge can give you up to five years in prison—and he's a hard ass, believe me, he'll do it. With a plea bargain I can get you out in less than two. You'll plead no contest."

***

Briley was right by my side for the arraignment, trying to do my attorney's job for him. We went over the details again as I straightened my tie.

"The judge will ask, 'How do you plead?' And you'll answer . . ."

"No contest, Your Honor."

Briley's gasp was audible, echoing off the deep hallway walls. "Why would you ask him to do that? It was self-defense on my part. He saved me from who-the-hell knows what."

Richard was patient with her as he answered, "Even if we had evidence that you were drugged, it wouldn't be admissible in court. The fight didn't take place on scene, it was hours later. Trust me, I'm doing what's best for Mr. Sterling."

She was in hysterics and knowing her, she was ready to find the judge and work things out on her own. I cupped her face in my palms. "B, he knows what he's doing. I trust him."

Being in that room, feeling like a bug under a microscope, was too much. It felt like time slowed but everyone's speech sped up. My stomach turned as the judge studied papers on his desk. By the looks of the man holding my fate in his hands, I was screwed. He probably had several reasons for the permanent scowl on his face, masked only by a pair of reading glasses sliding down his nose. His comb over was almost too thin to count for anything and his robe threatened to choke the life out of him if he gained another ounce.

My lawyer spoke first. "Your Honor, the DA and I have reached a plea deal."

The judge pulled on the material around his neck before glancing up at me briefly. "How do you plead?"

"No contest, Your Honor." I heard Briley groan behind me, or more like a growl.

Trying to look strong for Briley and my parents, I squared my shoulders and gripped the edge of the table in front of me. When the judge finally spoke, not having the decency to look up when he gave the crushing blow that I knew was coming but apparently wasn't ready for, my shoulders slumped.

"Third degree battery felony, punishable by up to but no more than five years in the state prison system."

The judge ruffled through more papers, pulled on his collar again, and glanced up through his readers. He slammed his gavel down onto the wooden plank and stood. I heard shuffling of feet behind me as everyone stood in obedience while the judge made his grand exit.

My father hugged me and I noticed his chin quiver. My mother was a mess, of course, crying and carrying on. But Briley's reaction was the one that nearly broke me. Her hands covered her face as she sobbed, apologizing and blaming herself for my punishment.

"Now you're going to be gone . . ." She swiped the length of her forearm under her nose, sniffling. "For what should've been the best five years of our lives."

"No, B. I won't be gone that long." I looked to my lawyer and pleaded, "Richard, explain it to her again."

"Our plea bargain agreement states that he'll only serve seventeen months."

My gaze back on Briley, I tried to speak calmly, convincing her everything would be okay. "See, everything's going to be fine."

"I'm sorry, Coop. So sorry."

"Nothing to be sorry about, B. I don't regret anything."

***

Present day...

The first year in prison was hell. Most of the guys respected my size and strength, but there was a group of four or five that wanted to test it. The plea bargain hadn't gone as well as my attorney had planned, so I was serving seventeen months in this hole. Don't misunderstand; I knew that it could've been a lot worse. I often thought about what I would've missed during a five year sentence. Still, it was hard to count myself lucky when

I was surrounded by guys who either wanted to kill me or fuck me.

Briley and Blake set a wedding date on month eleven of my incarceration and I almost lost it. She wanted a fall wedding so she could use orange flowers in her bouquet. If anyone had tempted me the least bit on the day I got her *"oh-so-exciting news,"* I'm sure I would've increased my sentence by at least another year. Instead, I upped my anger management sessions to three times a week and focused on getting out. I had to get to Briley before she made the biggest mistake of her life.

Lying on my cot, staring at the ceiling nearly drove me insane. I felt like I was rotting away while she planned her wedding. To Blake. Fucking faggot. My fist slammed hard against the concrete wall. At least I was smart enough to use the side of my hand, careful not to break any bones like last time. What she saw in Blake, I'd never understand. I knew she had a thing for villains in movies, but in real life, too? Briley-the-masochist, that didn't even sound right. I knew her better than she knew herself. She was trying to prove something by marrying Blake. *What* she was trying to prove . . . that stumped me.

Blake was a punk and everyone knew it. He was going to break her heart and I couldn't do a damn thing about it while I was behind bars. I pulled the letter back out and held it. It was too dark to see the words, but having it close seemed to make my thoughts clearer. Her letters had always been cheerful, even if she was putting on a front for me, encouraging me to hang in there and avoid trouble so I might get out early. But this letter was much different. I could've read through her words, feeling the desperation as she tried to hide it, but she hadn't tried at all. She made it clear that she needed to see me.

Blake had already broken her heart. That had to be it. And I was here instead of there, where she needed me. She had her mom. *Please, Briley. Go to your mom. Don't wait for me.*

Each minute passed, bringing the morning hour closer. I was going to be exhausted, but it was useless trying to sleep. Phone calls weren't permitted until after chores, so I'd get my ass in gear and see if I could get two calls in. One to my dad—feel him out and see if he had any news—and then Briley. I needed to know she was okay, that she had it in her to be strong.

***

As hard as it was to wait for the phone, I made sure I was last in line so my conversation was private. Last thing I needed was the guys' bullshit and sex noises behind me. I only had time for one call, so I gave the operator Briley's number.

I heard every word between her and Briley, although it sounded distant, as if I were eavesdropping on an accidentally connected line.

"Collect call from Polk County Correctional Institute, will you accept the call?"

"Yes, of course." The operator connected us and unplugged from her end, making the connection clear. "Cooper?"

All of the breath left my chest at once. I inhaled slowly, taking in the sound of her sweet voice. My delay provoked her impatience.

"Coop? Are you there? Hello? Can you hear me?"

I found my voice and cut her off. "I'm here." Clearing my throat, I continued, "How are you?"

"Good. How are you? I mean, I know you can't be—"

"I'm fine, B. I got your letter yesterday and it didn't sound like you. What's going on?"

"Nothing. Just an off day I guess." She sighed. "I'm fine, Coop. Really." Her voice cracked. "I'm so glad to hear your voice. Did you get my last care package? Did they let you have the cookies? Are you still getting out early for good behavior?"

"Yes to all and thanks, B." I couldn't tell her they tossed her treats every time. Cruel fuckers. "The cookies were the best thing I've had since . . . listen, I only have a few minutes, so let's stop bullshitting and get to the honesty." God, I missed her voice. She sounded so close. "I've known you all my life and I know something's wrong. What is it, B?"

"It's . . ." I heard a muffled sob. She was covering her mouth or the phone to hide from me.

"Don't hide from me, B. Cry if you need to. Get that shit out." My fist clenched beside me as I felt the anger rising. There was no doubt in my mind that Blake was behind her tears. Always was. *Fucking bastard. He has no idea what he has and he's fucking it up.* I'd always hoped she would see what a loser he was but I hadn't thought about the pain it might cause her. "What did he do?" I gritted out through clenched teeth.

"He—he—didn't do anything. Everything's fine, Coop. I just miss you. Please let me come see you."

I knew she was lying, I could hear it in her voice. Was she trying to protect him? "Why won't you tell me what's really going on? Are you afraid? Has he done something to you, B?" The anger in my voice easily matched the rising pulse thumping in my ears.

If he hurt her . . .

"No, no. Nothing like that." Her voice was too high, cartoonish. *Now* I was worried. "I'm just emotional. You know, hormones . . . that time of the month. TMI, but I miss you. You've been away too long. You can't blame a girl for wanting to talk to her best friend, can you? I mean, I'm a girl after all. We have fourteen thousand words to expel each day and that's hard to do . . ."

She was rambling like a crazed woman, unknowingly confirming that something was wrong. The guard's eyes bore into me as he tapped his watch with an index finger. "B, I gotta go."

"No, Cooper. I need you. Let me come see you this weekend. Please."

"Don't do this to me, B." I rested my head against my forearm and pressed against the wall, eyes shut. "You know you can't come here. Unless you want me to stay in here another year . . . do not come here."

She sighed heavily on the other end. "Okay. But you better get out of there soon and be ready to listen, because the fourteen thousand words a day are adding up. And . . . I need you, Coop."

I laughed. "Thatta girl. Wait for me, B. Just a few more months and I'm all fucking ears."

Another giggle. *Thank you for that one, B.*

"Bye Cooper. Hang in there. One-four-three."

"One-four-three, B."

Seven

Briley

With an ounce of renewed strength, I smiled to myself. All alone in the kitchen, I allowed a smirk and another piece of chocolate. It was funny how the same guy that cursed like a sailor still indulged me with our child-forged code. I thought back to the fort we made under the massive pine tree and the promises that were made under its branches.

"I'll always be there for you, B."

"Ditto." I had no idea what it meant at the time, but they said it in the movie Ghost.

"I love you, B."

"Eww."

"Not really 'love, love' . . . our kind of love. No one else knows about this kind of love. It's the kind that only the best of friends have."

"And there's no kissing involved, right?" I queried, scrunching my nose in disgust.

"No way!"

Now my best friend and savior from that awful night was in prison for a crime that I personally found justified.

***

Late into the night, I slipped into the oddest dream. *A dirt path in the woods. I wasn't afraid to be alone in the woods, the clean smell of pine surrounding me, birds singing songs of romance as a cool spring breeze pushed lightly on my back, urging me forward.*

Daylight faded into night, but I still roamed, unafraid. The songs of birds ceased while the crickets took over, playing a more solemn tune alongside the bass of a few bullfrogs. Smiling, enjoying the sounds of the lone forest, I strolled on. My feet grew heavy, the path sticky with mud that clung to my shoes. Lifting my legs became too difficult, so I pulled on the hem of my dress, an invisible string connected and tugging my leg upward with ease. After a few more steps, I realized someone else was pulling the strings now, guiding my steps. It was easier to walk, but they were leading me down the wrong path, away from any light source, toward a darker part of the forest.

No more green was visible on the pines, only dead limbs and gray. Everything so drab and gray. Turning around wasn't an option as the strings pulled, dragging me against my will. Tears pooled in my eyes but refused to fall . . . until I saw him.

"Daddy?" I whispered.

"It's all right, baby girl. Sometimes you have to take a road you don't wish to travel to protect the ones you love."

"What does that—?" I reached out to grab his hand before he faded away, but it was too late. "Daddy?" I whispered, the tears falling now, so furiously that my clothes became soaked. Looking around, I realized it was raining. The drops were soft and warm and sprayed over me like a shower, soaking me to the bone and making the road beneath me thick with sludge. Even the strings couldn't move me.

Cooper appeared, holding out a hand. I took it, unfazed as though it was the most normal thing in the world for him to be in the forest. He led me easily down the path to a lone cabin. It was a small, quaint cabin and the warmth of a wood burning fireplace relaxed my tense muscles. Fireplace to the left, small table for two in the center. A kitchen to the right and a bed in the back.

Without a word, Cooper scooped me into his arms and carried me to the bed. He peeled the drenched clothes off of me and warmed me with his body. His hands were everywhere at once, stroking, kneading, gripping at my hips. The embers in the fireplace were no match for the heat inside me. I wanted him. He kissed me—every square inch from head to toe—whispering praises until I was panting with need and close to begging him to end the torture and take me.

I sat up in bed, looking around my bedroom until my clarity returned. It wasn't the first sex dream I'd had about Cooper, but it was the most detailed.

My fingers absently touched my lips, as though unwilling to wake.

Eight

Briley

Three months had passed since our separation, but Blake's harassing attempts to get me back hadn't slowed. He wouldn't let go. Like any other woman, I loved to be chased. It should've brought me some kind of comfort knowing the man I gave my heart to still wanted me. Of course, deep down I knew he didn't want me for the right reasons. He didn't love me too much to lose me. He loved himself too much to lose . . . at anything.

Blake was a handsome man—wispy blond hair, dark blue eyes, and a lean runner's body that was worked five days a week. I fell in love, or at least I thought I had. In hindsight I realized I was in love with love, not Blake. Like most women raised without a father, I gave my heart and soul to the first person that turned my head.

I sniffled into a soaked tissue, sitting at my mother's kitchen table. "I'm sorry, Mom. I can't seem to get a hold of myself. Every time I start down the path to healing, Blake steamrolls right over me." Pulling out another tissue, I wiped the trail of tears from my raw, salty, wet cheeks.

"What's he done now?" My mother, painfully thin but beautifully dressed, asked as she swirled a spoon through her spiked coffee. The worry in her creased brows was enough to bring forth fresh tears. I hated unloading on my mother, but there was no one else and I needed to talk to someone.

The sound of my mother sipping her coffee through pursed lips brought me back to the conversation.

"Every time I turn the corner, he's there waiting and watching. I feel terrorized in my own home."

"You need to change the locks, Bee." She glowered at me, as if it was common sense and I should've already done it.

"That's a good idea, Mom." Although still too hot to drink, I blew the steam off my mug and sipped the liquid slowly through my lips. "He's been waiting in the driveway for me to come out. Yesterday he was actually sitting by the pool with two cocktails when I walked out. How did he know I was going for a swim?" Panic washed over me as I thought about how little I knew my own fiancé. Was he having me followed, or could he have hidden cameras throughout the house to spy on me? I cupped my hand over my mouth with too much force and tasted the copper bite of blood.

"What is it, Bee, what's wrong?"

"He's been watching me. He knows my every move, Mom. I think he has hidden cameras in the house . . . maybe in our bedroom."

"*Your* bedroom," she snapped.

I nodded and thought back to buying my first home—a foreclosure needing some work. Cooper and a few of his buddies helped get it move-in ready for me. I was so excited, focusing on getting the pool liner replaced so I could throw a thank you bash for the guys after they finished.

"Now, let's think this through. What makes you think he'd have a camera in your bedroom?"

"The other day . . . I didn't think anything about it when he said it—he says some crazy things lately. He said, 'I prefer the green dress.'" Blinking back the tears, I continued. "Mom, I changed out of the green dress and wore a navy one. I was in the navy dress when he saw me. How the hell did he know I changed?"

"Okay." She continued circling the spoon in her coffee, something she always did when she was nervous. "Maybe he knows you love that green dress and he was just letting you know he preferred it."

Lifting my head to meet her gaze, I choked out the words in a whisper. "I just bought the green dress last week. He's never seen it." I gulped back the lump in my throat, making a noise that sounded like an animal struggling for its last breath. "What if he's had other women in my bed? What if he was into videoing and has hit the jackpot by leaving them there?"

I stood, eager to get home and strip the sheets. It was too hot for a fire, but throwing them out wasn't good enough. I needed to watch them burn.

"No, no. Don't go there, Bee, it'll drive you insane. Don't let him have that power over you." She shifted in her seat and it was the first time I had ever noticed uncertainty on her face. My mother, Nina Sheffield, was confident and strong. Nothing fazed her, no one crossed her, and she always had a plan. Sitting across from her now, watching her resolve crumble away, left me shaking.

"Mom?" I asked, watching her face change as the beginnings of an idea surfaced.

"We'll have someone come in and go over the entire house. Then we'll get a restraining order. This'll all be behind you soon."

"If the cameras are in the house, I don't want anyone to know about them." My head dropped in humiliation at the thought of someone watching videos of what was supposed to be private. "Let's look ourselves first."

Mom squeezed my hand from across the table and gave me a reassuring nod. Her eyes displayed the pain I was feeling. We had a connection that not many would ever experience. She was either a great mother or I was a good kid—probably a mix of both—but whatever we had worked. I'd rarely got into trouble and managed good grades. She was my mother first, then my biggest supporter and friend. Mom was my rock when my father died. Instead of losing herself in sorrow, she turned her attention to me, making sure I was raised properly and didn't miss out on the things only a father could provide. She did her best to be mother and father and I'd say she mastered the feat.

My father, Gerald, was fun-loving and strong. He could build and fix anything and always made me feel important as I handed him the necessary tools. Not many girls my age knew the difference between a Phillips and flathead screwdriver or what a socket wrench was. As girly as my mother tried to make me—dresses and huge bows for my hair—I was a full-fledged, dirty-kneed tomboy.

"Don't look at me like that, Mom. I know what you're thinking. I rushed into things with Blake." I crumpled under her scrutiny, pulling my knees up and hugging them

"Actually, I wasn't going to go there, but now that you've mentioned it . . ."

"I was crazy about him. He was everything I wanted in a husband."

"You wanted to be married and start a family." She fixed her eyes on mine. "He was your means to getting what you wanted."

I remained silent for a moment, reeling over the implication that I would use a man to get something I wanted. My arms unwrapped from my knees, letting my legs drop down so I could sit up straight. "You think I used him?"

"Of course not, Bee. I'm just saying . . . you've always had the gift of nurturing. Remember all the stray animals you brought home and cared for until they were well? What about that boy from school that you used to sneak food to because you didn't think he had a good home life? After college, I watched you look for something or someone to take care of. At first, I thought that's why you chose Blake. Maybe he needed someone to look after him. Then it came to me. You wanted a child."

She knew me too well.

After taking the last sip from her mug, my mother looked inside, seemingly surprised that it was already empty. "More coffee?" she asked, gripping the arms of her chair and grimacing before pushing herself up to stand.

I jumped up, scooting my chair back. "I'll get it. Is your knee bothering you again?"

"A little. I just need some Aleve and it'll be fine."

Before pouring more coffee, I handed her two pills and a glass of water. She placed them in her mouth and jerked her head back before chasing them down with the liquid. I always wondered if they went sailing into the back of her throat. It seemed to me that would make a person gag, but she had done it all my life.

Setting the carafe on a pot holder in the middle of the table, I carried the Bailey's Irish cream liqueur over. Ignoring her request to leave out the Bailey's, I poured a two-count into each of our cups and topped it with fresh coffee. I *needed* the numbing effect of the liquor.

Nine

Briley

I was keenly aware of my masochistic tendencies as I reached for our engagement DVD. I didn't have the courage to go back to a possibly camera-infested house, so I decided to sleep over in my old bedroom. Surprisingly, my twin bed was cozy, with the familiar soft mattress and worn out pink toile comforter.

Pictures of me and then Blake, from birth until the day we met, flashed across the screen, all while some of our favorite love songs played in the background. Several pictures of my childhood included Cooper. Through tears, I grinned, remembering how pissed Blake had gotten that Cooper was included. He was my childhood friend—a huge part of my life—besides, if I'd cut Cooper out, there wouldn't have been more than five good pictures to use on my side.

Repositioning myself in bed and hugging Mr. Flippy-Flop, I continued the visual torture. After the picture montage, video footage followed. A light tap on the door had me fumbling with the remote, trying to stop the DVD.

My mother peeked around the frame. "Did I wake you?" she asked.

"No, come on in." I finally found the right button—too late— and shut the television off.

She scooted onto my bed next to me and stroked my hair, just like she did when I was a child. "I wish I could take this pain away, Bee. Just know that this will heal. Your heart will mend and you'll find love again."

My eyes widened and I sat up. "I'm over him, Mom. I don't even know why I'm crying. It's just . . . it's a mixture of everything. I hate that I've wasted so much time on someone like Blake. I hate that he's capable of instilling fear in me and I—I miss Cooper."

She wrapped an arm around my shoulders and pulled me in for a side squeeze. My head rested on her shoulder, something I'd found comfort in all my life. Her scent was unique, the way Givenchy's Ysatis blended with her skin. It smelled different on me—too strong with a touch of floral.

She didn't bother with words that tried to make me feel better. She just kept me company. We sat there for what seemed like forever before she got up, kissed the top of my head, and said goodnight. "I love you, Bee."

"I love you, too, Mom."

***

After an hour of staring at the water stain on the ceiling, the one that eerily resembled the profile of Elvis, I threw the covers aside and got out of bed. Anger seethed through me like a poison, eating away at my insides. Whoever said warm milk would help you sleep was wrong. However, a cup of Chamomile tea with honey seemed to at least calm the pain in my stomach. I sipped my steaming cup and replayed March seventeenth—Saint Patrick's Day—over again in my head.

"I'm sorry, Bee, I'm a shit. I need counseling or something. It's a problem, but we'll work it out. I'll do whatever I need to do, just tell me what to do," he had said, opening his arms for me to seek comfort as I crumbled.

But something inside of me died on that uncharacteristically warm night in March. Instead of crumbling, I backed away half a step and folded my arms across my chest. The reaction that followed surprised me. Blake's eyebrows sunk, causing the skin between his eyes and above his nose to crinkle. His eyes portrayed sadness and his lips curled into a frown so phony, I began to laugh. Hysterics overcame me—an all out guffaw—until the laughter turned to sobs. The kind of sobs that morphed into dry-heaving and had me running down the hall and into our guest bathroom. I slammed the toilet seat down, wondering—hoping—it would shatter. "Why can't you put the damn seat down?" I'd shouted. Trying to regain my sanity, I began with my breathing. Slow, deep breaths in through my nose and out from my mouth. I could feel the calm just outside my grasp. It didn't last long and before I could regain control, I started vomiting.

After what seemed like an eternity of my body purging the wasted time, with the stranger pleading forgiveness from the other side of the door, I collected myself. The cool water of the faucet refreshed my heated, red face and I drank from my cupped hands until my scorching throat was quenched. Standing at the door, I couldn't make myself unlock and turn the handle. Before I could face Blake, I needed to make some decisions. If it had been a one-night-stand, or the first time he had cheated, I might have been able to forgive him. But it was the third. I silently cursed myself for coming so far down this path of destruction.

The first time we went through this, I forgave him. How could I not? He drank too much and hooked up with a stranger at a bar. Everyone makes mistakes. We sat through countless sessions with a counselor, managed to finish our assigned homework, and reconnected as a couple. Neither of us had seen divorce first hand, so breaking our engagement wasn't an option I considered.

It was two months before we were intimate—the most emotionally cruel moment of my life. Was he was thinking of her or me. *I* couldn't help thinking of her. His hands roaming over her body as she moaned and urged him on. Imagining his reaction to her. Did she have skills I didn't possess?

Andi was an attractive blonde, but even at my most insecure I didn't feel threatened by her. She wasn't the striking beauty that men ogled over and she had the body of a twelve year old boy. What could she have possibly offered him that I couldn't? Most women might have cried from the emotional overload of their cheating fiancé moaning about their undying love as they found their release. I didn't. Instead I went over my grocery list, organizing it in my head according to aisle. I didn't feel anything. This should've been a red flag, but I was glad I wasn't torn up over it. Happy I could move on. I thought it was strength.

"Third time's a charm," as the saying goes. I wasn't stupid enough, or desperate enough to find out. Once was heartbreaking, twice sucked the life out of me. As much as he begged and promised to never hurt me again, it was too late. My feelings for Blake McGregor were gone.

***

The smell of bacon permeated the house and stirred me to get out of bed. My mother was in the kitchen busying herself with a breakfast large enough to feed a family of four. I leaned against the wall watching her whisk eggs in a large glass mixing bowl.

I cleared my throat entering the kitchen and was rewarded with the smile my mother had given me every day before school when I was younger. "Good morning, Bee. Sleep okay?"

"Yes." I lied. "Who's coming over for breakfast? I usually just have a piece of toast and coffee."

"I guess I got carried away."

"Here, let me stir the eggs." I manned the stove while she methodically buttered a stack of toasted wheat bread.

After breakfast, Mom eased up out of the chair, bracing herself to guard her left knee. After two surgeries, arthritis had set in and seemed to give her more trouble when it rained. It had been raining non-stop for two days.

"Do you feel up to going by my house today, Mom?"

"Yes," she began, swallowing back a dose of anti-inflammatory medicine. "The sooner, the better. If we do find something . . . well, let's just say your mama has some tricks of her own ready to unleash on that bastard."

My eyes rolled like a teenager, embarrassed and maybe a little concerned over what she might have in mind. However, I was thankful to have her by my side and there wasn't a doubt in my mind that she could whip him. I'd always heard about a mother's ability to protect her young in the wild. My mother protecting her child in Tampa, Florida was no different.

Ten

Briley

Dressing in black for our secret mission seemed appropriate. Sneaking around in my own house didn't. If Blake had cameras in the house and was watching us look around for them, he'd immediately know who we were by our shape and movements. Unless he was dense, which, given the circumstances of our situation, wasn't too hard for me to fathom.

The bedroom needed to be tackled first. "Look behind, under, and inside everything," I suggested as I made my way to the dresser first. "I've seen shows on television where they hide microscopic cameras in sunglasses and tubes of lipstick."

"You realize those are fictitious shows, right? Blake's a car salesman, not a CIA operative."

"He owns two successful dealerships and he's got friends in high places." I tip-toed over the tiled floor as if there were sensors waiting to trigger any noisy steps. "Besides, it's not that far-fetched that his job is a cover. He's been leading more than one life the past two years," I deadpanned.

"I've got the best idea!" She squealed, making me jump and drop the tube of lipstick I was inspecting. "We need to take a mother-daughter trip. Remember our last trip to Charleston?"

"Mom!" I scolded. "Can we focus, please?" On my hands and knees, I reached under the dresser, patting around like someone without sight, until my fingers wrapped around the object I desired. When I stood the absurdity of our situation hit me. My room was completely torn apart—jewelry strewn across the bed so we could inspect the inside compartments of the jewelry box, clothes all over the floor, picture frames disassembled. The bedroom represented the chaos of my life.

Sitting defeated on the edge of the bed, an idea popped into my head so clear and brilliant, I had to work hard not to giggle. Looking purposefully at my watch, I exaggerated an intake of breath. "I've got to get ready, Mom. We're not going to find anything here. Do you mind waiting for me to change? I can drop you off on my way out."

"You have plans tonight? Where are you—?"

"I've got a date." I interrupted, grinning like a school girl. "Remember that guy I was telling you about? The one I met at Black Thirteen? I'm meeting him for a drink tonight."

"Who?" she asked, twisting her face as she tried to recall any mention of it. If I had mentioned meeting someone—a man—she would have remembered. "I don't recall—"

"Gene," I sputtered. It was the only name I could think of on the fly as I slipped into my favorite jeans that hugged my curves just right and made me feel like a confident, sensual woman. "You were half asleep, but I told you about him. Tall, dark, handsome, and that accent . . . he's sexy as hell." Leaving that last adjective out would have been the smarter choice, but I needed to make Blake as green with jealousy as possible. I wanted to rile him enough to have him follow me. My mother was stunned and still trying to remember any mention of this hot foreigner. She leaned against the dresser and looked at me for answers. Using the opportunity for my advantage, I continued. "We're meeting at The Loft . . . eight-thirty. Do you think this top shows too much cleavage?"

"Yes, it does. What kind of message are you trying to send?"

"The right one." I winked. Lying to my mom was difficult, but if she could just hang on until we got in the car I would explain.

"You just met this guy, Bee." The concern on her face nearly broke me and foiled my plan. Grabbing her arm along with my makeup bag, I led her out of the house and to the car.

Once safely inside and away from any listening devices, I unfolded my plan.

"Mom, there is no hot guy. We weren't having any luck finding a camera, so I'm running a test. If Blake is watching or listening, he's crazed with jealousy right now. The Loft is secluded and not a place he would ever frequent. So if he shows up, we'll know he's watching." I threw my head back against the seat and grunted. "Damn him."

We drove in silence until I pulled into her driveway. She turned to face me and it was clear she didn't intend on getting out. "Are you sure about this, Bee?"

I nodded once, letting her know she didn't have a shot changing my mind.

"Then I'll ride along."

"Mom, you can't. I'll be fine. He's a cheat, not a villain."

"Do you even have a plan if he shows up? Are you just going to confront him?" Her voice raised an octave with each sentence. "You don't expect him to apologize and remove the hidden devices, do you? Where's your phone?"

"Jeez, Mom! Okay, what do you suggest?"

"If he shows up—and I don't think he will—have your phone on record. You'll need evidence for a restraining order."

"How many years have you been watching that crime show of yours?" I raised an eyebrow and cracked a slight smile. My mother was a lot wiser than I gave her credit. Shutting off the engine, I sat there a moment pondering. "All right, let's take your car. I'll drive."

"Afraid I'll ram him?" She unbuckled her seat belt and fished in her oversized purse for the keys.

***

My heart began to race as I pulled the car up to the curb, a block from The Loft. It wasn't as crowded as I'd hoped and I didn't want to take the chance of Blake seeing my mom's silver Ford Taurus. Inhaling deeply and letting my breath out all at once seemed to ease my nerves enough to manage the handle on the door. "Wish me luck." I gave my mom a quick smirk.

"Don't forget the record button," she whispered in her loudest tone, pressing her finger on her imaginary recorder.

"I won't." My eyes rolled but I saved myself by offering a quick chuckle before shutting the door behind me. I graduated college with honors, yet my mother felt it necessary to remind me how to perform the simplest of tasks.

Standing in front of the The Loft, pretending to check my phone for emails, I waited for my handsome phony date. Each time I heard footsteps coming close, I hit the record button. A gorgeous couple walked past me, into the bar. After that, two women—one with long, red hair, and the other a brunette pixie cut. Like all women, I distractedly studied the competition and debated adding red streaks to my dark brown hair.

I checked my phone once more, ignoring the footsteps closing in on the front door. When he stopped in front of me, I glanced up and swallowed the cuss word playing at my lips.

"What a surprise," Blake began. "I'm meeting someone for a drink. Are you here alone?"

"Keep your day job, dear. You're a terrible actor," I deadpanned and slyly hit the record button on my phone.

He feigned innocence, shrugged his shoulders, and dragged out each word as he spoke. *"Okaaay."* Looking down at the watch on his wrist, he checked the time. "I'm early."

He looked back up at me and smiled. It was the smile he used to capture my heart when I first saw him. Now I saw right through it and swallowed back the desire to slap it off his face.

"How've you been, Bee?" If he used that nickname just one more time, the daggers I was visually shooting him would turn into fists.

He threw up his hands in surrender. "Sorry. Bri-ley."

He was mocking me? *Punk.*

He didn't have to ask, he knew. He'd watched my every move. Watched me fall asleep each night. He knew that I watched our engagement video, drank too much wine, and soaked in the tub until my fingers looked like raisins. I wanted to dig my heel in his foot and grind as if putting out a cigarette, but my phone wouldn't record forever. We needed to get this show started.

"Great. Just fantastic." I smiled over gritted teeth. "I sold our bedroom suite. Gave it away actually. The neighbor across—"

"No you didn't. Why would you tell me tha—?"

"I knew it!" My finger was pointed half an inch from his freckled-from-too-much-sun nose. "You've been watching me. That's how you knew I was here tonight. You know when I'm going for a swim, when I've changed my dress . . . who the hell do you think you are?"

He grabbed my arm, causing my phone to fall to the sidewalk. "I'm your fiancé. I have a right to protect what's mine. Look at you, giving yourself away to some strange man from a third world country."

Jerking my arm from his grip, I picked up my phone and shoved it in my back pocket. If looks could kill, he would have been laid out on the pavement. "Ex fiancé," I began, my words coming out staccato. "You gave up your rights . . . and the only protection I need is keeping you away. I know you have cameras watching me, you sick bastard. Do you get off watching me . . . or do you and your whores—" I couldn't finish, the thought disgusted me and the degradation was more than I could bear. "You're busted, Blake."

Anger wasn't a strong enough word to describe the emotion running through me. It took all the strength I had not to let the tears spill over my lashes.

"There aren't any cameras, Briley. Have you gone nuts?" He backed up and pretended to check the time again. "I can see you're upset. I'll call my friend and tell him to meet me somewhere else. Be careful, Briley. You *really are* sending the wrong message dressed like that."

My legs barely held me upright as I watched him walk away. As soon as he rounded the corner, the dam opened and the tears flowed.

Startled, I jerked away when my mother's arms wrapped around my shoulders. She pulled me into her and held me like a child who'd lost her kitten.

"Why, mom? Why is he so stinking mean?"

"I don't know, Bee. He's a coward and a bully."

If I hadn't been so overcome with emotion, I might have thanked her for not interfering with my mission. It had to be hard for her not to jump the curb and run him over with the car.

"Let's get this video to the police. I'm ready to have Blake McGregor out of my life for good."

My mother turned toward the car, a quick clip in her step. "I'll drive."

Eleven

Briley

Having never stepped inside a police station, I immediately felt like I was walking into the principal's office. Not in a hurry to experience whatever awaited us through the double doors, I dug through my purse for gum and offered a piece to Mom.

"It's all right, Bee." My mom used her soothing voice. She did that when she wanted to ease my frazzled nerves. It worked when I was a child.

I reached for the door handle just as it flew open. A man came bustling out, his cigarette lighter already aimed and ready to fire. "S'cuse me."

I stepped inside and was surprised to see the opposite of what I had conjured up in my mind.

"It's clean," I whispered.

"What did you expect, prisoners handcuffed to their chairs?"

"Well," I shrugged my shoulders. "Yeah."

Two men in uniforms busied around the room while a woman in matching attire sat at the front desk. I approached the desk as my nerves battled the rage still swimming through my veins from the incident with Blake. My nerves were winning by a long shot and my hands trembled as I wrapped them around the evidence—my phone.

"May I help you?" The officer behind the desk asked, glancing up with a flat, unreadable expression.

"Yes. I—I . . ." *Get a hold of yourself, Bee! There's no crime in speaking.* I took a deep breath and exhaled audibly.

There was no point in pretending I wasn't scared, it was obvious by the shaking and stuttering.

She looked at me and her expression changed. It was softer, laced with a hint of compassion. Her hard features, most likely developed over time from what she'd seen, smoothed and displayed her more feminine side. Her voice was gentle, the way an adult would speak to a lost child. "Ma'am, it's all right. Take your time."

"I . . . my name is Briley Sheffield. My ex fiancé, Blake . . . well, I believe he's installed devices in my home to spy on me."

"Okay. Do you have any evidence? Has he hurt you in any way?"

"I recorded a conversation with him this evening. He confessed." Pulling out the phone, I clicked the camera app and scrolled until I found the video. "Here it is. Do you want me to play it for you?"

"Yes, go ahead."

We both focused our attention on the video. It was a shaky shot of the sidewalk, but the audio was clear.

"Great. Just fantastic. I sold our bedroom suite. Gave it away actually. The neighbor across—"

"No you didn't. Why would you tell me tha—"

"A-ha! You've been watching me. That's how you knew I was here tonight. You know when I'm going for a swim, when I've changed my dress . . . who the hell do you think you are?"

A sudden thud was heard and I explained to the officer how my phone dropped when he grabbed my arm. We waited for the audio to continue, but it never did.

"What—?" I hit the play button on my phone again, noticing the length of the recorded video. "It must have stopped when I dropped the phone. Is that enough evidence for a restraining order?" Tears welled up in my eyes.

"I'm afraid not. He never admitted anything. It's all speculation."

"But—"

The now-kind officer smiled in my direction. It was a smile telling me there was no point in going any further with my pleading. "Tell you what I can do," she began, shuffling papers around on her desk. "I'll send an officer to your home to check around for any surveillance-type equipment. Okay?"

Not able to speak without releasing the floodgates holding the tears at my lashes, I nodded my head and forced a crooked smile of thanks.

⁂

Officer Norcom's physique reminded me of Barney Fife. His personality, on the other hand, was more akin to Harvey Keitel. Smiling was not one of his gifts and I wondered if his tough guy routine was just an act or the real deal. Maybe he didn't have much to be happy about, or perhaps he was pissed that he was given this task. Although I took it seriously and was ready for the nightmare to end, he most likely saw it as the equivalent of crossing guard duty.

"I think there's something in the bedroom. He knew all the details of my plans tonight. Who I was meeting, where the guy was from."

Officer Norcom looked at me warily. "You sure he didn't overhear you at the coffee shop?"

"No!" My eyes widened. Did he think all women were stupid, or just me? "I made up the entire evening. I told my mother I was meeting someone tonight, just to prove that Blake would show up. It's not a coincidence. He played right into my hands, can't you see?"

Nothing. Not even movement from his eyebrows. *Sheesh.*

I continued, leading the way to the bedroom. *You'll see.* Standing in the bedroom, I looked around and gasped. "Someone's already been here."

"What makes you say that?" Officer Norcom asked flatly.

I wanted to take my hand to his chin and close his mouth that was smacking away loudly at a piece of chewing gum. "First of all, this picture frame is knocked over."

"Do you have a cat?"

"No," I answered, dumfounded at the question.

"Could've knocked it over on your way out?"

"What about the piece of tape I stuck over this drawer? It's been tampered with."

The officer looked at me and I swear I saw a smirk play on his lips. "Are you serious, ma'am? Don't tell me," he began, tracing his chin with thumb and forefinger. "James Bond fan?"

The smirk I glimpsed earlier turned into a full blown smile. The kind you flash at a child pretending to serve you the best cup of tea you've ever had from a plastic Disney set. Officer Norcom hadn't wanted to take me seriously from the start. There was no convincing him otherwise now.

"He was here and I'd bet my life that he removed any evidence before getting caught. Thank you for coming out here, but it looks like I've gotten my privacy back after all." My tone was curt, as hard as I tried to be polite. Emotionally exhausted, I didn't have it in me to be any kinder to him.

"I suggest changing your locks if you're concerned." He wrote down a number and handed it to me. "This is a good company. Ask for Curt." He tipped his head in my direction, and followed my mother to the door. I was aware of their mumbling, but continued to search for any clues of what had taken place while I was out. I heard the door shut at the same time I plopped myself onto the bed with my arms slung overhead.

"You okay?" my mother asked. She stood in the doorway, leaning against the frame. Her eyes seemed tired and heavy with concern. Somehow, when I felt stronger, I'd find a way to make Blake pay for this.

"I will be." I huffed. "I just don't understand. He doesn't want me . . . until I don't want him anymore. What the hell?"

"His pride's been tarnished and you've taken away any control he had over you."

I rolled off the bed and paced the floor as I spoke. "There should be a mood strip on everyone's forehead that shows what kind of person you are. I should've known. But where were the signs? Where's the justice?" My throat tightened with each question, making my voice squeak. I knew I sounded childish, but my head was spinning.

She had no answers for me, just motherly concern in her eyes.

"I'm gonna call this locksmith and then I'd like to sleep at your house tonight, is that okay?"

"You never have to ask, Bee. It'll always be your home, too."

"I know, Mom." My lips curled slightly in a smile of appreciation. It was all I could offer at the moment.

Twelve

Briley

There were new locks on all the doors, which meant new, stiff keys that had to be worked a little. *Dammit!* I rammed the toe of my shoe into the gold kick plate at the bottom of the door.

Not wanting to dawdle, I grabbed my black dress, heels, and panty hose from the closet and stuffed a strand of pearls with matching earrings into a silk bag. It was going to be a hard day but I'd known my parent's friend, Mr. Quinn, all my life and couldn't justify not going.

Once at my mother's house, I dressed and joined her in the bathroom to get ready. My father's shaving kit remained on his side of the counter and every now and then I'd take a whiff of his aftershave.

Getting ready in my childhood home had the usual effect on me . . . I was once again a child. The tiny room with tan and light blue striped wallpaper wasn't the only thing making me feel like a little girl. The thought of seeing Mr. Quinn in a coffin, the plastic effect of funeral home makeup, made me feel small and helpless.

My mother exited the room, leaving me to lean against the countertop and let my mind wander to Cooper. Before long, I was going over our last argument like a detective sorting through a crime scene.

"You can't marry him, B."

Giggling, I shoved him lightly. "You're ridiculous, Cooper. Now go on so I can finish getting ready." I twirled my engagement ring on my finger once before grabbing the tube of mascara and applying a thin coat to my lashes.

"Look at me, B." He lifted my chin and locked his eyes on mine. "He's not the right man for you. He's a selfish asshole."

"Don't say any more if you value our friendship, Cooper." My fists rested on my hips, showing my serious mood. "I'm in love with Blake and we're going to spend the rest of our lives together." Reaching out, I laid a hand on his arm. "You're my best friend, Cooper, and I know you're trying to look after me but trust me . . . he's a good guy and he loves me." I saw a flash of pain in his eyes before he turned away from me.

"Just promise me," he began, his back still to me. "Promise me you won't rush to the altar. Have a long engagement, B. Learn everything you can about him before you jump into anything."

On a heavy sigh, I nodded and tossed the capped mascara back into the drawer. I couldn't understand why Cooper hated Blake so much. Did he think our friendship would change once I was married? I'd have to convince him that wouldn't happen. But I was late for a movie date with my new fiancé so that talk would have to wait.

"I'm going to be late. We'll talk later?" I scooted past him, brushing against his statuesque frame. Stopping, I turned back around to face him. "I wish my best friend could be happy for me. Usually these things are celebrated."

A shiver ran over my skin, leaving goose bumps behind. The expression of pain on his face would forever be etched in my mind.

Mom and I drove in silence to the funeral home. After dropping off our chicken casserole and pecan pie in the hospitality room downstairs, we made our way to the front door and signed the guest book. Waves of familiar faces greeted us as we made our way toward the front of the chapel to pay our respects. I swallowed the growing lump in my throat and fished through my bag for a mint to help my case as my mother talked with a neighbor. Before I could get it unwrapped, a tap on my left shoulder made the mint drop into the black abyss of my purse.

Whipping my head around, I looked into familiar gray-green irises. Cooper's dad smiled and drew me into his arms for a hug. My own arms dangled by my sides, trapped by his squeeze.

"Mr. Sterling, good to see you."

"I have news," he whispered, ushering me away from the crowd to a more secluded spot. "Cooper's coming home." His voice cracked. In his eyes I saw such deep love for his son. That, mixed with the knowledge that my best friend was finally coming home, left goose bumps pebbling my flesh in response.

My eyebrows shot up, along with my heart rate. I whisper-squealed, "Are you serious? When?" Finally, he'd get his life back. Finally, I'd have *mine* back. I couldn't wait to dissolve into his arms.

"Two weeks. He's being released for good behavior. Can you—" He covered his mouth to stifle a chuckle, but his eyebrows shot up in excitement, giving him away. "Can you believe it? Cooper released for good behavior?"

I took his hands in mine and gave them a squeeze. My insides felt like they were filled with Mexican jumping beans soaked in Red Bull. "I *can* believe it, Mr. Sterling. He doesn't belong there. That's not who he is. He did the right thing that night. He saved me from—" I turned my head, trying to erase the memories that suddenly invaded my head.

"Oh, I know, sweet girl. But he was always in trouble." He shook his head disapprovingly, but pride was still evident in his eyes. "That boy throws his fists around like he's getting paid to do it. I just thought for sure he'd tack on extra time around some of those hooligans."

Hooligans? I tried not to laugh, but a giggle escaped before I could prevent it.

"I'm so excited. What can I do? A party?" My mind raced with ideas.

"I thought maybe you could pick him up?" His voice was quiet, almost a shy whisper. His eyes showed doubt and pleading.

"Sure, I'll go with you. But I don't want to be in the way. I know you're excited to see him."

He gave me a half-smile, the kind that told me I misunderstood. "No, I'm asking you to go alone."

I tried to protest, shaking my head. "But I—"

He raised a hand, stopping me in mid sentence. "Briley, I know you're frightened, but it's safe. You don't even have to go inside. You can wait in the car."

One eyebrow shot up. *He thinks I'm scared? He watched me grow up!*

"I'm not *scared*, Mr. Sterling. I just thought you and Mrs. Sterling would want the honor. Of course I'll pick him up. I'll walk right in there . . ." *Oh.* I could tell by his smile that he had tricked me. He knew the fear card would bully me into going. But why? Mrs. Sterling would have a fit if hers weren't the first arms around Cooper's neck.

"It's the best gift I can give him, Briley. He'll appreciate this much more than a party."

Thirteen

Cooper

Two weeks until I was out of this hell hole. Three things kept me from punching my cell mate, Butch, in the throat. A medium rare steak right off the grill, sleeping like a baby again on my thick mattress, and Briley. My mouth watered thinking about the taste of grilled meat. Real meat, not the processed kind. But my body and soul ached for Briley. I could almost smell the fresh scent of her body wash, a mild vanilla that lingered on her skin.

Damn, her body was perfect. Curves in all the right places, long, tapered legs, and an ass that drove a man insane. I imagined running my hands over her hips, winding around until her ass was in my firm grip. Wondering if her lips still tasted like strawberries. *Fantastic, now I'm hard.* Make that four things that kept me from punching that dude humming the same damn tune: the freedom to masturbate in private.

Instead, I had to lie there and listen to Drake's "Started From the Bottom." It was enough to make me lose my erection, thank God.

"Don't you know the rest of the words?" I shouted before covering my head with the postage stamp-sized pillow. Fucker kept singing the same seventeen words. Yes, I counted. Something had to help get my mind off Briley.

I had to tell her how I felt and find a way to shake some sense into her. Even if she didn't believe I was the one for her, she had to know Blake wasn't. Although I had tried in the past with no luck, I'd keep trying. She was worth the effort. One thing I learned in this cage, life was too short to dick around. I needed to go after what I wanted, and I wanted her. She belonged with me. I just needed to make her see the light.

That night I drifted to sleep thinking about her. The smile that lit up the room and the giggle I'd heard on the phone replayed over and over in my head. Tickling her to hear that laugh again, my hands on her soft flesh. Two weeks seemed like an eternity. And by the end of it, my balls would be as blue as Papa Smurf.

Fourteen

Briley

Two weeks, fourteen days, or three-hundred thirty-six hours. For some that might seem like an eternity, but I had planning to do. The timing was perfect, a welcome distraction to the Briley's-life-is-a-volcano-of-shit party.

A party! Not a bad idea. There were several ways to welcome Cooper home and they all swam through my head. A barbecue, pool party, or perhaps something more formal? No, Cooper would hate formal. My eyebrows scrunched, lips curling to the side. Cooper would hate any kind of attention that a party would bring. Maybe just a nice dinner with his parents, me, and my mom. Or would that make him feel like we didn't care? Welcoming him matter-of-factly, *"Hey, Coop. Glad you're back. Can you grab me a glass of tea on your way in here?"* Ugh! Think, Briley.

Running always opened my think tank. Before the temperature rose too much, I dressed and stretched. My iPod—fully charged, thank God—blasted "My Hero" by the Foo Fighters as I started out in a slow jog, allowing my muscles to warm up and become accustomed to the pounding I was about to unleash on them.

Usually the lyrics didn't register. The music was always background noise as I let my mind work out lists, life goals, and more recently, my screwed up life. But the words of this song made me think of Cooper. I agreed with the lyrics and nodded my head. Yes, Cooper was my hero. He was always there for me. This time he took a bullet—if you will—for me.

After my run, I had it all worked out. A family dinner the first night—something casual, home cooked. He'd surely appreciate the relaxed atmosphere and real food. I'd follow his lead if he needed to relax in sweat pants by the television, or was stir crazy and needed to take a drive afterwards. I couldn't begin to understand what it felt like to be trapped in a cage. Maybe he'd like to run around the block a few times?

The following week, once he'd gotten his bearings back, I'd have a barbecue with a few of our friends. I decided to stop by Madison Cull's house on the way back and see if she was available and would like to meet some of my friends. Acquaintances were more like it. I wasn't the type of girl who had many friends. I usually saw Madison on my morning run, but I hadn't been out lately and it was later than usual for a run.

She opened the door moments after I rang the bell.

"Briley!" She seemed genuinely happy to see me. "Come in."

"Are you busy?" I asked. She was still in her running clothes, wisps of sweat-dried hair framing her face."

"Nope. I was just about to have a cup of coffee. Like some?" It wasn't a question as she turned, not waiting for my answer, and led me to the kitchen.

Madison was new to the neighborhood. Divorced, no children. She'd never been to my house . . . that would've been like dangling meat in front of a wolf. Blake would've devoured her right in front of me. Madison was a knockout—long, blond hair, blue eyes, lean runner's body—your typical all-American Barbie-type with a vixen attitude.

"How do you like it?" she asked, filling two black mugs with coffee.

"Black is fine."

"Good run?" Her back was to me as she stirred sugar and cream into her cup.

"Eh." I shrugged. "Got a late start and had a lot on my mind." Taking the mug she offered, I nodded a thank you and took a sip. "You?"

"Yeah. Downloaded a new playlist and kept a good pace." She leaned against the counter, glancing up between sips. Our encounters were always awkward, but I was trying.

"What are your plans today?" I asked.

"Pure laziness. Absolutely nothing on the agenda except getting caught up on all the shows I've recorded. You?"

"Shopping. I need something new to wear in a couple of weeks. Something special. A good friend of mine is coming home and . . ."

"Ooh, something *special?* I'm guessing this friend is male?" She flashed a knowing grin.

"Yes." I smirked. "He's a guy, but we're just friends. Best friends."

"So, are we looking for country-girl-sweet, or city-girl-sexy?"

I sucked on my bottom lip. Hell if I knew which look I was going for. I wanted an outfit that said, *"Welcome home from jail."* But I wouldn't tell her that.

"I don't know."

"Okay, sure." She brought the mug to her lips so I couldn't read her expression. Was she saying *"Sure, I understand"* or *"Sure, I don't buy your story?"* Setting her coffee on the counter, she studied me. "He's been gone a while . . . military?"

I didn't answer and kept the mug to my lips, pretending to drink. "He probably hasn't seen a woman in who knows how long. Definitely go sexy."

"Gross! He's like my brother."

"Oh," she groaned. "I can't help you then. I don't have anything for the 'brother-type' guy."

He wasn't exactly the 'brother-type' guy she was probably thinking but I couldn't explain our relationship to her. Hell, it didn't make sense to me sometimes. "I'm sure I'll find something."

I took another sip of coffee and thought about inviting her over to lay out by the pool. I needed more friends—girls I could talk to about things you didn't want to share with your mother.

Gripping the mug in both hands, I offered, "We could lay by the pool at my house? It's supposed to be gorgeous today."

"Sounds good!" Her brows arched above blue eyes. "I'll bring drinks."

I checked my watch for the time. Nine twenty-two. "Eleven thirty?"

"See you then."

***

"This feels so good." Madison took a deep, satisfied breath before taking a sip of the concoction she had created for us.

We were both on floats in the pool, lapping up the warmth of the sun, enjoying the bliss of a relaxing, mind-numbing day.

I sipped on my straw. "This is good, what's in it?"

"You'll die. It's so easy. Blueberry vodka mixed with strawberry lemonade. You know, the Crystal Light mix?"

"Seriously? How much vodka? I can't even taste it."

"I know, right? But there's two shots in each, so you should feel it, even if you can't taste it, *doll*."

So far so good. Madison wasn't so hard to get along with. I hated that she called me *doll* though. She probably had pet names for everyone she talked to, like the waitress on Nebraska Avenue. *"What can I get you, baby? More coffee, sugar?"* Was she asking if I wanted more coffee *with* sugar, or more coffee my little sugar baby? Either way, I hated it, but I loved that diner and always asked for her section. She was the best and always brought me extra bacon.

"Are you dating anyone?" I didn't look up and for all I knew, neither did she.

"I've been on a few *really* bad dates. I had no idea there were so many losers out there." She chuckled, maybe remembering one of the dates. "What about you?"

"No, no. I'm in that all-men-are-assholes stage." I squirmed, adjusting my position on the float.

"You've got to get back on the horse before you chicken out. The longer you wait, the harder it will be, and they're not *all* jerks."

"Yet, you and I found jerks."

"True."

I heard her shift and then the water moved. My eyes opened, following her to the side of the pool. She rested her elbows on the edge behind her before continuing. "So, your man was an ass? Mind if I ask why?"

"An ugly baboon ass." I laughed. That felt good. "He's a whore. Couldn't keep it in his pants."

Suddenly I felt exposed, vulnerable. I'd told her too much. Now she probably assumed I couldn't keep him in our bed. I wasn't a good lover. Maybe I wasn't?

"That sucks. I've had my share of cheaters. The one that nearly destroyed me was Daniel Clark, my first love." I could see the pain in her eyes as she spilled his name. "I knew we'd marry. He was everything to me and I did everything in my power to show him how much I loved him.

"He cheated on me with Beth Fitzpatrick." She over-exaggerated a shiver. "I was way hotter than she ever was. It ate at me. I had to know why he would cheat on me with *her* of all people." She shook her head and smirked. Not a happy one, but the kind that admitted foolishness.

"Thanks for sharing that." I smiled and rolled off the float to cool off. I dunked under the water, getting my hair wet and came back up. "So, get back on the horse you say?"

"Immediately."

"Then we need to go out. A club or something."

"Hells yeah! Next weekend works for me."

"I can't go next weekend. In fact, that's the whole reason I came over this morning." I shook my head and chuckled. "I'm having a few friends over for drinks and food—probably something on the grill—you wanna come?"

"Yeah, what can I bring?"

"Bring the ingredients for these drinks? I'll have beer for the guys."

After refilling the lime green plastic cups, I set mine in the cup holder on the float and carefully shimmied on my belly across the plastic, balancing my weight.

"So, tell me about these awful dates." My words were lazy, almost slurred. Mostly from the relaxation, but a little from the alcohol.

"Oh my God. I'm telling you, some of the stuff that happened . . . well, you just can't make this shit up." She laughed and I laughed with her, the jostling of the float not the most comfortable feeling while lying on your stomach. "This one guy . . . Jack was his name. We met out for dinner. Rue. You know where that is?"

"Uh huh."

"Not only does he order for me, but he orders me a salad. That's it. I'm thinking maybe he can't afford much, so I don't complain. It's fine. But then *he* orders a steak. I think maybe he plans on sharing it with me. Like, we're going to split the steak and salad. Kind of sweet or romantic, right? No! He doesn't even offer me a bite." She huffs. "I'm not going to say anything, because . . . hell, I don't know. But I don't say anything. After dinner, when he's eaten every single frickin' bite, he says, 'Sorry I didn't offer you a bite. I figure you don't eat much to keep that smokin' body in shape.' Asshole."

"Wow." I let the word roll of my tongue slowly, feigning disbelief. Actually, her story wasn't that astonishing. I had better stories with my fiancé. *Ex-fiancé.*

"Your turn." She kept her eyes on me, waiting for me to spill.

"I don't have any bad date stories, but I remember some shitty moments." Not realizing how robotic I sounded, I listed off injustices served by the man who was prepared to vow in front of God, family, and friends to love and care for me forever. "Plates taken away after he thought I'd had enough. Wrecking plans between my mom and me by *accident.* Checking out other women when we were out together. Coming home marinated in someone else's perfume. Wrecking my freaking life."

"Sorry, but *why* did you fall for a guy like that?"

"He wasn't always like that. He was witty and fun." I couldn't help the smile that came along, reminiscing about the good times. "His personality demands attention. He's the life of the party and always has a crowd listening to his jokes and stories.

"I remember the first time I saw him—blond hair, blue eyes—the kind of good-looking that made people turn all the way around for a second look. When he walked away from the two girls he was talking to at The Phunky Grill and started flirting with me . . . I was toast. He could've told me he was a serial killer and I still would've gotten in the car with him.

"He wined and dined like he'd been bred for it. I'm talking flowers and compilation CD's . . . he was too good to be true." I shook my head. Another red flag.

"When did things change?"

"When I agreed to marry him." I twisted the tie of my bikini top around my finger. "I guess he thought when he put a ring on my finger, he owned me. Surprisingly, his rules didn't apply to him. I mean, demi-gods don't follow rules, right?" Sarcasm oozed from my lips like a chocolate fountain, except unlike chocolate, the aftertaste of Blake was bitter and poisoned my mood.

The atmosphere was sufficient to ease the anger percolating within. With the calming warmth of the sun and surrounding music, I intermittently dozed off.

It wasn't a bad way to waste a day.

Fifteen

Cooper

My emotions were all over the place when the guard came with the mail. Anticipation—would he pause at my cell? Elation—an envelope handed through the bars. It had been opened and read before my eyes could see its contents, but it was something to look forward to. Something to get me through at least two more days.

Briley was amazing, writing to me so often I was hardly ever without a letter. The longest I had to wait was four days because of a stupid holiday. She sent me her articles after they're published. It was never anything I was interested in—this last one on how to choose the best olive oil, including a recipe at the bottom—but I was proud of her. She was doing what she loves and actually really good at it. I wish she'd work on her novel though. I think it would give her the boost of confidence she needed knowing she'd finished something she's dreamed about for so long.

Always making the moment last, I studied the pages, lifting them to my nose for a chance smell of the outside world. She wasn't the type to spray perfume on the letter. We didn't have that kind of relationship . . . and Briley wasn't a girly-girl. A woman in every sense, but the thought of spraying perfume on a letter would make her laugh. I could imagine her nose crinkled up, rolling her eyes at the ridiculous thought.

Damn, I couldn't wait to get out of here. See my family. Make Briley laugh.

Stuffing the letter under my pillow for the night, my mind wandered to the beautiful brunette I'd loved my entire life. Her words claimed she was on my side, but would things change between us? Would she be afraid of me now that I had a criminal record . . . knowing what I did to that asshole? My stomach knotted at the thought and it was the first time since that night I was glad I hadn't killed him. I couldn't stand the thought of being less in her eyes. Matt needed that ass-kicking. Deserved it. I didn't regret messing him up. But if she was afraid of me . . .

My hands punched the pillow, taking out some of my frustrations and trying to add some fluff to the piece of shit under my head. *She's not afraid of you, dipshit.* She hadn't revealed even a hint of fear at the trial or in her letters, yet irrational fears popped into my head often. More often as my release date got closer.

I'd have to prove myself—I'd have to prove a lot of things to a lot of people—but right now all I cared about was her. Beautiful, sweet, Briley.

Sixteen

Briley

Only one week left until I picked Cooper up. Even after my morning run, my insides were unsettled. Nerves combined with an unplanned meeting at work had me on my second cup of coffee, which only added to the shakiness. I couldn't imagine what my boss needed to meet with me about. She usually emailed me assignments. I dreaded the forty minute drive, especially knowing something must be wrong. If I lost this job, it would devastate me.

Feeling as confident as one could fearing her job was in jeopardy, I pressed my hands down my sides, loosening any wrinkles that had worked their way into my gray pantsuit during the drive. My purse felt awkward on my shoulder, so I carried it like a briefcase . . . and then lifted it over my shoulder again before stepping off the elevator.

I was greeted immediately by the sweet, perky Sophie. "Hey, Briley! Haven't seen you in ages. How've you been?"

"Great, thanks." I lied. "How are your piano lessons?" My brows waggled teasingly. "Landed a date with the hottie yet?"

She blushed and cupped her hands around her mouth so the whisper would reach me. "We've been dating for six months!"

If I hadn't been nervous about my meeting, I might have reenacted the scene from *An Officer and a Gentleman, "Way to go, Sophie! Way to go!"* But I *was* nervous, so I settled for an under the radar high five.

"I've got a meeting with Angela." I watched Sophie's expression, hoping it would reveal a hint if something was wrong, but she didn't offer any clue.

"Yeah, she's ready for you. Said to send you in when you got here."

"Great, thanks." I threw up a hand and headed to her corner office.

Pausing outside the closed door, I took a deep breath, prepared for the worst scenario, and rapped on the wood.

"Come in," she called out.

Stepping through the door, I was greeted with a smile. *Good.* I took the seat across from her desk and set my bag on the floor.

"I'm sorry to make you drive all the way down here, Briley, but I thought it best to talk to you in person about this."

Shit. Here it comes. Her smile remained, which pissed me off a little. She'd been a nice person to work for, was I to see another side of her now?

With her chin resting in folded hands, propped up by elbows on her desk, she leaned forward slightly. "I've got an assignment. It's perfect for you and I'm counting on you to accept."

Way too excited, I almost blurted out, *"Yes! I'll do it!"* But remained calm. For all I knew it could be cleaning the staff bathrooms. Then again, at least I'd still have a job. *Hold tight, Bri.*

"You've been doing a brilliant job with your articles; we're lucky to have you with us. But I've got something a little different." She watched my face, my expression hidden beneath the concealed bundle of nerves and twitches.

"How would you feel about traveling for your next assignment?" She leaned back in her chair, eyes locked on mine. "The magazine is doing well, but I want great. I'm thinking instead of writing about the difference between prosciutto and pancetta—send you to a place that makes those products. Taste them, feel them, and then write about your experience. I'll send a photographer with you to capture everything." She searched my eyes for a moment, and then added. "You won't be in the pictures, just the products."

My stomach flip-flopped. Was she sending me to Italy? It was a dream of mine to visit the hills of Tuscany, taste wine from Chianti . . . a sigh escaped my lips, producing a wide smile from Angela.

"Well, what do you say?"

"Yes, it sounds like a great idea and a wonderful opportunity. I assume . . ." I hated to ask, but I'd learned the hard way to cover all my bases.

"Of course, expenses paid . . . as long as they are job related." She winked.

"This is exciting, Angela. Really exciting. Thank you."

"So, your first assignment isn't all that exciting, but we'll get there." She swiped through her iPad, trying to locate something. "Yes, your first trip will be Epcot."

My face fell. "Disney World? That seems too . . . I mean, I thought our magazine was right up there with Epicurious. Shouldn't I be focusing on something more . . . gourmet?"

"Hey, now. There are several high end restaurants in Epcot. A lot of people want to know what their dining opportunities are other than a pretzel stand, or a Mickey shaped ice cream." She swiped across her screen again. "Next, you'll travel to

Washington, D.C. If this idea takes off like I think it will, we'll look at sending you out of the country."

"Now you're talking." I shifted in my chair, my pulse racing with excitement.

An hour and a half later, we wrapped up the meeting. Nerves settled, worry dissolved, I hooked my arm around Sophie's and invited her to lunch. She took me to a new bistro within walking distance and we ordered salads topped with grilled chicken and roasted pears.

"Tell me all about . . ." I couldn't think of Mr. Hottie's name to save my life.

"Alex," she answered, her cheeks flaming as she spoke his name. "He's perfect."

"No one's perfect, Sophie," I warned. Relaxing my forehead, easing the crinkle between my eyebrows, I tried again. "But he's good to you? A gentleman?"

"Oh, yes. He opens doors, calls when he says he will, and the other day . . ." Her voice became background noise as I let my mind wander. Now that my freak-out was a thing of the past, I planned on dropping Sophie back off at work and doing some clothes shopping. My upcoming trip to the prison parking lot—a whole new source of excitement and anxiety—was a great excuse for something new.

I looked up to find Sophie looking at me expectantly. I must've missed a question and she was waiting for an answer. By the way she was grinning, looking hopeful; it was a safe bet to answer with a nod.

"Yeah, I think so, too," she answered. My curiosity played with me, desperate to find out what I just agreed with her about. Had she asked me if I thought he was the best looking guy on the planet? Or did I think he would propose? Soon? Oh, God, I should've paid attention.

After saying our goodbyes, I drove three blocks to a street lined with small boutiques. Surely I could find something feminine but not frilly, figure-enhancing but not slutty, and cheap enough for my budget.

Seventeen

Cooper

Writing letters was not my thing. I couldn't wait for the day I could send a text or voicemail again. A simple note—brief and to the point—was easy enough, but Briley complained. She wanted details. What was I supposed to tell her? This place sucked. The food wasn't fit for an animal, I was surrounded by men that either wanted to kick my ass or make me their bitch, and I hadn't had a decent night's sleep since I got here.

Instead, I'd commend her on her promotion. Tell her how proud I was of her writing. She needed to hear these things. I knew Blake never told her. He either didn't know what a fragile soul she was, or didn't care. I believed the latter. Prick.

Briley,

Congratulations! I'm so proud of you. This is a great opportunity for you and you deserve it. You're very talented.

Shit. My mind didn't want to be controlled. My fingers scribbled what was really on my mind.

Are you afraid of me? Do you know that I would never hurt you? The only reason I did what I did was because I was protecting you. I miss you, beautiful. I miss your big doe eyes, the way your long dark hair sweeps across your back when you walk, the sound of your laughter, and the way you fit perfectly in my arms. I love that we've been so close all our lives, but I want more. I need more. Are you afraid of me, B? Don't be. I would never hurt you.

After wadding the note up and tossing it into the trash bin, I wrote what she needed to hear—I was great, looking forward to a hot shower and my favorite jeans. I asked her if there were any good movies out because I was craving buttered popcorn. After addressing the envelope but not licking the seal—they would open it and read it anyway—I handed it to the guard and got ready for my shift.

***

The only good thing about laundry duty was the music. Harris was one of the cooler guards and played some pretty good jams while we worked. Hip hop was never my favorite, but it was growing on me and internally I rapped along with Wiz Khalifa. When the song ended, my mind took over and I started worrying about my job.

In a week I'd find out just how secure my position was. Colin Tyler, a buddy from college and I owned a construction business. He was overwhelmed, but running things on his own while I was incarcerated. According to my father, he'd hired some help, but hadn't replaced me and was keeping his word. No matter how close we said we were, I knew a man needed to watch out for himself. Especially when a girl was in the picture. A fiancé to be exact.

It's difficult for a man with a rap sheet to find a job, so I was counting on Colin to pull through for me. If we'd owned our company outright, it wouldn't be an issue, but we were still paying off a couple of small loans. Although my sources said I didn't have anything to worry about, there wasn't much else to do in this place. So I worried.

I was pulling a load of T-shirts out of the dryer when I heard the commotion. Two of Isaac Khan's gang members had Harris pinned against the wall while Khan drew back a fist and slammed it into his gut. He got in another punch to the gut and one to the face before I decided what to do. If I interfered, rescuing a guard, it would be as good as painting a target on my back. It would've been a no brainer if the playing field had been even but three against one set me off.

"I always knew you were a pussy, Khan, but needing so much help to throw a punch . . ." I shook my head as I walked closer. "What do you say we level the playing field?"

By the look on his face, I'd raised his rage level to a new height. He looked at the guys holding Harris and nodded in my direction. At the same time, as if they'd been programmed to follow his every command, they dropped Harris and came after me. Harris dropped to the floor, coughing and sputtering while trying to reach for his baton.

I knocked one of the Khan members out as he approached but the other two held their own. Before Harris and three more guards got control of the situation, I'd received a bloody lip and what would later be a swollen, black eye. The others were worse off but it'd been a long time since anyone had gotten that many blows in on me.

Eighteen

Briley

Disney World. By myself. The way I was moping as I walked toward the kitchen was despicable. All the years I begged my parents to take me to the Magic Kingdom and now I was complaining. But this was different and I should be grateful for the promotion. My passion for food and writing weighed equally on my balance scale, so I should be skipping through town like Buddy the Elf after landing this job. *I just wish Coop could go.* It was always better to experience things with someone else. Sunsets were always more magnificent when witnessed together and I felt the same about food.

With my hands wrapped around my favorite *Zombie Defense Serum* coffee mug, I blew the steam from the hot brew. After the first sip, I felt it working its magic, awakening my tired eyes first, then moving down to my limbs. Staring into the cup, maybe out of boredom or perhaps I thought it held wisdom, an idea sprouted.

Before I could second guess my brazenness, I dialed my boss.

"Angela Corbould."

"Hi, Angela, Briley Sheffield. I was wondering . . . would it be possible to swap the D.C. and Disney trip?"

"It shouldn't be a big deal, what's up?"

I don't want to go by myself. I mean, who goes to Disney alone? "I'm excited about D.C. and I feel like I can put out a great first article, starting there. There's a lot going on right now, like the national barbeque competition."

"I don't want an article on a rib cook-off, Briley," she warned.

"No, no, of course not. But if we need any fillers . . . you know, I could have Evan get some shots of the competition, maybe one with the winner. We could add some links at the bottom. Or maybe a top ten list of events in the area. We don't have to . . . just thinking it might be good to have extra rather than not enough material."

"It's a good idea. Make it happen. You have everything you need?"

"I do. I'll check flights now. Thanks."

Before I could take a seat in front of the computer, my cell vibrated.

"Hello?"

"Hey, it's Madison. Got plans today?"

"Sorry, I'm working today and trying to get a flight out this evening."

"Bummer." She sighed.

"I'm curious though, what did you have in mind?"

"Whatever. Shopping, lunch, or hanging out by the pool."

"Any of that sounds wonderful, but I'll have to take a rain check. I'll be back Thursday morning and still need to find an outfit. Wanna join me?" My lip was raw from all my nervous chewing. This trip came at the wrong time and it was stressing me out. I needed to find something to wear, get my head straight and my nerves calm before Friday but there wasn't time. Or, maybe it was good that I didn't have time to think about picking Cooper up. Wondering if all the prisoners would be standing around shouting obscenities or not had me on edge.

Madison took in a long breath and blew it out. "I have to work."

"You work odd hours, what do you do exactly?" I hoped that didn't sound as rude as it came out.

"I'm a nurse. I work three twelve hour shifts a week."

"Wow," I thought for a minute. "That's a fantastic schedule."

"Yeah, sometimes. Unless you're a masochist like me and do all three in a row. By the third day I've worked thirty nine hours and I'm a zombie."

Glancing down at my zombie mug, now refilled with my second cup of get-up-and-go, I smirked.

"We'll connect when I get back and make something work." *As long as it didn't interfere with Cooper's release day.* I'd also need some time with him to hang out, catch up.

"Sounds good. I liked hanging out with you the other day."

When our conversation ended, I sat down at my desk and waited for the computer to boot up. My new friendship with Madison was a good thing. Great, actually. Since Cooper had been gone, I'd craved friendship. Maybe Madison would be good for me. When Coop returned, he and I could still hang out, but he wouldn't feel obligated to be with me as much. He needed his friends—guys to shoot the shit with and have those pissing contests to prove their manhood against each other.

Coop also needed a girlfriend. I knew I was holding him back. Growing up he had very few girlfriends and I was to blame. People always got the wrong idea about us, thinking we were a couple. Blake, too, was concerned about my relationship with Cooper. He always came up with ways to foil any plans I had with him.

Blake . . . creepy bastard. I couldn't say his name anymore without tagging him to a nasty adjective. Blake-the-dickhead, Blake-the-S.O.B. I shook him out of my mind and concentrated on Cooper. He needed a girlfriend. Deserved the love of a woman. And coming out of prison . . . he was probably desperate for feminine affection.

Nineteen

Cooper

Three days left until my release and all I could think about was Briley. I tucked one of her letters—the one with her latest poem—in my sock and took it to the yard with me today. Since I only had two more days, I took advantage of the bars and got in a good workout. Fifty of each—pull ups, pushups, dips, and sit ups.

After the workout, I took a seat across the yard on a stone bench. It was nice to have some time to myself, away from the noise. I pulled out Briley's letter and read her poem.

As the rain dances on the pavement,
As the clouds blanket an otherwise
beautiful day,
I think of you and what you mean.

You mean to me sunlight,
peace on earth,
good will toward men,
sugar and spice and all things nice.
So that is why . . .
Without you there are only
thunderstorms, grayness, and faceless people.

Everything has lost its meaning:
Birds sing melancholy madness,

flowers' beauty quickly fades,
and now I know all too well,
that smiles and love are easily taken away.

The poem wasn't written for me, I knew that. But it was beautiful and transparent, giving me a glimpse into Briley's soul. It didn't hurt anyone to pretend the words were written for me.

Focused on the paper in my hands, I didn't notice the small group gathered nearby. Before I knew what was happening— Isaac Khan, the cocky little Asian from the laundry room fight had my letter in his hands.

"What the ever living fuck?" I spun around, facing Isaac and five of his boys.

"What's this?" He taunted, holding the note and sniffing along the center of it like a pair of lace panties. "She smells sweet."

Envisioning his black eyes rolling around in my bloodied hands, I squared my shoulders and faced him. "The letter. Now." I darted my eyes from his face to my open palm and back to his face again. "Now, motherfucker."

Enjoyment flashed through his eyes as he lifted the letter and began to read. "I think of you and what you mean." Raising the pitch of his voice, he mocked her words. "You mean to me sunlight, peace on earth, good will toward men, sugar . . ." He glanced at the guy on his left, including him in the game. "Sugar and spice? Pretty boy here's a faggot."

The jeering comments came from all five of them, bringing my blood to a boiling point. Snatching the letter, I shoved it in the back pocket of my pants. The sliver of composure I clung to was fading. Securing my focus on a bead of sweat trailing his forehead, I reminded myself, *three days. Three days until you're out. Don't blow it over this fucktard.*

"You get out Friday, pretty boy?" The punk shook his head. "Might as well put her outta your mind. I've got three more weeks and then I'm coming for her." He pumped his pelvis, fucking the air. "I'm gonna fuck her so good, she won't want your pansy ass."

The others made licking and sucking noises, but the sound of blood pumping in my ears drowned them out. My head pounded, begging me to unleash my fury on this little bald headed pussy. In a flash, my hands were wrapped around his throat, pulling him so close to my face that I could make out the pupils in his black eyes.

Through gritted teeth I spat, "If you so much as think about my girl, I'll slit your fucking throat."

Fear flashed in his eyes for a moment, then a smirk. My arms were jerked behind me, pinning me as Isaac's fist reared back and sank into my gut.

Cupping his crotch, he leered. "I'm gonna tear that pussy up."

Using the two guys holding my arms as leverage, I leaned back and kicked him, hard enough to knock him to the ground and loose the grip of my capturers. Like a snake, I was on him. One hand gripped his throat, holding him on the ground, while the other pounded into his face. His hands came up, blocking many of my blows, but I didn't stop until I felt warm, slick blood on my hands.

With an acid tongue, I growled each word, "I. will. kill. you. One *thought* and I'll fuck you up, Buddha."

I guess I should've been surprised that no one tried to pull me off him. Were they shocked or suddenly on my side?

Standing, I looked around and my questions were answered. One of the guards—Fitzpatrick—was walking toward us. I made eye contact with him and my body stiffened. *Fuck! If I don't get out of here on time, I'll fucking kill this Asian prick!* Fitzpatrick kept his knowing gaze on me for another moment before turning to talk to another guard. I knew at that moment I was screwed.

Yard time ended and we were all ushered back inside. Fitzpatrick stood at the gate, his eyes fixed on me. No one cared who started fights, how or why one was provoked, they only punished. They were bred for it. Actually got off on prolonging someone's sentence. When I passed by, I thought briefly of turning my head the other way. But I wasn't ashamed of finally giving that prick what was coming to him, so I stood tall.

I heard him whisper as I passed, "I've got your back."

Surprised and confused, I kept walking forward. What did that mean, he had my back? No one had my back after I protected the guard in the laundry room.

Questions for another day.

Twenty

Briley

Finally home from D.C., I dropped my suitcase by the door and collapsed onto the couch. Every part of me was exhausted. My legs were tired from walking, my arms and hands from writing, but mostly my brain was drained from the strings of thought spider-webbing through my head. A hot bath and a glass of wine were a necessity.

Peeling myself off the couch, I walked over to the suitcase by the door and rolled it into my bedroom. Moving like a robot, I put my toiletries back in their place, hung my dress clothes in the closet, placed my shoes on the rack, and dumped my dirty clothes into the hamper. After tucking my suitcase on a shelf in the guest room closet, I trekked back to the bathroom and started a lavender-infused bubble bath.

I poured a glass of Malbec while the tub filled, turned on my computer, and laid my notes from the trip on the desk beside it. I'd have to finish the article tonight, and hopefully I'd recover enough from the much needed soak to get it done.

Stepping into the hot water, I sighed as the water caressed my skin and eased the tension in my neck. My phone lay beside me on the edge of the vanity, pouring the sultry sounds of Sevyn Streeter into the room. Although the lyrics meant nothing to me, I loved the sway of the song.

Breaking the enchantment, my cell buzzed repeatedly with an incoming call. *Should've put it on silent.* It was probably my boss, wondering how the trip went. Or my mother. Reaching while trying to keep most of my body enveloped in the warmth of the water, I fingered for the edge of my phone. Stretching until I finally reached it, I swiped the answer button before checking the caller ID. *Mistake.*

I answered, trying but failing to keep annoyance out of my voice. "Hello?"

"How could someone so beautiful sound so irritable?" Blake's voice coursed through the phone, chilling me to the bone and ruining my bath.

"What-do-you-want?" I hissed through clenched teeth.

"I called to check on you, babe. I know you don't want to hear it, but I love you, Br—"

Without letting him finish, I ended the call. Just to be sure I wasn't bothered with the buzzing of incoming calls or texts again, I shut the phone off. Sinking back down into the water until only the tops of my shoulders were exposed, I cried. Not the sad cry of a girl with a broken heart. A full blown, all out wailing of someone who was hurt and thoroughly pissed.

After towel-drying my hair and body, I wrapped myself up in a thick robe, slid my feet into slippers, and poured another glass of wine. The crying jag had to be pushed aside. I had an article to finish.

Twenty-One

Cooper

Today was the day. Freedom at last. I should've been overjoyed, thinking about a hot shower, warm bed, and medium-rare steak. Instead I was as nervous as a kid in the principal's office. Being picked up by my father—surely Mom stayed behind, this was no place for her—had shame coursing through me like blistering lava.

After signing all of the papers, gathering my few belongings, and nodding a "fuck you" goodbye to the guards, I walked down the hall toward the door to "never-looking-back."

Stepping out into the sunlight every day in the yard didn't hold a candle to standing beneath the same rays outside the prison walls. I inhaled the fresh air, a smile creeping into the corners of my mouth, and closed my eyes to take it all in. Opening them, I took a step forward and my world began to spin.

It was one of those feelings that stuck, forming a memory so vivid and strong you didn't need to record it any other way. There she stood, fidgeting with the fabric of her pale blue dress. My legs defied me, refusing to move. Instead I stood there like a fool, studying her features. She was the complete package, sexy and angelic, sassy and sweet, soft with curves in all the right places. Her dark hair fell in loose waves around her shoulders, framing the face that held those large, almond shaped pools of dark chocolate and full lips of delicious ripe fruit.

Shit, it'd been a long time since I was around a woman. Whose idea was it to throw Briley at me first thing? Suddenly I felt like a sixth grade boy, unable to tame the hormones running through me. My palms were sweaty . . . hell, I could feel beads of sweat forming all over. Briley coming here was a cruel punishment and at the same time, the best gift.

Pull it together, Coop!

My body obeyed, causing my legs to take one halting step and then another in her direction. She looked timid, almost scared to move from her post against the white Maxima. It took forever to reach her, but when I did, she pushed herself off the car and stood tall before me.

"What are you doing here?" I asked, worried something had happened to one of my parents. It didn't make sense for her to be here.

"What kind of greeting is that?" She answered and flung herself into me so hard I nearly lost my balance. Her arms tightened around my waist as I held her, one hand on her back, the other stroking her hair.

She felt so good in my arms—her head cradled in the dip of my chest—a perfect fit. Inhaling her scent—freshly shampooed hair, the vanilla-scented lotion she'd used for years mingling with her skin—a scent that belonged solely to her. I closed my eyes taking her in. Whispering into her hair, I asked, "Is everything . . . everyone all right?"

I felt her nod against my chest. "Your dad said it'd be okay if I picked you up. I think he knew I . . ."

She trailed off and my instincts took over. I pulled her in tighter and kissed the top of her head. No telling how badly her asshole fiancé treated her while I was gone. With no one to hold him accountable, he was probably taking what he wanted and giving her leftovers. I shook the prick out of my mind and savored the feeling of Briley in my arms while she was mine. When her body began to tremble, reality along with my shoulders sank in. She was afraid of me.

Pulling back, I rested my hands gently on her shoulders.

"B? It's okay. I'm still me, don't be afraid."

She looked up, tears trailing down her porcelain cheeks and stared at me for a moment before punching me playfully in the gut.

"What're you talking about, you big idiot! I'm not afraid of you." She shook her head. "Did you lose your sanity in there or something?"

I gawked at her. Like the idiot she accused me of being, I just stood there wide-eyed and stared at her waiting for clarity.

"I'm happy to see you, Coop. These are tears of joy." She shook her head again and mumbled to herself. "Scared. Hmph. Of Coopy Sterling?"

I could've done without the added giggle. I wasn't a teddy bear after all. Most people *were* afraid of me. Briley never had a reason to fear me, but after what I'd done to Matt and spending the last seventeen months in prison, it wasn't that farfetched an idea.

"Hey now," I began, casually flexing my biceps. "I'm a big guy. You might show a little respect."

She rolled her eyes. "And I forgot about all those tattoos. You *are* dangerous." She feigned a shiver of fear.

"Damn straight, baby." I flashed a wink.

"Oh, Coop!" She flung her arms around me again. "It's so good to have you back."

After tossing my bag in the back, I climbed into the passenger seat. Her car was small compared to my truck and I preferred driving rather than riding, but I was so happy to be out of the joint, I was tempted to stick my head out the window like a dog, lapping up the air of freedom.

I watched her as she shifted gears and pulled out of the parking lot onto the main road. Everything about her was perfect, even the way her long, tapered fingers gripped the shift knob. When she was in fifth gear she relaxed, glancing over every now and then as she chattered about this and that.

"What did you miss most? What's the first thing you want to do or eat? Did you meet anyone in there? Was it like in the movies or much different? Why wouldn't you let me visit?"

"Good God, woman. One question at a time! I'm craving steak. And a beer. And shit, I could go for an ice cream."

"All at once?"

"No," I smirked. "Let's stop for an ice cream first."

Twenty-Two

Briley

Sitting across from Cooper in the ice cream shop, I watched him savor his two scoops of chocolate chunk ice cream while I poked my spoon around in a cup of pineapple sherbet. He'd lost weight, or it seemed he had. He looked bigger than he ever had but his jawline was more pronounced and when he smiled, his dimples sank deeper into his cheeks. As he brought the cone up to his mouth for another taste, I watched his tongue wipe the excess from his full lips. He glanced up and smiled an easy, playful smile that took me back fifteen years.

He was the same Cooper I'd known all my life, until I studied his eyes. His most dominant feature was vibrant, mountain meadow green eyes. All the girls swooned over them and I often made fun of him, calling him 'my little grasshopper.' But now they were pale—more chartreuse with flecks of yellow—and tired . . . or sad?

"Cooper, was it awful?"

He looked up from what was left of his devoured cone and shook his head. "Like camping without a fire. The beds were awful, food was crap, but it wasn't so bad."

I didn't believe him. After all these years, why did he think he could pull one over on me? Maybe he just didn't want to talk about it. I could understand that.

"Hey! I've made some plans and I hope you're on board."

He glowered. "C'mon, B, no parties. I don't want the attention."

"No parties." I held up my hands in surrender. "I thought we could have a family dinner tomorrow night."

"Now that sounds great. Meat . . . *real* meat and beer."

"Well, tomorrow night your mom wanted to fix all of your favorites, so it's Chicken parmesan." That brought a smile to his lips, popping those killer dimples again. "I'm bringing Key lime pie."

"Thanks, B. That sounds perfect."

"And then . . ." I twisted my hands in my lap nervously. "I've invited some friends over on Saturday?" It was a statement, I'd already invited them, but I presented it as a question. I guess if Cooper really hated the idea I could make something up, find a way to cancel.

He took a deep breath in, held it for a moment, and exhaled like he was savoring a joint. "Thanks, B, but—"

"It's just a barbecue, Coop," I pleaded. "Steaks and beer. I've only asked a few people over. Ryan and whoever he's currently dating, Colin and Claire, and my neighbor, Madison. It's really a get together for her. She's new in town and I wanted her to meet you."

"All right, B. You had me at steaks and beer." His lips twitched into a half smile, half smirk.

After tossing my half eaten sherbet, I grabbed my keys and hooked my arm through Cooper's as we walked to the car.

"Wanna drive?" I asked.

"Yes," he breathed. "Thank you."

***

Nearing town, panic set in. I guess that's what it was? My chest felt tight, my heart rate accelerated. For some reason, I didn't want to spend the night at my place alone. I'd just gotten my best friend back and had so many questions, so much to tell him.

In unison we called out each other's names.

"Go ahead," he urged.

"You're stopping by your parents?"

He nodded. "Want to come with?"

Working my lower lip between my teeth, I thought about crashing his reunion with Mr. and Mrs. Sterling. *C'mon, B, don't be so selfish.* "No." I shook my head, convincing the rest of me to agree. "But if you're not too tired afterwards, maybe you could stop by my place?" I didn't dare look at him. Of course he was exhausted. He'd just spent close to a year and a half in prison, sleeping on a cot. Probably had one eye open, making sure no one would knife him in his sleep. Jeez, what was I thinking? He needed a hot shower, a beer, and a good night's sleep. "Or if you're too tired, I understand. Forget I asked. We'll catch up tomorrow."

He pulled the car to a stop at the four-way and looked at me for a long time without saying a word. There was tension between us that I wasn't used to and honestly, I didn't care for the feeling. Cooper was the only one I'd ever felt completely at ease with. I could say anything, do anything, and wear anything around him without a care in the world. Even my mother gave me the worried eye if my hair was messy or I lounged in my favorite ratty sweats all day. But Cooper acted like everyone should be in ratty sweat pants all day.

"What's up with you, B?" Cooper asked.

"Nothing, why?"

"You're gnawing on your lip like a detoxing junkie."

"You can go now, Coop." I looked around, waiting for a car to pull up behind us and start honking.

"No one's in a hurry. What is this?" He waved his finger back and forth between us. "I feel like you're not telling me something."

An audible sigh left my lips without my permission, informing my cheeks to heat under the pressure. Too late for propriety, I let the words flow at leisure. "I know you're exhausted. Probably want a hot shower, cold beer, and a good porno. But selfishly, I want to hang out with you. I've missed you." After inhaling for another round, I let loose. "I'm sorry for being narcissistic, but it's been lonely without you, Coop." I risked looking into his eyes—a mistake. A glint of amusement flashed in them. At least the vibrancy of color was back, reminding me of the green meadow again. "S-D-F."

"What?"

"It's my new favorite curse word. Stands for shit, damn, fuck," I whispered the spellings as if my mother might overhear.

"For shit's sake, B. Are you still too timid to cuss?"

"No." I answered defiantly. If he only knew the obscenities I'd spewed to Blake in the past few months. I'd changed since Coop went away and Blake shattered my self esteem. Cursing was a newfound freedom I'd taken up and enjoyed more than I should have.

He laughed. More than was normal. I started to worry when a car behind us started honking, but Cooper didn't move. He was smacking the steering wheel as the laughter completely took hold of him.

"God, I needed that. There's no . . . laughing in . . . prison," he managed to say between chortles. "And I'd love to come over, on two conditions."

"Name it," I challenged.

"You have cold beer in the fridge and Blake's not there." His face grew serious when he spoke Blake's name. In the past, it was an off-the-table topic. He was obviously testing the waters.

Instead of explaining, I simply agreed, "It's a deal."

Twenty-Three

Cooper

Even a grown man feels like a kid again stepping through the door of his childhood home. My mother was dressed in dark slacks and a blue blouse, much too dressy for their night in front of the television. She stood on her tip toes, wrapping her arms around my neck in a tight, motherly squeeze. Lifting her off the ground, I spun her around, listening to her squeal.

"I'm so happy you're finally home! You look thin." She raced off to the kitchen, calling over her shoulder. "What can I fix you? Sandwich, leftover lasagna . . ."

"No, thanks, Mom. I've already eaten." I lied. Telling her I'd filled up on ice cream would not have been a smart move.

Dad and I shook hands before he pulled me in for one of those manly shake-hug-pat moves that men tend to share. It felt as awkward as it probably looked and the moment grew more uncomfortable as he looked at me. It was as if he knew how badly I wanted to get out of there and over to Briley's.

"How'd ya like the pickup arrangement?" My father winked. Things hadn't changed since Junior prom. He'd known I'd fallen in love with Briley way before I was clued in. Now he watched me expectantly, like he was waiting to hear I'd proposed in the car.

"It was nice to see Briley. She looks . . . good." I searched my father's eyes for insight into what might be bothering her. She did look amazing, but something was off. I assumed it was me, hoped it wasn't anything more. I could fix the tension between us if that's all it was.

"You have plans tonight?"

"I thought I'd stop by her place before heading home."

My father yawned. It was obvious and exaggerated and I almost called him on it. "Well, I'm sure you're exhausted. I know I am. You go on and we'll talk tomorrow. Your keys are in the truck, under the mat."

***

After leaving my parents', I stopped by my place for a quick shower and shave. The place hadn't changed, everything was just as I left it. *And why wouldn't it be?* I thought to myself as I looked around before stepping into the shower.

The only luxuries we were afforded in prison were deodorant and toothpaste. As much as I wanted to be with Briley, I was desperate for a hot shower and change of clothes.

Feeling human again, I rifled through my T-shirt drawer until I found the charcoal gray shirt and khaki board shorts I was hunting for. Damn, I didn't realize how much I'd missed flip-flops until I slipped them on.

Pulling into Briley's driveway, my heart began to race. Time in prison allowed for only one thing . . . being alone with your thoughts. What I'd learned in all that time was life was too fucking short to be a pussy. I'd always gone after what I wanted and why I didn't fight harder for Briley was beyond me. But I had every intention of making it right this time. I'd find a way to make her see that Blake was a prick and I was the man for her.

Squaring my shoulders, I stepped up to the door and rang the bell.

Twenty-Four

Briley

Hugging Cooper was the right thing to do and something I'd done a thousand times without a second thought. Bringing my arms up and around his neck, however, seemed like the most difficult task I would ever perform. My limbs felt heavy and awkward, as if they were robotic parts I had to control remotely. Too much time had passed. Twenty-five years of friendship instantly erased and replaced with something awkward in less than two years.

Cooper squeezed me tight, a second longer than was comfortable, and pulled back. He wore a smile that made me feel even less comfortable. Something stirred inside of me as I took in his appearance. His tight charcoal shirt clung to the ripples beneath and hugged his arms, covering only half of the new cross tattoo adorning his left shoulder.

With hands on my hips, I raked my eyes over his beautiful body, surprised by the effect it had on me. It had been at least four months since I'd been intimate with Blake . . . with anyone . . . and years—if you counted the hormone-raged make out session when we were teens—since I looked at Cooper in a sexual way. Yet, there it was, that lustful ping in the pit of my belly.

"I thought we were hanging out. You're dressed up and I'm in ratty sweats," I complained. I felt ugly and unkempt. "I'll change."

He grabbed my arm and spun me back around to face him. "Don't you dare. You look perfect. I haven't worn shorts in seventeen months, it feels good."

Looks good, too, I thought to myself, feeling the heat rise to my cheeks. "All right," I turned around so he couldn't see my cheeks. "Have a seat." I waved my hand toward the couch and began walking toward the kitchen. "I have Corona, Rolling Rock, or—" Before I could fish through the fridge, I felt his presence. He was standing too close behind me, peering through the open door.

"I'd love a Rolling Rock, thanks." He reached around me, grabbing one, along with a bottle of Corona for me. "You got a lime?"

"Jeez, you scared me. I thought you were in the living room. I'm the host, I'll serve the drinks."

His arms flew up in defense. "'Scuse me. Should I start calling you Mrs. Cleaver?" He laughed, a contagious sound that had me giggling too, releasing the uncomfortable air between us.

"Fine. I'll cut the lime while you search the pantry and find us some pretzels, or pop a bag of popcorn."

Cooper and I stood watching the microwave the entire three and a half minutes until the popcorn was finished. Standing there, I tried to think of something to start the conversation, but came up short. What did one say to someone just out of prison? *So, how was your mattress? Did you make any friends? Enemies? Do you have a law degree now?* It seemed that most prisoners these days were getting degrees. *You look amazing, I can tell you've been working out. Do you feel this electric buzz in the air between us or is it just me? Is that gross?*

We made our way to the living room, the bottles nearly drained already. He must have been as uncomfortable as I was. Or he was thirsty.

"Another beer?" I started to stand before the backs of my legs even hit the couch cushion.

"I'll get them."

I couldn't help looking at his ass as he walked away. *Cripes, what is wrong with me?* Cooper had changed, physically and most likely emotionally. I knew I had. I'd been through hell with Blake and it changed my perspective on things. Opened my eyes, to say the least. But that was no excuse for threatening a relationship built over the years on trust and transparency. I couldn't and wouldn't risk our friendship by testing the romantic waters. I must've been sex starved and half crazed but that wasn't a lasting situation. Like a virus, I'd get over it in time.

Cooper returned and set another Corona with a lime wedge on the coffee table in front of me. I downed half of it and held it between my palms like a security blanket.

"Christ, B, some reason you need to get drunk?"

My head whipped around. "No." My answer came out a little too defensively. "Just thirsty." I handed him the bowl of popcorn. "Here, have some."

He set it on the table before turning in his seat to face me. One leg was crossed, his ankle resting just below a massive thigh that strained against the dark denim. "How've you been, B?"

"Great," I answered with the perkiness of a Chihuahua. "My job is going well and I've been . . . great." As much as I wanted to fill him in on all of the bullshit that had happened while he was gone, it wasn't fair to pile it on him now. He just got out of prison and deserved at least one night to just relax and watch some mind numbing reality TV. I stood, walked over to the television, and grabbed the remote.

"*Great,*" he mocked me. "Now that we've gotten over the formalities, tell me how you've *really* been. And none of this *let's just chill and watch some television,* crap. You've got one shot to get your fourteen thousand words out." He winked, flashing a smile that had me fumbling to catch the remote I'd nearly dropped.

"I—well, you just cut straight through the bullshit, don't you?" I lowered myself gracefully onto the couch beside him, grabbing a cranberry and sage plaid throw pillow to hold on to.

"Always have. From what I remember, so do you. Have you changed that much?"

Yes, I thought as the sadness of my situation covered me like a blanket of soot. "No, but it looks like you have." My eyes defied me and traveled over his physique. "What've you done?"

"You've seen in the movies, prisoners so bored all they do is workout. Well, it's true. We had yard time to work out, and when you're in the cage, you can either read or work out. I'll give you two guesses which I preferred." He chuckled, revealing a smile that took me back ten years.

He had a brilliant mind, but he hated to read. Sure, he read to further his knowledge, but hand him a romance novel or mystery-thriller and his eyes glossed over.

"You look really good, Cooper." As hard as I tried to keep my eyes on his to avoid gawking at his marvelous new body, my eyes disobeyed and stole quick glimpses. He had changed drastically from the boy I'd played with and even from the college guy I'd played darts with.

Outwardly, he was a different man. Had he changed on the inside, too? In all our years together, my thoughts had never strayed from anything more than friendship. It wasn't that he was unattractive . . . he just didn't spark anything for me. Now, during the most inopportune moment—as I sat before him in sweats, my hair in a messy bun—I couldn't stop checking him out.

"You're as stunning as you've always been, B." His eyes locked on mine and remained there.

Coming from the man I had played with in the mud, taken baths with as a child, and trusted with my deepest secrets, his compliment shouldn't have affected me, but it did. Heat rushed to my cheeks and I felt it flaming down my neck. I studied the creases of my knuckles intently, waiting for my flesh to cool. The ridiculousness of it finally took hold of me—a movie slap moment—bringing me back to reality. Cooper and I were friends, buddies, nothing more. I knew everything about him, from the China-shaped—or moose-shaped, if I wanted to razz him—birthmark on his left calf, to his abnormal fear of snakes. I didn't want anything more than friendship from him.

What I felt was a response any woman in my situation would have. Cheated by love and wanting someone to make the hurt go away, I'd have to be careful who I took my frustration out on. A failed engagement was bad enough; losing my best friend would destroy me.

Before I could look up, he lifted my chin with his forefinger and tapped my nose, just as he did when we were kids. "What's going on, B?" He glanced around the living room. "Where's Blake, anyway?"

I shook my head, wanting to talk about anything other than Blake. But if I knew Cooper, he'd get it out of me sooner rather than later.

"I'm fine, Coop." I shifted, a sure giveaway that I wasn't telling the truth. Cooper was the better liar of the two of us. If we were ever caught doing something we shouldn't, he did the explaining.

"Cut the crap, B. Your ears still turn red when you lie, just like the night I split my lip and you got us busted for sneaking out. You remember that?"

Fourteen-year-old Cooper had been bleeding like a stuck pig and I caved like a cheap suitcase—admitting our transgression before our parents even asked. He ended up with three stitches and we were both grounded for two weeks. "I don't want to talk about it." I shrugged a shoulder and sucked on my bottom lip. "Besides, shouldn't we be talking about how *you're* doing?"

"I'm fine." His eyebrows knit together in frustration. "I've spent the last seventeen months in prison trying to figure out a way to get you away from this prick . . ." He raised his hand to stop me from interrupting. "I know, you don't want me bad mouthing your fiancé, but I won't sit back and watch him destroy the wom—destroy you, B. You know—"

"He's gone, Cooper. We're not engaged, we're not together, and you can say anything you want about him." It felt like all of the air had been sucked out of my lungs and I couldn't look at him. I felt stupid for not listening to him, humiliated that I wasn't even worthy of Blake's attention for a few months before he began cheating on me.

Cooper scooted closer, taking my hand in his. "What happened, baby?" He'd only called me that once before, when I was in the hospital after having my appendix removed. It was a foreign term to me, but I loved it. The single endearment made me feel cared for. The squeeze of his hands reiterated the sentiment.

"You tried to warn me, I know." My words came out like a sullen teenager awaiting her father's scolding *I told you so* speech.

"What did he do?" He let out a steady breath, obviously trying to reign in the building anger.

"He's a fucking cheater!" I regretted it as soon as I said it. Blake was the bad guy, yet I was the one marinating in shame, taking full responsibility for his actions.

"Are you serious?" he whispered. I couldn't tell if the flash in his eyes was pity or shock. Both made me feel worse. "Who the—?"

"I didn't want to tell you. I didn't want to talk about it at all." The only thing that could make this moment more humiliating was tears. Without warning, they began to fall.

"He's a damn fool, B. Anyone who—"

"Please, Coop. Can we talk about it another time?"

He pulled me in, shifting on the couch so I could settle into his side. We remained there for a time while I cried and released a little more of the sickness Blake had infected me with.

After drying the tears with the backs of my hands and catching my breath, I excused myself for a moment in the bathroom. A scattering of emotions collided inside of me. I recognized a few. I was elated to see Cooper, but at the same time I wanted to yell at him. Why did he have to pummel Matt's face and go away for so long? When I needed him most he wasn't there. The nagging question was why he was sending me vibes that had me all discombobulated, and why in the freaking hell did he have to smell the way he did . . . clean soap mixed with masculinity and topped off with a scent described only as *Cooper.*

Taking my time, I rearranged a small vase of orange zinnias on a side table. If I remembered correctly, they were Cooper's sister, Carleigh's, favorite flowers. Returning to the living room, I plopped down on the sofa next to Cooper and curled my legs up underneath me.

"Better?" he asked.

"Much, thanks. Hey, how's Carleigh?"

Cooper's sister was two years his senior and three years older than me. Growing up I'd envied her beauty and tried to mimic her feminine ways as I stumbled through puberty.

"Good. Did you know she's pregnant with twins?"

"Twins? I knew she was pregnant, but, wow! When is she due?"

"End of July."

"How exciting. You'll be an uncle!" I punched him playfully on the arm. "Uncle Cooper." I tried the name on my tongue. "Or Uncle C. That's it! Uncle C."

"I like it." His lips curled up on one side. "Mom and Dad are going to be G-Ma and G-Pa. They think it sounds cool." He chuckled and gave his best gangster impression. "I can see the babies now, 'What up, G?'"

We shared a hearty laugh and then another awkward silence that I decided needed to be broken. I searched my mind for something to talk about, but my brain resisted and shut down. Cooper's brain was kinder to him, and he spoke first. "How's your writing coming along?"

"Meh. The creativity train hasn't stopped by lately."

"Come on, the last couple of poems you sent were brilliant."

"You have to say that or I'll pour beer on your head," I teased him with the last few drops in the bottle. "I wrote to you about the new job. It pays great and you know I love to travel, but so far it's been dull and I'm having a hard time being passionate about trendy restaurants in towns that aren't that exciting to me. Every time I sit in front of the computer, it just stares at me. I feel like the cursor is tapping its foot impatiently chanting, 'I'm bored . . . I'm bored.'"

"You've been through a lot. It'll come back and you can make that rude cursor dance all over the page." He laughed contagiously and I caught the virus.

It wasn't that funny, but for some reason I couldn't stop laughing. I could hardly catch my breath when my phone interrupted us.

"It's my mom." I shrugged a shoulder and stood to take the call. "Hi, Mom. Yep. Actually, Cooper's here. Yep. Just catching up. I'll call you later, okay?"

Cooper stood and stretched before picking up our empties and carrying them to the kitchen. I loved how comfortable he was, like time hadn't passed.

I, on the other hand, was struggling.

Twenty-Five
Cooper

When I returned from the kitchen, I found Briley standing casually by the window, watching the day transform into twilight. The sky darkened, streaks of red and orange painting the horizon. With her hair piled up in a loose bun, I studied her, noticing all the little areas that I so desperately wanted to touch. The nape of her neck and small of her back. I couldn't take my eyes off her.

By the time she turned, I was right behind her. The proximity startled her at first, but when she flashed a shy smile, I knew it was time. I'd loved her all my life and that love held me back. The fear of losing her always greater than my desire, until now. I had to know if she felt anything. In that moment it seemed worth the risk.

"I'm glad you're here." She smiled. When Briley smiled, her face lit up and her dark eyes sparkled. It was intoxicating.

Those few simple words sent a jolt up my spine and had my heartbeat playing a fast tune inside my chest. Her mouth was so enticing, lips full and moist. She traced her tongue along her bottom lip and I had to take a deep breath to keep my body from igniting on the spot.

Without saying a word, I slid one arm around her waist and pulled her close to me. Our eyes locked and time stood still. I traced my thumb down her cheek and across her jawline before sliding my hand around to the back of her neck. I was desperate to taste her and feel her body against mine, but I took it slow so she had time to back away if she changed her mind.

Her eyes revealed a blend of desire and something else, was it . . . doubt? Eager to erase the latter, I pressed my lips to hers. They were soft and moist, just as I had imagined. What I hadn't anticipated was the electric current traveling through my body. We'd kissed before, years ago, but I didn't remember it feeling like this. My knees nearly buckled when her lips parted, inviting my tongue into her mouth for a slow, sensuous dance.

So many thoughts tried to race through my muddled mind as we stood there making out like teenagers. *She isn't fighting it. God, she tastes amazing. Fuck, I'm hard. I hope she doesn't freak out.* Pulling back, I looked into her eyes, dark with desire. Her chest heaved as she took in shallow, desperate breaths.

Before I could think, my mouth crashed into hers again. I leaned my body in, causing her to take a step back, and pressed her against the wall. With our mouths locked together, tongues continuing to explore with reckless abandon, my hands rested on her waist. I could feel her breasts against my chest, pressing into me with each breath. My right hand traveled under her shirt until I reached her lace bra.

Briley pulled away suddenly, her eyes wide with alarm and a glint of regret.

"Oh, god, what are we doing?" She wiped her mouth with the back of her hand and turned away from me.

"Don't do that, B. Look at me." I took her by the arm and tried to turn her around, but she shook me off. "Briley. Look at me."

Slowly, she turned and inch by inch she raised her eyes to find mine. "I'm sorry, Cooper. I shouldn't have . . . we . . . I think you should go."

"What happened, B? You felt something, you can't deny—"

"Please, Cooper. Please, go." Tears trailed down her cheeks, making me feel like an asshole. If you're lucky enough, one person will come into your life, remove the cobwebs of your filthy soul, extinguish the demons residing there, and fill it with light and love. Briley was that one person for me. I'd kill for her. I'd die for her. Instead, I'd made her cry.

"I'll go."

I walked to the front door and gripped the knob. Holding it for a moment, I turned to look at her once more before leaving. Her arms were crossed against her chest, hugging herself as she gently shook.

"Will you be all right?"

She nodded.

Driving home I replayed the evening over again in my head. *Everything felt so right; where did it go wrong? Was she really afraid of me, or did Blake hurt her more than she let on? Maybe she didn't have feelings beyond friendship . . . but the way she looked at me, the way she kissed me. Her feelings were real; I saw it in her eyes.*

Slamming my fist against the steering wheel, I cursed the air. We both needed a good night's sleep. All would be clear in the morning.

Before drifting off to sleep, I sent her a text. I wouldn't apologize for kissing her. She needed to be kissed, and by someone who loved her. But I was sorry for making her cry.

After erasing four texts that made me sound like a pussy, I settled on short and sweet and hit send:

1 4 3

Twenty-Six
Briley

Ignoring two texts and three phone messages wasn't helping my case in avoiding Cooper. I'd managed to avoid him for fifteen hours, but he infiltrated my thoughts like a bandit, robbing me of sleep and nourishment. Nothing satisfied my hunger or quenched my thirst and I'd tossed around the bed all night.

Curled up in my favorite chair with a blanket I'd had since college—a T-shirt collage Mom made me using shirts from various trips and races—I flipped through the channels and landed on Millionaire Matchmaker. The episode began with a male bachelor looking for love. He was a millionaire, and had earned his money from an accident. Apparently he was hit by a drunk truck driver, and sued the trucking company. He grew his wealth by investing in a few small companies, including a gadget invention that organized all of your chords and made them disappear under the desk or behind the television. It was obvious he came into money quickly and didn't know what to do with it, or himself. I could always spot the difference in new money versus old money. People who grew up with money didn't try as hard to show it off. They dressed comfortably, talked freely, and didn't really care which fork you were supposed to use, unless of course, they were attending a formal event.

The ones with new money always made sure the labels of their expensive shirts were visible, their watches looked too new, and they carried themselves differently. Trying too hard to be snobbish. I'd never met anyone with new money that didn't tell me what kind of car they drove or how much they paid for a piece of clothing they were wearing at the moment. Always taking advantage of the opportunity, it excited me to quip back with a remark, whether it was true or not. *"Love the dress. Mine was a hand me down from my dead sister."*

Until a commercial for pool liners interrupted, I was lost in the show, rooting for one of the couples and disgusted with the behavior of the other bachelor. In the background of the commercial, a man dove into a newly screened pool. He came out of the water and shook the moisture from his dark hair. He didn't resemble Cooper in the least, but my mind chose to focus on him anyway, bringing me back to the night before . . . yet again.

No longer able to concentrate on the show, I indulged my conscious and thought about Cooper's soft lips, gentle but urgent against mine. The way his arms wrapped around me, cocooning me in a net of warmth and safety. Was it so wrong to treat myself to the pleasure of Cooper Sterling? Even if it didn't work out, our friendship could survive . . . *couldn't it?*

No, it couldn't. How could I be so selfish? I knew he would never hurt me like Blake did. In fact, he'd stick it out even if he wasn't happy. *Oh, God, I'd make him miserable!* Still, my mind traveled down the forbidden road. An electric current surged through me as I recalled his hands roaming over my body, hungry for . . . *jeez, he's been in prison! Of course! He hasn't been with a woman in almost two years.* Not sure if I should be pissed or feel sorry for him, I threw the blanket off, walked into my office, and took a seat in front of the computer. Work was piling up. It was the perfect anecdote for getting my mind off Cooper.

Tapping my fingernails on the marble topped desk, matching the beat of the impatient cursor, I doubted my capabilities as a writer. Nothing made sense anymore. Did people really care about the difference in olive oils or how to choose good caviar? Would they visit a restaurant because *I* said the lamb was cooked to perfection or the sweet breads were to die for? My fist slammed onto the desk, making a loud noise, but not helping my mood. *I'm a failure . . . at everything. I can't write. I can't think. I can't hold onto a man.*

Just as the tears started to flow, but right before the ugly cry ensued, my phone dinged with an incoming text.

Missing you . . .

Blake! I typed my reply:

WASTE OF TIME

He texted right back:

I love you

Before I could type a nasty reply, my phone dinged again. *You stupid, stupid man! Leave me the hell alone!* I turned my phone upside down on the desk while I thought of my clever, mean-but-not-too-vulgar response. As mad as I was, I'd probably break the glass with my thumbs before I could get the text sent, but I'd try and then turn the thing off before he could get another one out.

The last text that was displayed on my screen made my chest cavity feel as if it were filled with Mexican jumping beans. It wasn't from Blake. It was Cooper.

On my way over. Need to talk to U

Crap! Typing in a response, I lifted my shoulder to wipe a rogue tear from my cheek.

Not a good time. Working.

I raced around the house, picking up dirty dishes and shoes that I'd walked out of and left wherever, knowing he wouldn't listen to me.

2 bad

Too bad? Too bad? I repeated to myself, partly in question, mostly in astonishment. Since when was Cooper so demanding? Okay, always. Glancing at myself in the hall mirror, I ran to the bathroom to run a brush through my hair and a toothbrush over as many teeth as I could hit in two swipes.

I wasn't sure why I cared what I looked like. Cooper and I were friends. I nodded my head as I processed the thought. And we would remain that way, as far as I was concerned. In fact, I should have slipped my sweats back on and eaten a piece of garlic. He deserved better than me. Someone who wouldn't bore him, someone without all of the baggage I came with. I loved him too much to ruin his chance at happiness. But I couldn't help wanting to at least look decent around him.

The doorbell rang and I took in a calming breath, then ran my hands down my white tank and pink shorts, smoothing out as many wrinkles possible, before opening the door.

"Come in." I greeted, hoping my nostrils weren't flaring from the adrenaline rush. "Want some coffee?" I asked, not sure what else to say after our make out-turned-crying-jag session last night.

"Sure. Actually, no, thanks. I came here to say something to you and I'd like to get on with it."

"Okay." We took a seat in the living room, me in my favorite cream-colored overstuffed chair, and Coop across from me on the couch. After sharing an uncomfortable silence and watching him take in the room for the third time, he began.

"You're avoiding me, B and we—"

"I'm not avoiding you," I interrupted. Shifting in my seat, I tucked my legs around in the chair, hoping to appear casual. "I've been working."

"We've known each other too long. I can still read you like a book." He held up a hand, asking me to let him finish. "I know why you freaked out last night."

Picking at a piece of thread on his jeans, he was clearly as uncomfortable with this conversation as I was. Neither of us was good at the polite small talk that spider-webbed around until a point was finally understood. Usually we got right to the point. However, things felt different and I didn't know how to be honest with myself, let alone him.

"I'm sure you don't." I pulled the throw pillow out from behind my back and straightened the decorative tassels.

Cooper let out a long breath, then chewed on his bottom lip while contemplating his answer. "Then enlighten me, B, please."

I shook my head, chin resting in my right palm. "We're not right for each other, Coop." I sat up and leaned back in the seat. Suddenly the room felt too hot and the air was thick. "Can't we just forget last night and go back to being friends? I don't want to lose what we had."

"B," Cooper ran a hand through his hair and I could tell he was struggling to say what he wanted. "No. I don't want to forget. It was good. We're good together."

"Cooper," I stood and threw the pillow onto the chair. Pacing the room, I spoke in short, choppy sentences, trying to relay what I needed to say. "We're good together. As friends. Best friends. But . . . more than that . . . won't work." Pausing long enough to sit on the arm of the chair, I popped up again and resumed pacing the floor. "Move on, Cooper. Date someone. Fall in love. Be happy. Let me be the one you hang out with, watching the game. The girl that you have belching contests with." Finally, I plopped back down into the chair sideways, letting my legs dangle over the arms.

Now it was Cooper's turn to stand and walk around the room. He didn't speak for a while, instead he picked up a monogrammed coaster and rolled it between his palms.

"When you . . . fell for Blake . . ." His words picked up a fast pace, along with his frustration, and he unleashed a madness on me I wasn't expecting. "You changed. You got all squishy-girly on me. Everything was Blake this and Blake that. We drifted, B. I didn't want to lose our friendship, but you couldn't see or hear anything around you unless it had Blake's lousy scent on it." He sat back down on the couch and crossed his right ankle over the opposite knee. "What did you even see in that asshole?" He shook his head. "Anyway, I saw you in a different light. I've always loved you, you know that. But the way you started smiling and . . . your eyes sparkled. I knew I had fallen in love with you. Not just the one-four-three, but the kind of love that makes you look forward to growing old, so you can sit on the porch with the one you love and watch the sun set."

Tears stung my eyes and pooled in the corners. I had a sudden urge to run to my car and drive away. That was my usual modus operandi. When things got tough . . . run away.

"Great, I've made you cry . . . again." He was in front of me within seconds, pulling me out of the chair and into his arms.

"I'm not crying," I muffled into his chest. Overwhelmed by being wrapped up in his arms, an all-out ugly cry was about to ensue. "I just wish life wasn't so freaking hard."

"But it *is* hard. Let me walk through it with you."

I nodded my head. "That's what friends do." The implication was too obvious and I grimaced against his shirt. But he needed the movie slap moment. He needed to know that a relationship with me was off the table.

He sighed, rubbing my arms up and down and I kept my body plastered to his. "Sure," he mumbled on a whisper so low I almost didn't hear him.

"Why can't we just rewind and forget? Pretend the last three years of my life didn't happen. Wouldn't you prefer that, too? Erase the horrible memories of prison?"

"Wouldn't that be nice? Let's start by rewinding and pretending I wasn't a complete asshole, mentioning the past." He paused for a minute, pulled back, and searched my eyes. "Your eyes are still moist. Didn't work. Guess we'll have to face it, embrace it, and move on."

He could always make me laugh and the stupider he sounded, the harder I cackled. "Did you hear that in a building seminar?" I lowered my voice, trying to mimic him. "Face it, embrace it, and move on, guys. Even if the dang building falls down."

"Yup. It's our motto. In fact, I brought a stack of bumper stickers for you to pass out to your friends." He smiled and it covered his entire face, making its way to his eyes.

His hands were still gripping my arms as the laughter faded. My lips curled into a slight smile.

"You know I loathe bumper stickers." I hated uncomfortable moments and felt the need to fill the silence with words.

He released me. "I used to know everything about you. But I've missed out on a lot."

Twenty-Seven

Cooper

So much had changed in seventeen months. You could only talk about so much in letters, especially knowing how many eyes were on those letters before they reached the intended party. I tried to control the rage that raced through my veins, begging to be released by smashing my fist into a wall or taking Briley into my arms and kissing her until her head was screwed back on.

Why didn't she think we could make it work as a couple? Because I had a record? I shook the thought as soon as it entered. I knew Briley, that wasn't the reason. She was broken. I could see it in her eyes and in the way she carried herself. She'd been marinated in sadness, it seeped from her pores. Being a man, I wanted to fix it. Immediately.

"Catch me up, B. Why didn't you tell me about the split in your letters?" She turned away from me, but I took her hand in mine. "Talk to me."

"You had enough to deal with, Coop. I wouldn't have dared to share my problems with you. It was nothing compared—"

"It was everything, baby. I wish you'd have unleashed everything. I thought that's what friends did?" It was a jab and it felt as bad as it sounded, but fuck it. I wasn't used to not getting what I wanted. "And prison was cake." I shrugged. "Sitting around, working on these guns . . ." I pumped my biceps, eliciting the laugh I'd hoped for.

"Sheesh! You gonna tell me the food was to die for, too, Alan Abel?"

I racked my brain trying to figure out who she was talking about. "Who?"

"Alan Abel. He's infamous for his tales and pranks. You know the guy that published his obituary in the New York Times . . . false." She laughed, slapping her hand on her thigh. "He wrote an article in the paper called 'The Society for Indecency to Naked Animals,' demanding that animals be provided with clothing."

"What? Why?"

"I don't know? But it's funny."

"Fine, the food was awful. Happy? Now, catch me up. You're not yourself, B."

Backing up, she felt for the arm of the chair and leaned against it. "I can sum it all up in a few sentences." The arm of the chair received her as she plopped down. "I gave up everything . . . my identity, personality. *He* greedily took it all and shoved it down the garbage disposal. For a redhead with big boobs and then a blonde who probably can't even read." She took a couple of deep breaths and apologized. "That was ugly. She can probably read a little." She tried to hide the worry taunting her eyebrows, unsuccessfully.

"That was mild."

She stood there, studying me with an expression I hadn't seen before. Either she was trying to think of something worse to say, or didn't understand my reaction. Why were women so hard to read?

"What?" I asked, truly dumfounded by her expression.

"What what?"

"You're looking at me like . . . like you're waiting for something."

"No, I . . ." Her focus became suctioned to the floor as if she spotted a stain that needed to be cleaned.

"Ah," I began, the light bulb finally connecting with the needed voltage. "There's more. Spill."

She sighed, but kept her gaze fixed on the invisible stain. "I don't know what he wants or why. He made it clear I wasn't enough for him, yet he's still harassing me."

"What do you mean?" I could feel the rage I was all too familiar with, pulsing thickly in a neck vein.

"Nothing serious. Calling, texting . . . you know." She exhaled the words like she was reciting a tediously long legal form and didn't have enough breath to finish it.

"Red ears. Lack of eye contact. C'mon, B."

Her eyes shot up, meeting mine. "Fine. He had cameras in the house. Got off spying on me, I guess."

"What the fuck, B?" My knuckles whitened as I gripped the chair. "I swear, I'm gonna—"

"You won't do anything, Cooper Hayden Sterling!" Rising from her position, she poked a finger into my chest. "Leave it alone. If you earn a place in prison again, I—I'll hate you until I die!" The words flew out of her mouth like poisonous darts. "I'm sorry, Coop, but I can't lose you again. Especially because of something that's my fault. I can't tell you how awful I feel. I—I'll never forgive myself for sending you to prison."

"Oh, now *you've* sent me to prison? When will you get it through your head, that night wasn't your fault? I could've called the cops, I could've let it go. It was *my* decision." *A decision I'd make again.*

"Just promise me you won't do anything. Besides, I don't want any part of him back in my life, not even the blood from his broken nose."

Just like a woman, she dragged me onto a roller coaster of tortuous climbs and free falls. One minute she had my heart beating with promise and the very next we were back in the friend zone. My mind was struggling to keep up. *"I hate you. I can't lose you . . ."*

"Fine." I raised my hands in surrender. "But the next time he texts or calls, let me answer."

"We'll see," she pulled the corner of her mouth up into a questioning smirk and mumbled, "If you're around."

"Stubborn little girl," I answered on a matching mumble. Looking up movie times on my phone, I found what I was looking for. If we left soon, we could make the next showing. "If we leave now, we can make the afternoon show."

"I'm not in the mood to go out. Why don't you catch up with Devi?" She sang, pretending to swoon. "I'm sure she'd love to see you."

"Seriously? I haven't liked Devi since fifth grade. And stop trying to push me away. I only have eyes for you." I waggled my eyebrows, trying to solicit a laugh, but she held on to her annoyed expression. *Too far, too fast? Who cares. It's fucking liberating to finally tell her how I feel.*

"Eat more carrots for better vision. This," she pointed back and forth between us. "Is not happening."

What-the-fuck-ever. I rolled my eyes. She was mine, she had always been mine. It would just take a little work on my part to make her see it. "C'mon, that new Sci-fi is out. You'll love it. Go change into some jeans and let's go."

"Please, Coop, not today. I'm a mess and I—"

"We'll stay in then. What've you got on DVD?"

"I wasn't expecting . . . I don't have any good movies or food."

"We'll order in then and catch a movie on Netflix." I settled back down on the couch, not taking no for an answer, and searched through my phone for a restaurant. "Does China Kitchen still deliver?"

Her arms were folded across her chest, right hip jutted out while the opposite leg held a firm stance. "Has anyone ever called you a persistent ass?"

"Only you."

"You understand this isn't a date."

"You're the only one being weird about this, B."

"I just don't have a lot of fight in me right now, Coop, so please . . . I need . . ."

"I know what you need, B." I turned around in my seat to face her. Her stance was relaxed. She had her hands shoved into her shorts pockets which pulled them down enough to glimpse the smooth flesh of her stomach. "You need. Period. I understand that and I can be patient. Besides the anticipation is exhilarating."

Twenty-Eight

Briley

I locked eyes with him, regretting it as soon as I did. Those emerald soul-snatchers drew me in, making me forget the speech I'd just delivered. Was it asking too much to unravel in his arms—pretending for a moment that someone had my best interest at heart—while keeping the line between friendship and love darkly drawn and underlined?

As if reading my mind, he patted the seat next to him on the couch. Hesitant, but powerless to say no, I joined him. All it took was one arm around my shoulders to release the dam of emotion. "Jeez, I'm like Old Faithful, erupting on cue."

Cooper handed me a handkerchief, which turned my blubbering into giggles. "Are you joking? Why the hell do you have a handkerchief?"

"It's not a handkerchief, Miss Know-it-all, it's a bandana."

"Oh." I turned it over in my hands, noticing the navy blue paisley design. After wiping my face, I folded it and handed it back. With my best Scarlett O'Hara impersonation I said, "Why, thank you kindly, Rhett."

"There she is." He smiled and squeezed my knee. "I'm starved, let's order. You still like spicy tofu and veggies?"

My stomach growled in response. "Yes. And get an order of the crab rangoons, too. I'll be right back."

After a few minutes putting myself back together, my crying jag was hardly noticeable. When I entered the living room, Cooper had already found the remotes and was flipping through movie choices. "What looks good?" I asked, plopping down beside him.

"I haven't seen a movie in ages, so they all look good to me. You pick."

"Nope." I slapped his knee playfully. "You invited yourself over, you're picking the movie," As I stood and walked into the kitchen, I noticed there was a bounce in my step, a lightness in my aire. Maybe that's what I needed—a good cry and my best friend back in my life. "What do you want to drink?"

"Whatcha got?"

"Tea, lemonade, and one Rolling Rock."

"Iced tea. I hope you like the movie I picked . . . *Dumb and Dumber.*"

"You did not! I hate that movie." Rounding the corner with two glasses of tea and a scowl, I met his face, crinkled with laughter.

"I know. I couldn't even enjoy it, you were so audibly critical." He raised his voice, doing a horrible impersonation of me the last time we watched it. *"No one's that stupid. This is awful. Seriously? Are you falling for this?"*

***

Inception played in the background, but it didn't hold our interest. Between bites, we tried to catch up on the seventeen months since we'd seen each other.

"Have you checked in with work? Everything as it should be?" I asked, stirring my container until I found a mushroom.

"Yeah, looks like everything's going to be fine. My team's working on that new hotel downtown that's been on the news. The Stuart. You've heard of it, right?"

"I have. That's a big deal. Do you think it'll be awkward jumping in on it, or will you work on something else?"

"I was there yesterday. Colin filled me in. Unless I'm reading things wrong, I think we're cool." He smirked. "Guys don't do awkward."

I shook my head before poking my chop sticks down into the spicy tofu dish. "I'm so glad, Coop. I mean, he knows why you did what you did. It's not like you committed a crime."

"A third degree felony charge . . . is a crime, B."

"You know what I mean, Coop. You didn't rob anyone or sell drugs. You brought the whoop-ass on an . . . ass. Matt should've been the one serving time, not you." Sticking my chopsticks in the container before setting it down, I turned to face Cooper. "I know you're getting sick of hearing this, but I'm so sorry, Cooper."

"That's the last time." He gripped my chin between his fingers. "I'd do it again and again, even if it meant spending the rest of my life in prison. It was not your fault."

"Okay, Coopy."

He grimaced. "Ugh, you haven't called me that since we were kids. Don't bring that back."

"Fine. I have a few more," I teased.

"If it rhymes with poop, forget it." He glowered. "Now, why Super-Cooper didn't stick . . ."

"I don't know *why* that one didn't stick. One would've thought the red cape—"

"Don't start." He interrupted. "I remember your many nicknames and something about a wand and magic fairy dust."

"It *was* magic." My eyes grew serious and then I giggled. "Those were good times. Nothing to worry about, no

responsibility. Bad decisions didn't exist in our fairy tale world
. . ."

"My favorite was Yelirb and Repooc," he replied, trying to
shift the conversation back to something happier.

"Oh my goodness," I breathed out the words one at a time.
"I forgot all about that. Our names spelled backwards. I
remember thinking we were brilliant coming up with those
secret names."

"We were great together, weren't we?" Cooper set his
empty carton on the coffee table and stretched his arms on the
back of the couch. He didn't have to finish the thought. I could
do it for him.

*But it all evaporated because I fell in love with Blake. No
fairy dust, magic wands, or secret nicknames could've
prevented it.*

I didn't want to spend any more of our time together talking
about my mistakes, so I changed the subject. "I think I've got
my next idea for a book. 'The Adventures of Yelirb and
Repooc.'"

"You're nuts, B."

I stood, collecting our dishes and taking them to the kitchen
as I talked over my shoulder. "When do you go back to work?"

"Monday."

"And we're still on for dinner tonight at your parent's
house?"

"No, Mom cancelled. Said something about you being rude
to her the last time you spoke."

"Seriously?" Water dripped from my hands as I whipped my
head around and watched his face contort, trying to stifle a
chuckle.

"Of course not. I can't believe you fell for that so easily. Have you *ever* been rude to her? Have you ever been rude to *anyone*, sweetness?"

I squinted my eyes, feigning exasperation. Before grabbing a towel, I flicked my wet fingers in his face. "Ha-freaking-ha."

"Yeah, we're still on for tonight."

"Then either make your own Key lime pie, or leave me so I can shower and still have time to slave over your dessert!"

"Slave? I've seen you make that pie a hundred times. Five minutes tops. But I can see where you'd need to prepare mentally for the baking challenge." He smirked.

"If I could lift you, I'd toss you into the pool, Cooper Sterling."

"If you have time for a swim, I'll toss myself in."

"I don't." Pushing him toward the door, he did a great job of acting like a toddler not wanting to leave the toy store. "Thanks for lunch. I'll see you later."

***

Foul mood lifted, I was able to get some things done while my pie set. After showering and blowing my hair dry, I stayed in my cream silk robe and changed the bedding. Moving to the bathroom, I wiped down the counters and mirror and set out the new tube of toothpaste I'd picked up from the store. The next twenty minutes were spent in the closet. The entire space was now mine, there were no more suits hanging on one side, or a rotating tie rack to take up a chunk of my clothes room. Still, I couldn't find anything to wear.

After trying on three pair of shorts, skinny jeans, loose fitting jeans, and two different sundresses, I finally chose a pair of dressy white Bermuda shorts and a navy blouse, tucked in and trimmed with a pink and white plaid belt. I looked and felt like a character from Strawberry Shortcake. Sliding the belt back out of the loops, I donned a slim gold one instead.

***

Dinner lacked the awkwardness I had prepared myself for. It was a relief to sit around the table with people I loved, talking about stuff that didn't matter in the scheme of things while we dined on Mrs. Sterling's specialties.

Cooper, despite his large, tattoo-embellished, muscular frame, reminded me of the muddy, skinned-knees-and-elbows kid I'd climbed trees with back in the day. He thought he was so tough—and I knew he could be when he needed to—but he was also kind and gentle. A son, a little brother, and the best friend anyone could hope for.

Watching his eyes light up as he spoke to his father about landing tickets to a big game, I knew his happiness was more important than mine.

Twenty-Nine
Briley

Pulling my sunglasses out of my purse, I slid them over my eyes, blocking the harsh rays of the afternoon sun. Cooper had to help me into his black GMC Sierra because it was so big. He shut the door before jogging around the back to the driver's side. I was going to pay for putting my article off until the last minute, but there was no way I was sitting in front of the computer on a gorgeous Sunday afternoon.

"I think you need a bigger truck." Sarcasm oozed. "This one's a little on the feminine side."

"It hauls my tools and gets me from A to B."

"It's really nice." Stretching forward, I turned the vents away from me. May wasn't hot enough for full-blast air conditioning that could freeze meat.

"Cold?" He raised a brow and turned the temperature to seventy-five.

Following my directions, we pulled into the parking lot of my favorite gourmet sandwich shop, Relish. The old country house was painted blue and had been transformed into a quaint restaurant on the inside. Outside, they kept the cottage-style feel with a white front porch swing and picket fence.

"Oh, Lord, you're taking me to a tea room?"

"No." I shoved him lightly. "It's a sandwich shop."

"Looks girly." He held the door open and waited for me to pass through. "And smells girly."

I took in an exploratory breath of cinnamon-infused air. "It smells divine."

Cooper grimaced.

"C'mon. Payback for making me endure *Dumb and Dumber*. Besides, you'll love it, I promise."

"That was years ago. I'm sure you've thoroughly paid me back with all those period films."

"I was helping expand your horizons, friend. You'll thank me one day."

Soft notes of a familiar tune danced through the room along with a warm breeze coming through the windows. The hostess stepped behind her podium and greeted us with a smile.

"Two for lunch?"

"Please," I answered. "Do you have anything on the veranda?"

"I do." She grabbed two menus. "Follow me."

We were seated by the glass, facing the garden. A small glass votive sat next to a vase holding a single white tulip. I had to touch it to see if it was silk or fresh. Holding my nose to the fresh flower, I inhaled. I knew tulips weren't fragrant, but I had to try anyway.

"Try the Roast Beast. I think you'll like it."

"What the—?" Cooper looked over the menu—a single sheet of parchment paper.

"It's a roast beef sandwich with a horseradish cream sauce."

"Oh, sounds good."

"Or the Miss Piggy—ham and Swiss. But you don't like Swiss. Never mind."

Our server brought waters and asked for our order. She was covered in tattoos and I couldn't help staring. Everyone had tats these days and I'd been thinking seriously about getting something small myself. After ordering, I asked about the tattoo process, how bad it hurt, and if she regretted any of them. Cooper gawked at me, but I managed to ignore him.

"The dolphin on my ankle. If you're going to get one, make sure it's not something trendy that you'll hate in ten years."

"Does it hurt as bad as they say?"

"It hurts, but obviously not bad enough for me not to get more," she laughed. "You can do it. Ribs, feet, and calves hurt the most. So, if you're not good with pain, avoid those areas."

I nodded, thanking her for the advice.

"First, what the hell did you order?"

"A Gettin' Figgy With It with a side of broccoli salad."

"What's that, Will Smith on sourdough?"

His comment caused a cackle that had me doubled over. "It's a Panini with prosciutto, fig preserves, caramelized onions, and brie. It's delicious, but honestly, I just like saying the name."

"And what's this new interest in tattoos? You've always hated them."

"I dunno?" I shrugged and took a sip of water. "I just want one. I need to experience it. You're not going to try to talk me out of it, are you?"

"No, but why don't you wait a while, make sure it's not the heartache talking."

I smirked. "I hear you and I won't make a rash decision, but I'm pretty set on it."

"So what's holding you back? Why haven't you gotten it?"

"You know me, I have to make sure. Think of how it will look in twenty years, thirty years . . . Jeez, Cooper, why can't I just jump on something? I have to run it through the presses a million times. It's insane."

"With everything else, I agree. But this . . . think long and hard. If you get Tinkerbell on your shoulder, you're going to hate it when you're sixty."

"Tink? Good grief, you know I'm not fourteen anymore, right? I've grown up . . . moved on to bigger, more mature things. I was thinking Minnie Mouse."

"B, you—"

"I'm kidding! I was thinking of script. Written across my hip, either above or below where my bikini bottoms hit. What do you think?" I searched his eyes, waiting for an answer. Big mistake. My cheeks flushed under his intense gaze, the heat moving down my neck, caressing my limbs. I was lost in his eyes, enticed by the mossy green discs, pulling me deeper into an abyss I wouldn't be able to escape from. Hell, I didn't want to escape. Not yet. Sitting across from him in a room full of motionless people, all sound muted, I reveled in the insatiable longing for a brief, indulgent moment.

Miss Tattoos set our plates down, the glass clinking against the metal table. "Can I get you anything else?" she asked.

"Um . . ." *Crap, where was my tongue?*

"I think we're good, thank you." Cooper answered. It amazed me and pissed me off that he could so easily snap out of a moment like that.

***

"You up for a walk?" he asked, pulling into the local park.

"For sure. It's a perfect day."

Walking along the boardwalks as they snaked through lush foliage and alligator-laden marshes, we did our best to catch up on all we'd missed in each other's lives. Stopping to snap a picture of an osprey devouring a fish, I took a moment to collect myself. *Pull it together, Briley. You're no good for him.*

When I turned, he swiped a strand of hair off my face and tucked it behind my ear. The way his fingers grazed my cheek ever so lightly filled my body with warmth, surely exposing my reaction with reddened cheeks. I reached for my purse, shoving my phone back into the small pocket inside, hoping the heat would vanish before he noticed. Cooper's eyes remained locked on me and instead of cooling off, I kept getting warmer.

There was no doubt my desire for him was evident in my eyes. I was giving off every signal that I wanted him to kiss me, but he didn't make a move, --- although I swear I saw the edges of his lips curl up in a slight smile. Instead of pulling me into his arms, he took my hand and led me further down the path.

Sadness wasn't welcome on the long walk in the park. The sun peeked from behind the clouds just enough to warm the air without being uncomfortably hot. It was a perfect day in May and I silently scolded the hours for passing too quickly.

***

It was late afternoon on Tuesday when Madison showed up without notice. Fully consumed in my work, I hadn't realized how late it was. Or the fact that I'd skipped lunch, until my stomach growled angrily at the neglect. Before I peeled myself from the leather chair, I assembled the chaos of sticky notes I'd accumulated into a stack that I could easily retrieve when I was ready to dive in again.

The only downside to working from home? Greeting a gorgeous blonde in a gray pencil skirt and spike heels while dressed in cut off sweats and a Seaside tank top.

"Hi, Madison." My greeting was a mix of statement and question. It was one of those open-ended statements that could have continued with *"What are you doing here?"* Or just as easily implied *"I'm so glad to see you."*

She moved past me into the foyer, letting me know it wasn't a front porch visit after all.

"I'm glad you're home." She took a seat in one of the barstools against the kitchen counter. "I had a horrible day at work. My boss is an ass bitch from hell. Would it be rude if I asked for a stiff drink?"

Yes. "No, we're friends. But it's slim pickings. I've got vodka and . . ." I searched the fridge, trying to find something to mix with it. "Orange juice."

"Perfect. Thanks."

I assembled the drinks while Madison recounted the details of her day. When I set hers down in front of her, she hit me with a question that made me appreciate the fact I was sitting down.

"Who's the hottie I saw hanging out here all weekend?"

My drink was lodged in my throat, not willing to move. A loud gulp forced it down the wrong tube, causing one of those strangling coughs that made your eyes water.

"Sorry." I choked out. "Wrong way."

She waited patiently until I got hold of myself and could speak intelligibly again, offering me a tissue to wipe the tears from my eyes.

"That's the friend I was telling you about. He's been out of town for a while." It wasn't a complete lie. He was one county over, which *was* out of town. "He got in Friday."

She waggled her eyebrows. "How friendly is this *friend?*"

"Not at all. It's not like that between us. We've known each other our whole lives."

She narrowed her eyes. "Men and women cannot be friends. Haven't you seen *When Harry Met Sally*?"

"I have and I disagree. Harry and Sally met in college. I met Cooper while we were still in diapers. There's nothing sexy about a guy that's peeing himself in front of you."

"Gross." She drained her glass and got up to make another. "However," she began, pausing to shake the orange juice and vodka together before straining it into our glasses. "He's not in diapers anymore. I'll admit, I only saw him from a distance, but unless he's got some weird thing going on with his face that I couldn't see . . . the dude is wicked hot."

I shrugged, letting her words fall around me like wasted breath.

"Briley?" She snapped her fingers, bringing my focus back to her. She held up her phone, wrapped in a hot pink case. "What color is this case?"

"Pink," I answered, not able to help the frustration on my face. I didn't have time for drinks, let alone games. I had more work to get done before my favorite show came on at eight.

"So you're not blind." She sighed. "What do you think about Henry Cavill?"

"The guy from the newest Superman movie? He's smokin.' Why?"

"Just making sure."

I looked at her quizzically while she finished her second drink. The woman could hold her own with liquor. I was already feeling a buzz after one glass and knew I wouldn't touch my refill.

"Making sure of what?"

"That you were into dudes. I guess I'll have to meet your friend and see for myself if he's as hot up close as he is from a distance."

"Well, you'll get your chance on Saturday."

Thirty
Briley

I awoke with a start, nearly falling off the pool float when I heard my phone ring. Not able to sleep the night before, I was exhausted and must have dozed. With my article turned in, I had decided to take some *me* time before attempting to work on any personal writing. The latest poem I'd started was so dark and dreary, it sucked the life out of me. I'd have to work on it in bits so it didn't consume me.

Dipping my hands in the water, I paddled to the edge of the pool and picked up my cell phone, answering breathlessly on the fourth ring. "Hello?"

"Hey, Bri. My boss invited a few people over tomorrow night for dinner. You remember, Chuck?"

My blood boiled as he spoke. "No, Blake."

"You know how much he likes you. Please, Bri."

"Take Andi or Candy or Cinder-freaking-Ella for all I care." Son-of-a-gun, I couldn't finish the poem I'd been working on for weeks, but could slam out silly ones over the phone with ease. "Stop calling me!" I shouted before slamming the phone down.

Within seconds, it rang again. I almost threw it into the pool, but knew I couldn't afford to replace it right now, even if it was one of the cheapest on the market. I should've ignored the call, but I was fuming and wanted to take my anger out on him—say things that I normally wouldn't say—vulgarities my mother would've washed my mouth out with Dial soap for, even at my age.

I clicked answer and shouted into the phone as I brought it up to my ear. "Listen, asshole, I'm recording all of your calls! So, *please,* keep calling you lousy, limp-dick, worthless mistake from a faulty condom, douche-bag, piece of shit!" *Wow that felt fantastic.*

"Whoa!" The sound of the voice on the other end of the line had me wobbling on my float, almost falling in. "Briley?"

I drew in a sharp breath. "Cooper?"

"I'm assuming, since my dick is in great shape and I was— according to my parents—a planned conception, you thought I was someone else?"

I groaned, embarrassed that Cooper had gotten an earful of my lousy insults. If I could've written and edited my mouthful of chaos, I'm sure it would've sounded better. "Of course. I—"

"He's been calling you today?" His tone was deep, raspy, and even. I pictured his teeth clenched as he spoke and the thick vein on the left side of his neck pulsing.

I remained silent. Cooper couldn't sneeze the wrong way right now, let alone get into an altercation with Blake or he'd earn his flimsy cot in prison again. I was a terrible liar, but I said the first thing that came to mind.

"Nah, I was just practicing my insults for when and *if* he called." My voice cracked and I silently scolded myself for being such a terrible teller of tales.

"*Who* were you practicing on?" He drew out the words like a father scolding a child. I would've been irritated if I wasn't scrambling for another lie. "Your mother would slap your mouth if you spoke to her like that, practicing or not. So, tell me, B, how many times has he called today?"

"Cooper, *really*." My eyes rolled for effect, even though he couldn't see them. "I have other people to talk to besides you and my mother. Sheesh!" *Another lie. Keep 'em coming, Briley.* "It was my friend, Madison. She's been helping me. You don't honestly think I could say those things without some help?"

"You're a terrible liar, but I'll give you points for trying." He paused and I heard heavy scraping in the background. He seemed to be moving things around as he talked. "And I have no doubt in your ability to throw a verbal punch when you need to. You're sweet, B and I love that about you. But you're strong, too. Don't doubt it for a moment."

"How's work going?" I asked, changing the subject. Getting his mind off Blake was the best option. "Any new projects?"

"It's going. A little tense, as expected, but it could be worse. At least I still have my job. In fact, we just landed a huge deal this morning."

My phone buzzed against my ear, alerting me that someone was ringing in. A groan escaped my lips before I could swallow it.

"Don't answer it," he commanded.

How did he know I was groaning over a phone call? I very easily could've been bored with our conversation. *What was the conversation? Something about a deal?* Choosing not to play my hand at stories again, I obeyed his command and tried to resume our conversation. "What were you saying about a deal?"

"We landed a huge deal. Fifty-nine hundred square feet in Harbour Island. At least one point nine."

"One-point-nine, what?"

"Million. The buyers want five bedrooms, a theater room, home office, gourmet kitchen, the works."

"Who throws around that kind of money? What do these people do?" I asked, astounded and green with envy. I loved my office, my desk hidden in a nook by the window of my guest bedroom, but a whole room sounded glorious. Maybe not as elegant as the theater room. As much as I loved movies—or cinematic experiences, as I called them—a theater room would be divine. I shook my head and giggled to myself, thinking of how fat I'd become sitting with a bowl of popcorn for hours on end watching movies. *Note to self . . . never have a theater room.* Not that I could afford one anyway.

"I don't know. He owns a company. They all own a company of some sort."

Maneuvering to the steps, I managed to climb off of my float without dropping my phone into the water. I picked up a large white towel, trying to wrap it around myself with one hand. The sound of a car slowing, too close to my house, made me steel myself and listen. Not being able to see the road from the thick hedge surrounding the screened pool area, I waited, listening for it to pass.

A car door slammed. The car was in the driveway. *Blake!* My pulse beat so fiercely my head felt woozy.

"Cooper," I whispered. My voice sounded small and I barely recognized it as my own. "I think he's here." My words were shaky, tumbling out in a chaotic pattern. "Bl-a-ke." I wasn't necessarily scared of him, but he'd done enough to shake me and it was clear I had no idea what kind of man he really was.

"It's me, B. I'm sorry I scared you. I just pulled into the driveway. It's just me."

"You're here?" I asked, still not sure what was happening. How could Cooper be at work *and* be in my driveway?

"Yes. I was driving while we were talking. I'm about to ring the doorbell. You're not going to have a heart attack on me, are you? I'll knock three times. Listen . . ."

I heard him knock three times, but the sound came through the phone.

"I'm out back by the pool." I was still whispering for some odd reason. "Come around."

Cooper stood by the locked gate and waited for me to come to him.

"See. It's me." He smiled sheepishly.

My pulse slowed, but not by much. After unlocking the gate, Cooper stepped through and I quickly locked it behind him, followed by locking the screen door to the pool.

"What are you doing here?" I asked.

"I was in the car already. Just finished up with the appointment I was telling you about. Are you okay?"

"Yes, I'm fine."

"You were upset when you thought it was Blake. What aren't you telling me, B?"

"Nothing. I'm exhausted." I dropped my head. "I'm sick and tired of feeling like this, Coop. It's my house. I should be able to relax in *my* house. Instead, Blake plays his games, stirring up as much shit as he can . . . as often as he wants. He has to stop at some point." I felt sure of my statement for a good three seconds. "Right?"

He pulled me into his arms and kissed the top of my head. "Let me handle him."

Shaking my head, I pulled away. "It's not a big deal, really. You know how I dramatize things." Sizing him up through squinted eyes, I pursed my lips and playfully scolded, "You came to answer my phone, didn't you?"

"I came to see you. But if he calls back, I'd be glad to answer your phone." Even in a suit, his cockiness came through. That was Cooper for you.

"Mm hmm." My fists rested in balls on my hips. When I noticed his eyes roam over my body, I realized I'd never gotten that towel wrapped around me. I was standing in front of him with nothing but a skimpy black and white polka dot bikini. It was my least favorite one, ill-fitting. One I wore when I was alone and wanted the sun to hit places I wasn't willing to show in public.

"Want something to drink?" I asked, turning to grab the towel. I wrapped it around, tucking the tail in tightly under my armpit. *Don't you dare lead him on, B.* I reminded myself of why Blake and I split. *You can't make him happy. You'll ruin everything.*

"I'll take a beer if you've got one." He leaned against one of the columns, positioning himself on the side shaded by the porch roof. "So, tell me about the calls. What did he say that had you so upset?"

"Do we have to talk about Blake?" Opening the mini fridge, I pulled out two Rolling Rocks. "I was enjoying a few moments in the pool." He didn't move, his gaze fixed on me, waiting for the answer. I popped the cap on both beers and handed him one. "He invited me to dinner. He has a work thing and wanted me there."

"What a douche." He took a sip of his beer and wiped his mouth. "What else did he say? You sounded pretty upset."

"That's it. He kept pushing and I snapped." If making my blood boil for the second time in one day was the goal, it was easily achieved as I replayed the short but effective conversation between me and my ex-fiancé.

"Now you've done it," I began, setting my beer down and re-tightening my towel around my body. "I'm mad as a hornet again." *At least now I have an excuse for the flushed cheeks. Keep it light, B. Friends. What would you do before you 'noticed' him?*

Squaring my shoulders, I moved toward Cooper. Instinctively he moved away from the column and stepped back into the open space, arms up in surrender, pretending like he truly feared my wrath. I closed the space between us, poking my index finger into his chest.

"Why can't a girl get a break once in a while? Lay by the pool . . . soak up some vitamin D . . . without *someone* coming in and stirring up trouble?"

He was so close to the edge of the pool, I couldn't help myself. With both hands, I shoved against his chest until he wobbled backward into the water. In the few seconds before he fell, his right arm slid around my waist and held tight, taking me with him.

Thirty-One

Cooper

She should've known better. I could read her like a book and knew her next move before she did. Sure, I played along. I'd finished at the office, and didn't mind getting wet and cooling off. The shock on her face made treading water in slacks and a dress shirt worth it. I was just surprised she didn't catch on when I removed my billfold and cell phone from my pocket and slipped off my shoes.

I chuckled, helping her to the side of the pool. "That'll cool you off."

"Cooper!" she gasped, unable to swim while holding on to her towel. "You got beer in the pool!"

With little effort, I gripped her by the waist and hoisted her up onto the tiled pool deck. She looked pitiful sitting there, trying to maneuver the heavy cotton towel to cover her.

"Give up on the towel, B," I commanded, pulling it from her and tossing it aside. "I've seen you naked."

She gave me a fierce glare. "Not recently."

"What, something's changed since you were five?" I teased, getting the response I sought. She hurled a fist at me, landing it against the side of my shoulder.

"Right back at ya, little Coopy." She lifted one eyebrow and smirked.

No man liked his manhood tested, no matter if it was a joke and no matter how long we'd been friends. After grabbing the now-empty, floating beer bottle, I pulled myself out of the pool.

Keeping my eyes locked on hers, I pulled my shirt over my head, popping a couple of buttons. She didn't flinch. That surprised me. When I unbuckled my belt, I lost her. She turned her head and held up her hands.

"Okay, okay! You don't have to show me your junk. Jeez, Coop!"

I proceeded to remove my belt, pants, and socks until I was standing in nothing but black boxer briefs. Claiming the seat next to her, I cleared my throat.

"I'm not naked, B."

She turned her head slowly, her gaze fixed on my bare chest for a long, breathtaking moment.

"You got a new tat." She traced a finger over the design on my right shoulder. "I like it."

Next she flicked her eyes down to my boxers and immediately back up to my eyes. Her cheeks flushed slightly. Before I could come up with a smart-ass comment, she pushed off the edge of the pool and sank into the water.

When she came back up, her hair was slicked back against her head and beads of water trailed down her face and neck. I longed to follow them as they traveled between her full breasts.

"Well, if you're swimming, get in," she ordered, her voice musical with a hint of playfulness.

Without hesitation, I stood, walked to the deeper end of the pool, and dove in. We spent a good hour splashing and goofing around. After the third time racing the length of the pool, I let her win. She studied me for a moment as she clung to the edge of the pool beneath the diving board.

"You slowed on purpose, didn't you? I can beat you fair and square, you know. I'm just out of practice."

Her chest heaved as she tried to catch her breath, her breasts begging to be released from two tiny triangles of polka dot material. My brain didn't register that what I was about to do might be a bad idea. Instinctively I trailed a runaway bead of water down her cheek with my thumb. My eyes locked on hers and I could feel my soul being enticed by the deep, dark pools of innocence.

When she didn't shy away, I leaned in. Sliding one arm around her waist while the other held onto the side of the pool, I pulled her to me. Moving closer, I felt her breath as her lips parted, taking in shallow, intermittent breaths. She was nervous. Excitement raged through my veins as I closed the small space between us and felt her soft lips against mine. Her lips parted on a sigh and I took the opportunity to explore the sweet taste of her mouth fully. Our tongues mingled, teased, and taunted, playing a wicked game and making me lose all sense of reality.

Even soaked in chlorine, she was intoxicating. Moving my mouth along the line of her jaw, nipping and kissing until I reached her throat, I found a spot behind her ear that elicited a low groan. I stayed there, reveling in the way it felt to have her fingers twisting in my hair. Losing control with each of her lust-filled moans.

Her flesh pebbled with goose bumps. A gentleman would've asked her if she was cold and wanted to move this out of the water. But I knew better. No way in hell was I interrupting the mood, even for a second.

The most amazing feeling—one that would forever be burned to memory—was Briley's legs wrapping around my waist. Her mouth crashed into mine hungrily and it was all I could do not to let go of the edge of the pool.

"Let's move this poolside," I exhaled.

A nod, barely visible, gave me the go ahead. Hoisting her up out of the water, I set her down and climbed out. The heat behind her eyes remained, bordered by rosy cheeks. My skull was a useless compartment of mush, as my brain went on autopilot, and I scooped her up to lay her on a chaise lounge. No way was that going to work unless I knelt beside her or climbed on top.

At the last minute, the synapses fired and I thought to pull the cushion off the chair, onto the ground. I set her down, crawling over her to find her lips again. This was where I belonged. We fit and she knew it as well as I did. The moment was almost interrupted by an incoming text, the sound of a donkey screaming "Hee haw, hee haw," but she was happy to ignore it. The joke wasn't lost on me but I wondered why she had gone to the trouble to change Blake's ringtone instead of blocking his number. Women were difficult to understand. I'd have to ask her about it later, but it would take some work peeling layer after layer to get to the real reason she kept his number.

Careful not to put too much weight on her, I lowered myself onto an elbow and let my right hand travel where it wanted. Starting with her cheek, I grazed my thumb down and across, finding her bottom lip. I moved slowly, her lip tugging gently to the side beneath my touch. I followed with a kiss, soft yet persistent. Not able to break my lips from hers, I let my hand roam down the smooth, damp column of her throat.

She felt so good melded to me. I could feel her body relax, letting the moment consume her. With fingers splayed, I traveled between her breasts, pushing the material of her bikini top to the side, teasing a nipple with the edge of my thumb. She took in a sharp breath and writhed beneath me, her hips making contact with my throbbing desire. Rather than easing the ache, it intensified. I couldn't remember being harder than I was at that moment.

My fingers moved over her smooth stomach and circled her belly button before dipping down between her legs. Fuck, the heat radiating from her nearly undid me. Arching her back, a long moan drifted from her mouth, vibrating on my tongue. I needed to be inside of her, my body on the verge of explosion, my heart as full as it had ever been.

Her phone went off again, playing a haunting tune that barely registered in my brain. I was too caught up in the moment to try to figure out what the tune was. By the third time the damn song played, as if determined to ruin the mood, I had it figured out. It was the theme song from *The Exorcist*.

I needed to put an end to this asshole calling, so I reached for her phone. She tried to stop me, scrambling to get it from my hands, mumbling something about leaving it alone or letting it go.

"Stop calling, motherfucker!" I waited for Blake to choke on his own tongue, silently prayed he would.

"I—I," he cleared his throat. "Let me speak to Briley."

"Every time you try to reach Briley, you're gonna get me."

"Who the hell do you—?"

"Every time, fuck face. Don't call, don't text, don't even *think* about her. She's with me now . . . and I *always* protect what's mine." I pressed end and set the phone down on the table.

When I turned, Briley was on her feet. She stood still, her eyes fixed on me intently. I waited for her smile and readied myself to wave off her praise for taking care of her loser ex. Instead her features were hard, unfriendly. I crossed my arms, studying her body language. She looked pissed, which had me completely confused. Did she still have feelings for that douche bag?

"What?" I asked.

"Thank you for handling him, Coop, but . . ." She twisted her hands as if she were wringing water from them and whispered, "I'm not *with* you."

"It sure as hell felt like it a few minutes ago." The words slipped out, taking a detour away from my filter. Just like I suspected, it wasn't the right thing to say at that moment. Briley's eyes widened at my words and then she turned and stormed into the house.

What. Just. Happened? I didn't follow her into the house right away. She needed time to cool down and it wouldn't do any good to chase after her like a love-sick pansy. Shit, I'd never had trouble getting a girl. Why did it have to be so difficult with Briley? Exhaling a long, steady breath, I grabbed my pants and jerked them on. They were mostly dry from the sun, with a few damp spots at the seams and pockets. Gathering the rest of my belongings in a heap, I entered the house.

Briley was in the kitchen, rummaging through the fridge. Her island was covered in empty produce bags. An assortment of vegetables spilled out next to them. I stood watching her silently for a moment. She looked comfortable in the sweats and T-shirt that swallowed her petite frame. Her hair was piled on top of her head in a messy bun . . . my favorite.

"What happened?" I asked.

"Why did you say that I belonged to you? I don't *belong* to anyone."

"It's a figure of speech, B." I shook my head. "You know that. What is this? You don't really care what I said to that asswipe." I closed the space between us, taking her hands in mine. "What's going on in that complicated mind of yours?"

She shook her hands loose and backed away from me like I was infected with the plague.

"I had way too much to drink, Cooper. I got caught up . . . I shouldn't have let things go that far." She paced the kitchen, wiping an already clean countertop with a dishrag. "I'm sorry. I know you call women like me a cock tease. I—I shouldn't have. I'm sorry." She stopped pretend cleaning and looked at me. "It was the liquor talking. I'm sorry if I gave you the wrong idea."

"Why the excuses? What are you so afraid of, B?"

"I'm not afraid of anything!" She defended herself, taking the stance of a teenager caught in a lie. "It was the liquor!"

"Bullshit!" I thundered. "You had half a beer. Try being honest, it feels pretty good."

"You want honest, Coop?" she yelled, her face and neck catching up with the redness around her ears. "I don't want you like that. I liked what we had and if we're not careful, we're going to ruin it!"

"Again, I call bullshit. You wanted me. I felt it in the way you kissed me, the way you moaned when I found that spot behind your ear. You can't hide desire, B. It was in your eyes."

"How dare you mock me? It was the alcohol, you conceited bastard!"

"Mock you? How—"

"I tried to warn, you, Cooper. We had something great and now it's awkward." Her eyes glistened with tears, but she was too stubborn to let any fall. I could see her mind working, trying to focus on being pissed rather than letting any other emotion seep in. If I pushed her hard enough she'd either crumble into my arms or add another layer of mortar to the already thick wall.

"You're the only one making it awkward, B. We had something great but we could have something amazing."

"Or we can have something awkward and messed up. Which is what we have." She uncrossed her arms and started taking things off of the island countertop and slamming them back into the fridge.

"Why can't you understand? I'm not ready for this!"

I stood there a moment, shocked that an equal amount of hate and love could battle inside of me. My teeth were clenched as tightly as the fists that hung by my sides. After a moment of glaring—a childish standoff between the two of us—I turned and walked away.

"Lock the door," I commanded, not turning to look at her before I stormed out and slammed the door behind me.

Thirty-Two

Briley

It had been years since I'd written in the caramel brocade-covered journal my mother gave me for college graduation. I saved it for my poetry and for detailing memories worthy of the treasured book. The fight that had my nerves twisted in knots wouldn't make it into the journal. Neither would the fact that I lied to Cooper about alcohol weakening my inhibitions. Truth be told, I hadn't taken a single sip of alcohol today . . . until now.

Lying was necessary, justified. Telling him the truth wouldn't have gotten either of us anywhere. Well, except that he would've won the argument. He'd be lying next to me right now and life would be more splendid than any fairytale written. For a while at least. Then it would all be wrecked and I'd make his life a living hell. No, I needed to get myself straightened out, heal, and have a rebound relationship or two before I could even toss around the idea of something with Cooper. He was too important for a risk that great.

My subconscious battled with me over penning this particular poem in the journal, but it was an important one. A milestone as I hit the depth of my depressive state.

With a second glass of wine poured and waiting on the night table next to my bed, I opened the journal and let my soul bleed onto the pages.

Pretended Wisdom
"Life isn't always fair."

I've heard it at least a million times.
But it never seems to help.
"Life goes on."
If anything, it's kinda' sad
to think that life does go on.
All the hurt, all the pain,
all the clouds and the rain,
over and
over and
over again.
When will it be fair?
Where is the finish line?
What is at the end of the colorless rainbow?
Someday I'll know.
But for now I must endure the endless clichés
of pretended wisdom.

A tear dropped onto the page, leaving a burst design over the 'm' in wisdom. It was one of the saddest poems I'd ever written and as I read back over it my heart ached.

Tonight my grief was heightened. With the roller coaster ride of Blake . . . making out with Cooper . . . Blake . . . fighting with Cooper. For someone who loved coasters, I was ready to get off that one. No photo op, no fast pass, thank you very much.

After the second glass of Chianti, I felt better. It made perfect sense that a third glass would tip me over the edge, into the land of bliss, right? Wrong. There should be an app for your phone that doesn't allow you to text until you've passed a breathalyzer.

My first text was to Cooper:

U there?

When he didn't reply, I tried to imagine where he was, what he was doing. He was probably out with some buddies, playing pool or darts. I allowed a brief flash of an idea that he might be on a date. The thought was quickly pushed aside as it made my stomach feel queasy. I texted him again:

I wish I was right for you. I backspaced until the entire line disappeared.

I want U. I let this one sit in my text window for a while before deleting it.

Cripes, why wasn't he answering my texts? Where the hell was he? In bed with some floozy? The thought pervaded every part of me, taking over like a horror movie fog. I was helpless beneath the heaviness of it, desperate to get out. Frantic. The first idea that came seemed to lift enough of the darkness for me to catch my breath. Sure, it was foolish and I'd regret it later, but like I said, I was desperate. I found the last message from Blake and typed in each comment separately so his phone would ding enough times to hopefully interrupt whatever or whoever he was doing.

Pencil penis

He Bitch

Man whore

I was on a roll. My phone dinged with a reply:

??? You ok ???

It was from Madison. I slapped my hand over my mouth, staring at the phone, mentally willing my previous texts to disappear. *And this is why you don't text drunk!* I scolded myself. *How did those texts go to her instead of Blake?*

oops. mistake. sorry.

She replied with a smiley face.

After switching it to silent mode, I set the phone on the nightstand, vowing not to pick it up again until morning. Turning off the lamp, I slid down, deep into the bed until the covers were pulled up to my chin. Once the room stopped spinning, I was able to drift off to sleep and dream . . . of Cooper.

Thirty-Three

Cooper

Instead of turning left on South Falkenburg road, I took a right and drove around for at least an hour. I set Pandora to Kings of Leon and listened as Caleb Followill sang haunting lyrics, written for such a time as this. He sang about a beautiful war and how love didn't mean a thing unless there was something worth fighting for.

It was true, Briley was worth fighting for . . . up to a point. A man could only fight so long without reciprocation and she wasn't giving anything back. It was time I started listening. Friends it was, then.

Driving down Bloomingdale Avenue, I spotted the Wet Whistle. Recognizing a buddy's car, I pulled in and parked. Before entering the building, I slung my favorite ball cap—a worn out orange one with the Harley Davidson logo on the side—onto my head. The place was crowded, but it didn't take long to locate a few friends gathered around a pool table.

"Cooper! Hey, man, I thought you couldn't make it?" Justin Mullane asked.

"Change of plans." I ordered a lager on tap from the waitress and leaned back against the wall, watching the worst game of pool in history. Justin was stripes and it clearly wasn't his night. He was a good guy, average build, dull brown hair, and a personality to match.

After Garrett Evans sank the two ball, he followed with a great bank shot into the far right corner, but after the six went in, the cue ball followed.

"Awe, nice shot, though," I exclaimed, taking his outstretched hand firmly in mine for a polite shake.

"Take my spot after this. I'm ready for a break."

"You sure?"

Garrett nodded, his hair falling over his eyes. He slung it back every now and then, a habit that was already getting on my nerves. But the ladies seemed to love it. He always had a girl on his arm. Just as I glanced at the strawberry blonde next to him, he introduced me.

"Cooper, this is Wendy. Wendy, this is a good buddy of mine."

She smiled and stuck out slim fingers topped with long, hot pink fingernails. "Nice to meet you."

With each lager, the empty feeling in my heart dissipated a little. By round three, I had captured the attention of a woman with copper-streaked dark hair and clear blue eyes. I can't say she was my type. The amount of makeup she used and the way her jeans looked painted-on made her look dirty. Not the opposite of clean, but the kind of dirty that makes a man wonder just what she wouldn't be willing to do behind closed doors. She obviously wasn't looking for anything long term and if you hooked up with her, you might want to double up on condoms.

No, she wasn't my type, but it felt good to be noticed, or rather eye-fucked from across a room. My brain warned, but my body begged. It was a battle I'd lose if I had another drink.

"Another round, fellas?" The waitress asked.

"Please," I answered.

***

With Savannah—the blue-eyed sex kitten—rubbing against me at every chance, I was losing the fight to sleep alone. Something I wasn't too pissed about. She was sexy as hell, but I could've done without all the perfume. Did she bathe in it, for chrissakes? But the night was looking up and I was doing a damn good job of keeping Briley out of my mind.

"Want another?" I nodded toward her empty martini glass, the sugared rim partially gone and replaced with fire engine red lipstick marks.

"Mmm hmm," she answered.

Halfway through her drink, her lips were on my neck. Warm breath fired up my senses. I was ready to blow this joint and peel the tight blue sweater off her body. Enjoying the feel of her ass on my thigh as she leaned against me, my hands twitched, wanting to squeeze her firm tits. Fuck me, I might regret it in the morning, but what man could resist this temptation?

My phone buzzed in my pocket, causing her to scoot away from me slightly so I could reach it. I considered ignoring the intrusion.

"I'm going to the ladies room," Savannah said. I watched her hips sway dramatically as she walked away, throwing a glance over her shoulder in my direction to make sure I was watching the show. Once she was out of sight, I pulled the phone out and slid the bar across, opening the incoming message.

Nothing will sober you up faster than a text from the woman you're trying to get out of your mind.

U there?

I didn't respond, but her message was impossible to ignore. It crept in and wrecked any chance I had for scoring a one night stand. Her moods were all over the place lately, leaving me confused and wondering if the ground was beneath or above me. It was time to stop the games.

With my buzz gone, I paid the tab and waited for Savannah to return. Watching her walk back to the high-top table wasn't nearly as intoxicating as watching her before. I wasn't that guy. Never wanted to be. Not that I was a cuddler or anything, but hooking up with someone you hoped left before the sun came up wasn't a good idea—even for me.

"Ready?" she asked.

"I'm sorry, Savannah. It's been a rough night and you were a nice distraction, but it's time for me to go. I've paid the tab. Have a good night." I tipped my head, topped it with my favorite ball cap, and turned away from her livid glare. I was on a roll, pissing off two women in one day.

I was only sorry about one.

Thirty-Four

Briley

Why did the sun have to rise so early? Didn't it ever drink too much and want to sleep in? I tried to snuggle deeper under the covers, but the bells wouldn't stop pounding in my head.

"For Pete's freaking sake, stop!" I mumbled into the empty air.

Finally, stirring to life enough to figure out my doorbell was being harassed by some jerk who didn't respect morning hours, I flung the covers off and sat on the side of the bed. Monkeys were taking turns with a miniature hammer inside my head, pounding to the beat of my heart.

"I'm coming," I whispered in the snippiest tone I could muster. Anything louder would've made my head explode.

Looking through the decorative glass on the side of the door, I saw Cooper standing there, his hand reaching for the doorbell once again. *No!* I unlocked the door and opened it before he could inflict the tortuous sound once again.

Cooper barged in, set two large coffees on the foyer table, and looked me over like I'd been found in a ditch after being missing for three days.

"Where the hell have you been?" he asked, his words clipped and harsh. A mixture of anger and worry tinged his tone.

"Here. Home." I dug my thumbs into the sides of my head, trying to massage the pain. "Why?"

"I've been calling you all night. I stopped by, but all the lights were out. Your car was here, so I knocked *and* rang the doorbell." He paced the floor, grabbed a chunk of his hair with one hand and held onto it. "Fuck, B, I was worried . . . I thought that . . . what the hell?"

"I must've slept through the doorbell." I walked away from him, made my way into the kitchen, and fished through the cabinet for Motrin.

"Why didn't you answer your phone?"

"I put it on silent so I could sleep." I tossed three tablets in my mouth and chased them with a full cup of water. "Besides, you didn't answer *my* text. What makes you think I'm obligated to answer you?"

He sighed heavily before handing me a large cup of coffee. "Caramel latte?"

"Thanks."

"I told you I had plans last night. I was out and didn't get your text until late. If you had your phone on, you'd see that I did answer."

I wracked my brain, trying to remember what I'd actually sent. Hoping I'd erased the ones I never intended to send. I wanted to know where he'd been last night. Not that it was my business, but the curiosity was overwhelming. I started to ask, but instead pulled the cup to my lips for another sip of the sugary brew.

After Cooper was satisfied that I wasn't abducted by aliens and taken to the mother ship for probing, he left for work and I retrieved my phone. Sure enough, he had answered, at two fifty in the morning.

I'm here
Always

U there?

Hello?

Where r u? Safe?

Answer the damn phone!

I'm coming over.

What had he been so worried about? It dawned on me suddenly, a chill snaking over my flesh as the thought bloomed. Blake had gotten to me. He either feared we were back together, or . . . he'd taken me.

***

The day ticked by. Wednesdays weren't my favorite anyway, but this one had an especially large hump to get over before the weekend closed in. A weekend I was no longer looking forward to. I tried to work, jotting down prose that didn't make sense. Everything that poured out of me was dark and depressing. I felt a deep connection to Edgar Allen Poe, but the creativity that was supposed to come with that link was lost in translation.

After wasting most of the morning typing and backspacing, saving and deleting, making notes and tossing them into the trash bin, I gave up and decided on a bath.

As the tub filled, I lit a few candles and found a playlist worthy of a relaxing soak. The hot water, along with Lana Del Ray's sultry voice, was just what I needed to wash my cares away. The feeling didn't last long as Sia began a sad tune. The lyrics seemed written just for me.

She summed it up perfectly. Although I was five feet seven barefoot, I felt small and needy. I had passed the heartache off as anger and fooled most, including myself at times. But the truth was I hurt. Bubbles could only take away so much sorrow.

What I really longed for was someone to unfold me and wrap me up in their arms, soothing the ache inside of my chest. I wanted that someone to be Cooper. But if I gave him the wrong impression and we crossed a line, there would be no turning back. I couldn't take a chance on hurting him . . . or losing him for good.

Perhaps I had already lost him for good. I knew he was angry, but we'd never gone long without either making up or continuing our fight. This was torture, pulling me in different directions. Anger, sadness, worry, grief. Sadness won in the end as I laid my head back on the bath pillow and pondered the situation.

I'd managed to royally screw up the best thing I had in my life. Trying to protect our friendship, I'd destroyed it instead.

Thirty-Five

Cooper

Wednesday took me down like a bulldozer. I was on my third cup of coffee before the day even started.

With mug in hand, I sat back in my desk chair, blowing the steam across the surface before taking a sip. A stack of papers waited to be signed, filed, or discarded. Instead, after setting my cup down, I folded my arms across my chest, leaned back in the leather chair, and reflected. *I've never chased a woman.* My face contorted into a defiant smirk. If anyone had been watching my expressions change as my mind battled the dilemma of Briley, I'd be committed. *You chased Briley. Chased her and gave up at the first sign of defeat.*

Distracted by the commotion across the hall, I sat up straight. Frank Arincini, a big time builder and A-1 asshole, eyed me through open blinds as he talked to my partner, Colin, in his office across the hall. Whatever they were talking about wasn't going well. Colin looked nervous, almost desperate, as he ran his hand through his hair and loosened his tie.

After straightening a few papers and signing the office paychecks, I looked across the hall again. Frank stormed out of the office, slamming the door behind him. Colin stood alone, disappointment evident in his stance.

I walked to his door and leaned against the frame. "What was that about?"

After a long sigh, "Frank wants out of the contract. He's hiring Goodman to do the job."

"Why? He knows we'll do a better job." I knew the answer before I finished my question. I shot him a knowing nod. "He doesn't want my name connected with him."

"He's a pompous ass," Colin barked. "It wasn't going to pay much anyway. Fuck him."

"Still, it would've paid something. Tell him you're in charge of the project. He doesn't have to work with me at all."

"I tried every angle. He won't work with Sterling & Tyler at all." He stood, smoothing his tie back into place. "Shrug it off, man. It was going to be hell working with him, anyway. He's as unsteady as a nuke on a gravel road."

"I can relate. It's what got me in this mess."

"I'm starving. Let's grab some lunch."

I drove, pulling into Taco Mamacita. We sat ourselves near the jukebox and snacked on chips and beer while we waited for our lunch.

Colin held up his Corona. "Here's to new beginnings."

"And doubling our clientele." I lifted my bottle. "Cheers."

Colin's gaze landed on a hot little blonde passing our table. An intake of air hissed through his teeth. "Smokin' body."

"She's tight. Too bad you're off the market."

"I can still appreciate a beautiful woman. I'm not dead."

"Touché." I took another swig of beer and popped a chip into my mouth. "How ya like playing house?"

"It's good, man. Claire's amazing. I mean, I miss hanging out, talking smack. But I wouldn't trade what we've got going on for another meaningless fling. Well, maybe one . . ." he mumbled, following the blonde with a hungry gaze.

"I'm glad you're happy, dude."

"You got your eyes on anyone? What about Briley? I heard she and that shithead finally split."

"They did." I drained my beer right before the waitress set our plates down.

"Ready for another?" she asked.

"No, I'm good. Bring me a water, please."

Colin talked as he filled a tortilla with fajita meat.

"You gonna make a move?"

His timing was impeccable, as I'd just filled my mouth. I shook my head while I chewed.

"Did," I answered, wiping sour cream from the corner of my mouth. "Not going to work out."

"Come on man, you gotta give me more than that."

The jukebox changed over to the next song, *Holding On For Life* by Broken Bells. It reminded me of the Bee Gees.

"I don't know what to tell you. One minute she's into me, the next she's freaked out and just wants to be friends. It's making me crazy."

"So move on. There's more where she came from." He leaned back, arms resting against the red faux leather booth. "Enjoy the freedom, brother."

"I plan to." I pushed my plate to the side. "I met a girl a couple of nights ago. Hot as fuck and couldn't say yes fast enough."

"And?" he encouraged.

"And, we went our separate ways." I leaned back, exhaled a heavy breath. "I can't get Briley out of my head. She's completely fucked my world."

I picked up the check and Colin threw a few bills on the table, covering the tip. After paying, we got in the truck and headed back to work.

"You're screwed." He shook his head. "What's your next move?"

"Leave her alone for a while. Let her get her shit together. I'm sick of the games and it's getting close to wrecking our friendship."

***

I melted into the sofa, popped the cap on a Rolling Rock, and took a long, much needed drink. After a stressful day at work, the only thing I wanted to do was watch mind-numbing television. Flipping through the channels, I skipped over several shows that usually would have interested me. *Hawaii Five-O, Shark Tank. Wedding Crashers* was on Starz, so I landed there for a minute until I was bored and turned the television off.

My Taylor 316ce rested against the wall next to the gaming system. Flicking my eyes from one to the other, trying to decide which one called the loudest. I couldn't remember the last time I gave my guitar any attention, so I pulled it onto my lap and picked at the keys, adjusting the tuning pegs until everything sounded as it should. Unplugging and playing acoustic made me feel naked, but it was too late for electric guitar and I was too rusty to risk busting out a loud, screeching tune.

Once I felt warmed up with a version of Creed's *With Arms Wide Open,* I was able to coax a range of rich tones from the neglected Sitka spruce and Sapele instrument. Nothing relaxed me more than Led Zepplin's *Stairway to Heaven,* although it sounded much better on the Gibson Byrdland. Finishing with the Goo Goo Dolls, I sang a few lines under my breath and thought of Briley. The lyrics rolling off my tongue, causing me to question every word. Wondering if she lost herself out there, if she was sad knowing that life was more than this. Was she lonely where she was?

Setting the guitar next to me on the couch, I picked up my phone and let my thumb hover over her picture. All I had to do was press my finger on her image and I could hear her voice. Instead, I sent her a text.

We good?

I didn't need to hear her voice to hear the clipped, harsh tone of her return message.

Yep

Party Saturday? I asked.

Yep

That settled it. Saturday would be uncomfortable, full of games and messages hidden beneath a sweet smile that wanted to bite my head off. Was it too difficult for women to say what they wanted to say instead of making us guess and play along? I believed they were taught how to play these games since birth. Make the man feel and look like an idiot . . . a monkey scratching his ass, wondering what the fuck was happening.

And she was good at it.

Thirty-Six
Briley

Being jolted out of a deep, glorious sleep at three in the morning wasn't my idea of fun, but it was a sure way to test a strong heart.

Wide-eyed, I glanced around the room to get my bearings. The house alarm was sounding and my heart launched into overdrive as it flipped around in my chest.

My mother's plan worked like a charm. She convinced me to call the alarm company and have the numeric code changed. Nothing had happened for a long time and I had given up on her plan.

How to handle the outcome wasn't discussed and went a lot differently in my head than it played out in reality.

Before my brain communicated the command to my muscles to move, the phone rang. Fumbling to pick it up with trembling hands, I took a long, shaky breath before answering. "Hello?"

"We've been alerted of your alarm sounding. Do you need police assistance?"

"I don't know?" Frozen in place, I couldn't move or think of how to handle the situation. It would have put a wild grin on my face to see Blake's face, but I'd already given him enough time to flee.

"Okay." She spoke in calm, clear sentences. "Two officers have been dispatched to your home. They'll be there soon. May I have your code, please?"

Crap! My mind went blank. "I can't remember. Can you give me a hint?"

"It's okay, this happens. Take your time, breathe . . . It'll come to you."

Obeying her command to calm down, I inhaled three audible cleansing breaths. It almost made me giggle as I felt like I was practicing Lamaze. "It has something to do with golf. Par? Ball? Boo . . . boogie . . . bogie! Is it bogie?"

"Yes, ma'am, that's it."

The alarm stopped, but my ears were still ringing. "What do we do now? Hang up?"

"No, wait on the phone until the police arrive."

"Okay." I felt compelled to make conversation with the stranger at the other end of the line. "Do you enjoy working the late shift?" Before she could answer, I heard the police sirens getting closer. "They're here. Thank you for your help."

Walking toward the front door was more daunting than I expected. Although I was certain this whole mess had Blake written all over it, the idea that a stranger could be hiding in my home played with my psyche.

I reached the door and opened it to an officer's hand in mid-knock. "Hi. I'm sorry." I hoped my apology covered all the possible reasons I needed to apologize—for making them come out so late, for my ex-fiancé's behavior, for the game I was playing by changing the code without telling him.

"Are you all right?" The first officer asked.

"Yes." I nodded.

"I'm Deputy Spielman from the Tampa Police Department." He held his beefy hand out to me and I shook it with the energy of an uncooked biscuit. "This is my partner, Pappano. May we come in and look around?"

Pappano's gaze lingered on my face, assessing me. I ignored it, realizing they had to be on guard for everything, trusting no one. "Of course, please." I stepped aside and they entered the foyer. "How does this work, do I show you around or let you do your thing?"

"We'll do the searching," Pappano said with his auburn hair and freckles that made him look too young to have a gun holstered. "Do you have any animals inside the home?"

"Nope, it's just me."

They were back in a flash, more relaxed and personable than before. Still, nothing like the Starsky and Hutch duo I had pictured before they arrived. The young one appeared nervous. I assumed he was a rookie. His partner, Deputy Spielman, must have been the more seasoned of the two. Friendliness wasn't something he offered that night, but I could tell there was a sad story behind his crystal blue eyes.

"Everything is clear. There's no one in or around the house," he began. "We saw no sign of forced entry. Whoever it was had a key. You'll want to get your locks changed."

"I just did that!" I growled. "My ex-fiancé doesn't understand the meaning of breakup, so I had the alarm code changed. After that, I redid the locks, so how the hell did he—" As soon as the words came out of my mouth, I knew. "The hideaway key?"

Stepping outside, I looked around, automatically assuming Blake's eyes were on me. My privacy was taken away months ago and even with the police inside my home, I didn't feel safe. I lifted the planter on the front porch to see the key in its place.

"It's here."

Deputy Spielman shook his head. "Don't leave a key on your front porch, ma'am. It's an open invitation. Your ex could've easily tried to use the key and replaced it when the alarm went off." He picked up the key and handed it to me. "Give it to a neighbor you trust if you must have an extra key."

I took the key, flipping it over in my hand as if it had evidence of foul play, eagerly awaiting my discovery.

"Is he a danger to you? We can file a restraining order if he's a threat." Officer Pappano, even at three-thirty in the morning, when most were exhausted, spoke hastily with a hint of excitement in his tone. He had the personality of Barney Fife, but definitely not the body. Instinctively I looked for a wedding ring. He'd make a fine husband once he settled into some confidence.

"No, he's never hurt me. He crosses the line just enough to make me miserable." I pushed myself off of the door frame and started for the kitchen. "I'll make some coffee."

Officer Pappano followed behind me, but his partner stopped him. "No, thank you, we've gotta get going."

"You'll be all right tonight." Pappano tipped his hat. I couldn't tell if he was asking or telling me I'd be all right.

"Sure. Thanks so much for coming by and making sure of that." Before shutting the door, I wished them a good night.

So now it was another sleepless night and I was flipping through the channels. I landed on an episode of I Love Lucy and wrapped the blanket tighter around my shoulders, trying to get comfortable.

Overtired and partly crazed, I laughed aloud into the empty bedroom. Within seconds, the laughter turned to sobs.

***

Concealer worked wonders for my tired eyes. I chose the sage-colored sundress rather than the navy one that threatened to enhance the dark circles beneath my lower lashes. When the doorbell rang, I turned around in front of the full-length bedroom mirror, taking one last look at my appearance. Happy with the result, I answered the door.

"Hi, Mom, come on in." Stepping aside, I waited for her to enter the foyer and closed the door behind us. "I made coffee."

We took a seat at the kitchen table, sipping coffee and catching up on her neighborhood gossip. Rudely, I yawned while she was telling me about Mrs. Cavasin's toilet papered front lawn.

"Everything was covered. Tissue in the trees, bushes . . . and you know her husband's gone. She had to clean—" She set her cup down, cocked her head sideways and studied me. "Why are you so tired? You look awful."

I took a deep breath, filling my lungs completely before exhaling. "Blake tried to get in last night." My mother's eyes widened, an over exaggerated expression on her face that was almost comical. "The alarm went off like we thought it would and the police showed up."

"Did they get him?"

"Of course not. He was gone before they got here."

"This has to stop. There has to be something they can do." She shook her head. "Maybe it's best that your new job requires travel. You can get away for a while. That reminds me," she began as she fished through her purse. "You said you needed your birth certificate to apply for a passport?" She pulled out a single gold key and handed it to me. "Your father was in charge of all the finances . . ." Her voice trailed off and I assumed she was thinking of my father. After a moment, she perked up and continued. "He kept all our important documents in a safe deposit box. Your birth certificate, social security cards, and your grandmother's pearls."

She snuck that tidbit of information in, making me feel like a loser for not being married at the ripe old age of twenty-five. I was sure it wasn't ill-willed, so I bit my tongue and didn't say what I wanted. It was tradition to wear the family pearls on your wedding day. My maternal grandmother wore them, then my mother, and I apparently should've already taken my turn with them.

***

Stepping into the vault, I felt like a character from *Ocean's Eleven*. Denying myself the craving to slide against the wall, avoiding the eye of the camera, I walked to the wall of metal boxes and scrolled down until I found number three twenty-seven. Inserting the oddly shaped key into the slot, I turned it until it clicked, slid the long box from its home, and set it on the table.

The box contained two manila envelopes and the precious family jewels. I pulled the velvet box out first, tracing my fingers over the smooth, cream stones. Imagining walking down the aisle in them, tears pooled in my eyes knowing my father wouldn't be there to give me away. I snapped the box shut, stored them safely in their place, and pulled out the two manila envelopes.

The first one held what I needed—two copies of my birth certificate—along with my parent's marriage license and a few bonds. Curiosity got the best of me as I pulled the contents of the second envelope out. Another sealed, legal-sized envelope and a key were inside. Turning it over, I realized the envelope wasn't labeled or addressed. I held it up to the light, trying to get an idea of its contents. I couldn't tell if it was handwritten or typed. It took me fifteen minutes to decide not to open the letter. Certain it was something legal like my mother's last will and testament, I let the curiosity die.

Turning the key over in my hand, I studied the engraved numbers. It matched the safety deposit key I used, but had the numbers one-seventeen carved on it. After locating the matching box, I tried the key. It didn't fit.

After replacing everything except the key and my birth certificate, I locked the box in its metal compartment, shut the vault door, and found the bank manager in his office.

"May I help you?"

"I hope so. I found this in my safety deposit box, but it doesn't fit the box."

He looked at the key, studying it as I had only moments ago. "This isn't our key. It's for another bank."

"Can you tell me which one?"

"Sorry, I can't. But I can narrow it down for you." He scribbled a list on a sheet of paper and handed it to me. The names of ten local banks were written down.

Thirty-Seven

Briley

Saturday evening rolled in on a clear, warm breeze. A perfect night for an outdoor party. I was nervous about seeing Cooper. We hadn't spoken since Wednesday, except for a few impersonal texts.

Before dressing, I prepped the patio area. The automatic pool vacuum had worked all day and the water was clear and sparkling, even though no one would be swimming. After lighting a few candles for ambiance, I rearranged the drink glasses, set out platters of prosciutto-wrapped melon balls, veggies and dip, and a fruit tray. The meat for grilling was marinating in the fridge and the potatoes were resting in the oven.

Checking over everything, I remembered the beer. I wouldn't have enough ice for drinks and to fill the large tub that would hold the bottles of Rolling Rock and Corona. Against my better judgment, I texted Cooper for help.

Can u pick up a bag of ice pls?

He responded immediately.

Yes

I chose a pair of short, cuffed white dress shorts to go with my new strapless turquoise top. Letting my hair air dry instead of blowing it straight, I piled the curls on top of my head, letting a few loose locks mingled with ringlets escape around the neckline before securing it in place.

When the doorbell rang, I smeared a layer of lip gloss across my lips and hurried to greet the first guest.

"Madison, I'm glad you're here!" I took a platter of brownies from her hands and studied her outfit as we made our way to the patio. A strapless, slate gray, very short jumper showed off long, bronzed legs. Her sleek, straight blond hair fell down the middle of her back and I felt a pang of jealousy run through me.

"I'm going to mix a pitcher of my famous drink, want one now?" she asked, setting up shop behind the wet bar.

"Yes, please. That sounds wonderful." The doorbell rang again just as I flipped the switch for the pool fountain. "On or off?" I asked for Madison's input.

"On. Where's the music?"

"Shit! Behind you. Do you mind?"

"Nope. I'll find something good."

Cooper stood at the door with a bag of ice and a case of Rolling Rock. After taking in a deep breath, I squared my shoulders, smoothed the material of my blouse, and opened the door. His dramatic green eyes disarmed me, making me lose the ability to speak.

"Hey, Briley." He stepped into the foyer, one hand shoved deep into his pocket while the other held a bag of ice over his shoulder. "You look good." He took me in with a quick glance before fixing his eyes back on my face.

"Thank you for getting the ice." I rubbed my lips together, feeling the slippery gloss glide across them.

I wasn't bold enough to risk moving my eyes from his, letting them wander downward to see what he was wearing or how his jeans fit on his amazing body. Just the thought warmed my insides, liquefying my muscles. We either needed to get that ice over the awaiting bottles of beer . . . or me.

Since he led the way, I checked him out from behind. His crisp white oxford was tucked into Rock and Republic jeans that sat low on his hips, hugging his ass better than my imagination had allowed. *Stop looking at his ass! It's Cooper, not Adam Levine, for Pete's sake. I know, I know . . . he's much hotter than Levine.* Shaking my head, I let an audible breath escape.

He turned. "What is it? Did you forget something else?"

"Nope. I think we're all set."

As soon as we were outside, I introduced him to Madison. "Madison Cull, this is Cooper Sterling."

He set the beer and ice down, wiped his hand on his jeans, and offered it to her. "Nice to meet you, Madison."

I watched her eyes fall on him, studying the way his lips moved when he spoke. She was entranced, as I knew she would be. What I didn't expect was the change in Cooper. Sure, she was pretty, but *come on,* did he have to be so obvious?

The doorbell rang again and I was tempted to ask Madison to answer it. With a huff, I turned and greeted the guests as they flowed in. Ryan Evans, one of Cooper's old band mates, was overly excited to see me, the smell of a few already-consumed beers wafting through the air as he wrapped me in a tight squeeze.

"Jeez, it's been too long, Briley."

"Good to see you, Ryan." I glanced at the petite brunette next to him. We had been formally introduced before, but had never shared a conversation.

"Where are my manners? This is Julia. Julia, this is a good friend of mine, Briley Sheffield."

Julia Parsons worked with Blake, which meant she would relay every detail of the night's events to my ex on Monday morning. I forced a smile and held out my hand to shake hers. "We've met before." Probably too formal for a cookout, but the whole situation made me uneasy. "Come in." I stepped aside to let them in. Others were walking up the sidewalk, so I pointed to the party. "Party's by the pool. Straight back."

Cooper's partner Colin and his fiancée Claire walked up. Claire was holding a large cake box.

"Hi guys! Glad you could make it." My eyes fixed on the cake box, praying it wasn't a cake penned with *Congratulations on your prison release.* "What's in the box?"

"Chocolate covered strawberries." Claire smirked. "Store bought. You know I can't bake."

"Perfect. Hide them in the kitchen and we'll eat them all ourselves." I teased. "Everyone's out back. You know the way. I'll join you as soon as I can."

After greeting a few more guests, I shut and locked the front door. It had become a habit to lock both locks, even if I was home. As I made my way to the back of the house, I paused in the doorway, taking in the scene.

Several people dotted the lawn. It reminded me of middle school dances, the sexes grouped together on opposite sides. Females held Madison's concoction or a glass of white wine, swirling their glasses in the air animatedly as they chatted. Males gathered around the grill—manned by the master, Colin—drinking beer.

I spotted the one person I wanted to be near. Cooper. He was still talking to Madison, so I sidled up and slid my arm through Cooper's. Not sure where it came from, I suddenly felt the need to make it clear he wasn't available. Although he was.

What was I thinking? A more correct statement was that he wasn't available for Madison. She wasn't right for him.

Cooper acknowledged me kindly, but pulled loose. "I'm gonna grab another beer and check the grill. Can I get either of you a drink?"

"Yes, a glass of Chardonnay sounds wonderful. Thank you." I looked at him possessively, cursing myself as soon as I did. *What the hell are you doing, Briley?*

Madison turned to face me. "Great turnout."

"Yeah. Let me introduce you to a few people. Graham's a good guy." I nodded my head toward him. "He's the blond in the white shirt. Good looking, right?"

"Not bad." She planted herself against the stucco wall of the house. "I want to know more about Cooper."

"What do you want to—?"

Before I could finish my sentence, Cooper was back, delivering our drinks. He lifted a Rolling Rock longneck to his lips, tipped it up, and took a long drink. Ryan called me over, asking for a platter to set the grilled meat on, so I had no choice but to leave Cooper alone with Madison again.

She was on him like death to a sick man, full-flirt mode engaged. I rolled my eyes as I watched her tilt her head back, laughing at something he said. A little too animatedly, in my opinion. The more I watched her go after him, the more I disliked her. She had been a good neighbor and she was the closest thing to a girlfriend I had. Definitely not the type of girlfriend other women had—sharing clothes, shoes, and intimate details of their relationship woes—but we shared morning jogs and an occasional cup of coffee. It felt like friendship.

My stomach churned as a thick cloud of jealousy swept through me, poisoning my mood and bringing a dull throb to my temples. Pressing my fingers inward, I massaged the ache, hoping it would go away. It was like fifth grade all over again, me wanting to rip out Savannah's strawberry blond pigtails. This time I wanted to be a bit more adult about the situation, slapping a hand over Madison's shrill, bubbly voice, making her shut up. If Cooper was going to have a woman in his life, one that developed into more than friendship, he'd have to be more selective.

When I announced dinner, everyone lined up buffet style to fill their plates. Colin and Ryan flanked Cooper at one of the tables, so Madison was forced to take a breather. She sat by me, most likely eager to prod me for information. Luckily, Claire and Julia dominated the conversation at our table, talking about the last book they'd read in the local book club.

"You should join, Briley. The next book sounds really good," Julia pleaded.

"Which book?" I asked.

"*We Were Watching Downton Abbey.*"

I waited for her to continue, but she never did.

"I love that show. What happened?"

"That's the name of the book. *We Were Watching Downton Abbey* by Wendy Wax. Have you heard of it?" she asked, cutting into her steak.

"No, I haven't."

Since Julia was chewing, Claire jumped in. "It's about three women who live in the same building. One of them is a writer, like you. Anyway, they come together and watch Downton Abbey. Oh, and there's a hot, British concierge. It got great reviews."

"I'll check it out."

"Madison, you in?" Claire asked.

Madison looked uninterested, distracted. "Maybe. Can I let you know?"

"Sure."

Conversations flowed as easily as the drinks throughout the evening. By the end of the party, I was exhausted trying to come up with ways to keep Madison away from Cooper. Finally, I was out of ideas and drained of energy. It didn't help matters when my head began throbbing with one of the second worst headaches of my life.

My vision blurred and I was unable to focus on anything. The effort enhanced the pain, making my eyes feel like they would explode. I took a seat in a back corner, as far away from the noise as possible, trying to ignore the fact that the blood was pulsing angrily in my head to the same beat Drake was playing over the speakers. Closing my eyes, I rubbed my temples, trying to sooth my head enough for the nausea to dissipate. This was not how I wanted to be remembered at the end of the night.

Thirty-Eight
Cooper

I almost felt bad, watching Briley busy around while I enjoyed myself. But the party *was* for me. I'll admit I was rather surprised when she introduced me to Madison. Was this her way of pushing me away, into the arms of a hot blonde so I'd leave her alone? What a shitty move. Not that I was complaining. Madison was hot and willing. It would take more than easy sex to get her out of my mind, but hell, I'd take the bait if that's what Briley wanted. Fickle woman.

While Madison chattered about something relating to movies, I searched the back yard for the master manipulator. I spotted her at a small table in the back corner. Head in her hands, fingers digging into her temples, she looked terrible. Almost sick.

"Excuse me." I brushed my hand across Madison's lower back, interrupting her ramblings and walked away.

Briley didn't flinch when I rested my hands on her shoulders, massaging lightly.

"You all right?" I asked.

She nodded slowly. "I'm fine. How are you getting along?" She grimaced in pain with each word.

"You don't look fine, B. C'mon, let's get you to bed."

"I can't, Coop. I've—"

"Shh, don't argue with me. It's turned into a full-blown migraine, hasn't it?"

She looked up at me, pleading. Her eyes, glazed in pain, blinked slowly as if she was only waiting for permission to pass out. I could tell she was fighting it, wanting the party to be a hit and not wanting anyone to leave on her account.

"I'll take care of everyone, B. There's not much cleaning up to do since you couldn't sit still. I'll make sure everything is locked up when the guests leave. No problem."

"Okay," she whispered, rising from her seat. I held her arm as she stood and then looped mine around her waist until she was steady.

Several eyes landed on us as I walked her inside. I'd have to explain after I got her settled. Her bedroom was dark and I wanted to leave it that way considering the headache. Since I wasn't familiar with her room, I let her lead the way, walking slowly as I was a blind man in new territory.

"Get undressed and get in bed. I'll be right back. Where do you keep the medicine?"

"Kitchen. Cabinet. Above sink."

I felt my way out of the bedroom and into the light again. The cabinet above the sink held a first aid kit, bandages, hydrogen peroxide, Motrin, and Excedrin Migraine. I grabbed the green bottle of migraine medicine, read the back of the bottle, and fished out the correct dosage.

Looking through every cabinet and drawer, I finally found a Ziploc bag and filled it with crushed ice. Last, I poured a glass of water and headed back to her bedroom, using the light from my phone to see in the darkness.

Briley was in bed, curled up on her side.

"Here, baby, sit up." I handed her the glass of water and set the pills in her hand. "Excedrin Migraine."

She swallowed the pills obediently, handed me the glass, and slinked back down under the covers.

"I've got some ice for your head." I waited for her to lay flat on her back and set the ice on her forehead.

Before leaving, I took a moment to sit with her, stroking her hair until I thought she was asleep. Standing slowly, trying not to move the bed, I started for the door. I was tugged back by my shirt tail.

"Coop?"

"Yeah?"

"Don't leave. The party. After . . ."

She wasn't making sense, speaking in choppy one and two-word sentences. I tried to help her out, guessing what she was trying to say.

"I won't leave the guests. I'll lock up after everyone leaves."

"After. Come back."

"I'll check on you before I leave, B." I placed her cell phone next to her hand on the bed. "Call if you need me sooner."

Making my way back to the party, I turned the music down and got everyone's attention.

"I just wanted to thank you all for coming tonight. I hope you had a good time, I did. Briley wasn't feeling well, so she turned in for the night. Please, stay as long as you like."

I turned the music back on, but a lot lower than it was so it wouldn't disturb Briley. The hint was taken by everyone, even though I invited everyone to stay, and they trickled out, sending well wishes to their host.

Madison stayed behind, helping me clean up. We put leftover liquor in the cabinet, extinguished candles, turned off lights, and flipped a switch to stop the pool fountain. Madison handed me a beer and leaned against the stucco beside me as we finished.

"I hope Briley will be okay." She gripped the longneck in one hand, drawing circles through the condensation with the other.

"She'll be fine. It's been a long time since she had a migraine. She just needs to sleep it off." I tipped my ice cold beer up, enjoying the feel of it as it slid down my throat.

"I'm gonna head home."

The way she ran her tongue across her bottom lip was an obvious invitation. One I'd kick myself for not taking. It would've been easy enough to lock up and head out myself, but I'd never seen Briley this sick and didn't feel right about leaving her alone all night.

"You live close?"

"Yeah, across the street and a few houses down." She pushed off the wall and smoothed her hair, pulling it around her shoulder to rest over one breast.

"I'll watch to make sure you've made it in."

Holding the back gate open for her, I followed behind, closing the gate cautiously so the click wouldn't disturb Briley. Madison stood there, fishing through her clutch for keys. Once they were in hand, she turned, her body language inviting and enticing me to dive in. I knew nothing about this girl except that she was a friend of Briley's.

Taking a moment to enjoy the view, I let my eyes wander over perky breasts peeking seductively from a strapless outfit. That's as far as I got before headlights came around the corner, lighting us up like we were in a Broadway show. After the car passed, she reached in her purse and pulled out a business card.

"Give me a call sometime."

I flashed a grin and watched the sway of her hips as she walked away. Murmuring a list of curse words after she was safely to her door, I turned, locked the gate behind me, and went inside to check on Briley.

Fucking masochist.

After turning out the house lamps, I turned on my cell, using the light again to find my way to Briley. Her house was quiet, the silence so strong it was deafening. Not even the sound of her breathing was audible. When I found her, I shut off my phone and let my eyes adjust to the darkness. Dim moonlight shot through the window, illuminating her face with a soft glow. She was asleep, but absent of peace as her eyebrows turned inward, grimacing from the pain.

The ice pack was next to her, mostly melted. I made my way to the kitchen, set the bag in the sink, and grabbed a package of peas from the freezer. She woke up when I placed them on her head, but I hushed her back to sleep.

With arms folded across my chest, I stood next to her bed and watched her sleep. She was a classic, rare beauty. Her olive skin and dark eyes a stark contrast to her sweet disposition. She was as stubborn as they came, a tough exterior fooling everyone, but inside she was as fragile as a china doll.

She stirred, opening her eyes to look at me. "Is everyone gone?"

"Yes." I squatted down beside her. "How are you feeling?"

"Like little minions are trying to crack my skull open." She moaned and closed her eyes.

I stroked my fingers down her arm. "Get some rest."

Thirty-Nine

Briley

Cooper turned to leave and desperation took hold of me. He was slipping away from me. Our friendship—the only thing of importance in my life—was on the line. With my last bit of strength, I clawed at the air, finding my target and pulling his shirt toward me.

"Wait." My voice faltered. It was the only word I could get out without vomiting.

I was vaguely aware of him sliding in next to me and adjusting the bag of relief on my head. It felt different than the bag of ice, forming to my head more comfortably. I wanted to thank him for taking care of me—for taking care of everything—and not bailing on me after I'd been a jerk. Maybe our friendship could survive after all.

Falling asleep while thinking of Cooper brought forth a marvelous dream. I was rewarded—or plagued—with emotions and feelings that couldn't be understood in reality . . . only in dreams.

Heat surrounded me like a blanket still warm from a cycle in the dyer. Although too far away, the sound of the waves matched my pace as I walked along the beach.

At first I was alone, enjoying the view as the sun set over the water. Normally the deserted scene would have disturbed me, but the time alone and serenity seemed appointed.

I felt a hand slide into mine. Not a glance was shared or a word spoken, but I knew whose hand it was. Our fingers intertwined, symbolic of belonging, possession . . . home.

Cooper's eyes were stunning in the fading sunlight—bottle green with flecks of gold around the pupils. I knew I was staring, but couldn't look away. Inching forward, I longed to feel his lips touch mine for the first time. As much as I tried to rush the moment, push myself to close the space between us, my body wouldn't move any faster than a snail's pace.

Flashing red lights followed by ear-piercing sirens jolted me backward. Cooper began to fade before me and his hand turned to sand as it slipped through my fingers. The moment, along with the dream, vanished.

***

My body jerked upright in bed, looking around the room for the source of an ear-piercing noise. *William Tell Overture* filled the room as I slapped my hand across the nightstand, trying to make it stop. Once I had my phone in hand, I slid the bar across and answered, "Hello?" I made a mental note to change my mother's ringtone to something softer, if she kept calling so early.

"Hey, Bee. You up?"

"I am now." I rubbed my eyes, thankful the headache was gone.

"What've you got planned today? I thought we could go shopping. I've been looking through the sale papers and . . ."

"Sorry, mom. Can't today." The frozen bag from the night before had worked its way down and underneath me. I picked it up and smiled when I saw it was a bag of peas. *Cooper!* I looked around the room, trying to remember if he had stayed. I thought he had, but there was no trace of him. Maybe he left after I fell asleep. Distracted, I continued. "I have to work today."

"It's Sunday." I could hear the disappointment in her voice. It was almost a tradition to shop together on Sunday, or at least do *something* together.

"I know, but I've got a deadline that I keep putting off. Next Sunday?" The spot next to me had definitely been slept in. The covers were crumpled and something was different. The pillow was missing. *Strange, maybe I knocked it off onto the other side?*

"Of course, I understand." My mother was too perky for this time of morning. After all these years, she refused to accept the fact I wasn't a morning person. "How did the party go last night? Did you have a nice time with Cooper? Just like old times?" Her voice cracked as she spoke, raising an octave. She reminded me of Andy Griffith's aunt.

"Yeah, good party. But not like old times. We've both changed." I paused, assessing my head for any trace of the pain that had incapacitated me last night. My headache was gone, but my eyes felt puffy and sore.

"He's very . . . healthy now, isn't he?" She was so obvious; I chuckled at her attempt to be demure.

I sat up, resting my back against the headboard as we talked. "By healthy, you mean hot?" I laughed, imagining my mother's scolding eyes.

"Briley Beatrice Sheffield!" Her disapproving *tsk* came through the phone and I slapped a hand over my mouth to muffle my giggle as she carefully asked, "Do *you* think he's handsome?"

"Of course he is, Mother! He's worked hard for that body and I can appreciate a good-looking man."

"What are you saying, Bee?" She drew in a sharp breath. "You've finally realized you have feelings for him?" It wasn't a question, it was a statement. She presented it as a truth that everyone knew but me and now that I'd finally caught on, a bell should be rung in the town square. *"Ding, dong! She's finally got it!"*

Pausing to let my mind recall the dream she woke me from, I thought about what it all meant. Yes, I *had* developed feelings for Cooper. Feelings that needed to be shaken out of my mind immediately. Too much damage had poisoned my heart for me to think rationally and play with someone else's emotions. Especially the one person who meant more to me than . . . me.

"Jeez, Mom! We're just friends. I can't ever think of Cooper as more than that. He's my buddy, my pal, comrade, someone to kick around with. I can admit that he looks great without wanting to marry him."

"Okay, okay. I get it." Her attention was pulled away by something and our conversation withered. "I'll talk to you later. Those shoes I passed up last weekend are forty percent off. If I see anything I think you'll love . . ." She faded again, leaving the sentence for me to finish.

"Enjoy your day shopping. Love you."

"Love you, too, Bee."

***

Feeling refreshed after last night's debacle, I was eager to get outside and breathe in the fresh air. A day at the park seemed like the perfect way to spend the day writing. Dressed in shorts and a T-shirt, I pulled on my tennis shoes and grabbed my satchel, stuffing my notepad and laptop inside.

I debated making coffee, or stopping by the local coffee shop for a caramel latte. Remembering Madison in her little outfit, all legs and boobs, helped make the decision to avoid the extra calories in a latte.

Making my way to the kitchen, I stopped in my tracks, my heart unable to keep any type of regular tempo as it pulsed in frenzied chaos. A magnificent creature was sprawled out on my couch . . . shirtless. My eyes burned up his flesh, inch by inch, traveling over every molecule that came together to form Cooper Sterling. Starting with the mop of disheveled dark hair atop his head, I moved down over his sculpted shoulders, inked arms and back, down to . . . oh God, where were his jeans? My knees turned weak as I let my eyes devour his firm ass, hugged by white boxer briefs. I'd seen this same person naked, it shouldn't have affected me to see him in underwear. Of course, he was just a kid then and he sure as hell didn't have a body like that. I couldn't look away, even if I had wanted to, I couldn't move.

He groaned, hugging the pillow that was missing from my bed. The movement startled me, causing an intake of air to fill my lungs more loudly than I appreciated. *Smooth, B!* Before I could escape, he turned over and faced me.

"Good morning." His voice was groggy with sleep, turning me on like a tea kettle ready to howl. "How are you feeling?"

"Uh . . . fantastic. Great." I couldn't look at his face for more than two seconds at a time, or stop fidgeting. *Calm the hell down! Or, totally work the Tourette syndrome—a much better excuse for why you're acting like this.*

He sat up, still holding the pillow over his crotch, out of respect for me, I assumed. A cocky grin wrinkled his sleepy features as he stood, still holding the pillow like a cowboy with a hat over his nakedness.

He shrugged one shoulder, "Morning wood. Can't be helped."

"Oh my God, Coop!" My hands flew over my eyes, blocking the view of something I desperately wanted a sneak peak of. I had to move—go in the kitchen, start the coffee. I could speak more intelligently if I wasn't looking at him, half naked, wondering how hard my pillow was working to cover his morning wood.

"Thanks for staying last night," I called over my shoulder. "Why are you on the couch?" I answered myself silently, *because you made it clear nothing was going to happen. Why torture each other?* "I mean, the guest room would've been a lot more comfortable."

I heard the zipper of his jeans. *Thank God.* When he walked into the kitchen, I realized the jeans hadn't helped my case at all. *Son of a bitch, put a shirt on . . . please.* He leaned against the counter, hands shoved into his pockets so deep it pulled his jeans down, revealing enough skin to steal my focus. Looking down, I fixed my gaze on his bare feet, hoping to find my calm there. Even his toes did something to me, and I hated feet.

"The couch was fine. Very comfortable."

"Coffee," I reminded myself, turning to get two mugs from the cabinet.

"What are your plans today?" he asked, taking a mug from me. He pursed his lips and blew over the liquid before taking a sip.

"I was planning on taking my work to the park." Gripping my mug with both hands, I found the courage to say more. "Or, if you're free, we could hang out. Watch a movie, eat a bunch of crap?"

"I don't eat crap anymore." He smirked.

"You could come to the park with me? Shoot some baskets while I worked?"

There was definitely tension between us, thick with awkwardness. I wondered if he hated it as much as I did.

"Can't. I've got plans today." He traced the rim of the cup with his index finger, seemingly deep in thought.

I let my eyes roam over his body, a daring, stupid move on my part. His chiseled body beckoned me to press against it, feeling his strong arms wrap me in a protective embrace. Memories of us together less than a week ago flashed through my mind, tampering with my ability to reason.

When my cell phone played the familiar bray, alerting me to a text from The Ass, my clarity returned.

His head jerked up, eyes squinted in the direction of my phone. "Blake?"

One shoulder shrugged in agreement, laced with an attitude of carelessness.

"Want me to—?"

"Nope." I shot him a look that I hoped portrayed the fact that Blake wasn't worth either of our time, but his reaction said he misread me.

I tried to smooth things over. "I'm done." A heavy sigh released some of the tension in my shoulders as I rubbed a sore spot with my thumb. "I just want to move on with my life already. Enjoy being free and single. Jeez!" I picked up my satchel and slung it over my shoulder, stuffing the phone in a side pocket.

Cooper handed me his cup, scooped his shirt and keys in one hand, and flashed me a sympathetic smile before heading out the door. I stood there, my mind battling over what had just taken place. The same couch that housed Cooper's exquisite, almost-naked body called to me, pulling me deep into its cushions as I sat down. I clutched the pillow he'd borrowed, inhaling his scent and allowing myself to daydream about a life with him. Waking up in his arms, sharing coffee before he left for work in the morning, having a cold beer waiting for him when he got home, watching the sun set from the back porch each night.

Another text came through, this time from Madison. I read hers first, asking if I was home. Next was Blake's. A short audio clip of two people moaning, obviously enjoying a sexual experience, preceded the text:

A man has needs & U were stale.

Tears filled my eyes, bringing my mood crashing down to the level of my self-esteem. I thought about replying with a snide comment about his penis size or how it took two to tango, but I needed to be done with him.

Forty

Cooper

Work was my only hope. I hopped in my truck and headed to the hardware store. I needed to keep busy and distract myself from Briley. My heart was broken and a sinking feeling swept over me, threatening to take me down.

I bought enough to fix all of the things that had been on my list since I moved in. A new part for the garage door, material to fix a few broken tiles around the pool, a replacement head for one of the sprinklers, and enough lumber to not only fix the fence, but replace the whole thing if needed.

As soon as all of the material was unloaded from the truck, I grabbed a beer from the fridge and popped the cap off using the edge of the table. After a drink to ease my nerves, I started on the pool tile, chipping away the broken tile and readying it for new ones. I worked for an hour in the hot sun, wiping the sweat off my forehead with the back of my hand. Once my forearms were wet with sweat, I remembered the handkerchief in my back pocket.

All the tools were gathered for mixing the mortar when my phone rang. I thought about ignoring it, eager to get the tile project finished, but answered anyway.

"Hello?"

"You're out of breath, did I interrupt something?"

"Hey, Ryan. I'm replacing some tiles around the pool."

"Oh. Well, hurry and finish up. Chesterfield's, eight o'clock sharp. Bring your guitar."

"I don't know—"

"What do you mean, you don't know? Have your sorry ass there at eight or I'll drag you there. Will's doing us a favor, letting us play tonight."

"It's been a while." I'd only dabbled on the acoustic a few times. "What are we covering?"

"Who knows? Bring both guitars and we'll see where the night takes us."

Hell, I wanted to keep busy, get my mind off Briley. This seemed as good a way as any.

"All right, I'm in."

Forty-One

Briley

Taking my work to the park turned out to be a good idea, and I was able to finish the article due the next morning. Since I finished it sooner than anticipated, I started on the next assignment which I'd been looking forward to. I was tasked with a personal article for the magazine—something that hadn't been done before—compiling old recipes from generations past, one or two from the magazine's editorial staff.

My mother was a culinary genius and accredited her mother and grandmother for most of the recipes, so I compiled some of my favorites along with those my colleagues had sent in. Each recipe would include a short bio and photo of the four generations.

My final task was researching my grandmother and great grandmother. My mother provided me a lot of information: birth and death dates, where they were born, and cooking stories to use in the magazine. But I needed more. Wanted more.

When I couldn't find anything on the Tremblay name—my mother's maiden name—I paid for an ancestry search site. Since my mother was from Canada, I assumed I'd have trouble finding information and this site promised results from across the globe. I had several names to research, maiden and married names of all three generations. After hours of research, I came up empty handed. None of the names matched any of the information or photos I was given.

I dialed my mom for answers. "Am I spelling this last name correctly, T-r-a-m-b-l-a-y?"

"Yes, that's right."

"I can't find anything on the internet for any of the last names you've given me."

"Probably because they were immigrants. I can tell you anything you need to know."

"Okay. I'll come by soon."

It was scorching by the time I left the park, but I was back home by one o'clock. I was enjoying an ice cold glass of tea, when Madison rang my doorbell.

"Come in." I stepped aside and shut the door behind her. It was like having an oven door open.

Madison took a seat on one of the barstools, leaning her elbows on the island. She was fidgety and nervous, which made me uneasy.

"How are you feeling?" she asked, her expression completely lacking concern.

"Perfect. Thanks for asking. It's been a long time since I've had a migraine like that."

"Good." She nodded her head one too many times.

"What's going on?" I asked over my shoulder as I grabbed another glass from the cabinet and poured her some iced tea. The tension in the air was thick and I wondered what had her so unnerved.

As I expected, she had at least a thousand words she needed to get out and they began bubbling out of her before my own lips touched the cool glass gripped between my palms.

"Tell me everything about Cooper. He's so . . . funny and smart and . . . God, those green eyes."

My headache from last night could easily be brought back with her breathless ramblings, at least one pitch too high. I rubbed my temples, trying to block her words.

"You sure you're feeling better?" she asked, assessing my mood.

"Yeah, just sore." Trying to change the subject, I added, "I'm sorry I had to cut the evening short."

"It was perfect, a very successful party." She tapped her fingernails on the granite countertop, but stopped once she remembered my head. "So . . . Cooper. He wouldn't leave you to walk me home, but he was sweet to watch and make sure I got home all right."

I breathed a sigh of relief, trying to play it off as a stretch. "Cooper's great." I raised my arms, feeling the pull of each muscle. "A perfect gentleman." All the things I loved about him poured out of me freely. "He's kind and considerate, good to his parents. He always puts everyone's needs before his own. I swear if there was only one banana left on a stranded island, he'd . . ." My voice faded as I recalled the last laugh we shared. "And he can make you laugh until you can't breathe."

She studied my face. "So *why* aren't you dating him?"

"Oh," I laughed. "I've seen Cooper naked." My body stiffened. "That didn't come out right. I mean, I've known him my entire life. I'm talking naked toddler. I haven't seen him naked recently . . ." There I went again, shoving my foot in my mouth, and the more I tried to make it better, it kept getting worse. The point was to turn her off of him, not make him sound more appealing.

Thankfully, I was saved from further reckless banter as my phone buzzed with an incoming text.

"We're friends," I mumbled, reaching for my phone. "Just friends."

I read the text from my mom that included a picture of strappy sandals that tied around the ankles, and typed in a reply.

No, I don't think I'd wear those. Thanks, though.

I couldn't blame Madison for noticing Cooper. He was quite a catch. Even though he was rough around the edges, he had a great job, captivating personality, and he was the most trustworthy person I knew. Of course, there was the obvious—tall, dark, and handsome. A sculpted body with enough ink to make your mind teeter on the edge of good guy and bad boy.

"So tell me everything. It's so hard to find a good man these days with all the creeps out there. Finally, I meet a nice guy *and* he's yummy." My head was spinning. Did she really just call Cooper yummy? "My God, I couldn't stop thinking about him. How you've managed to remain 'just friends' is beyond me." She made air quotes over her head. "You've never had feelings for each other?"

This question would have to be answered carefully. Yes, we had feelings for each other. But there were two reasons I wouldn't share that with her. One, she and I weren't close enough for that kind of sharing. Two, I wasn't about to play the role of fickle princess. I'd made my choice and I'd deal with it like an adult. However, as I stood across from a woman I'd summed up as competition, I had a strong desire to make her believe we were together. She wasn't his type—*yeah, right! Gorgeous, busty blonde. Keep telling yourself that, B*—so I should've felt secure knowing Cooper wouldn't go near her. Instead, I played it safe, hovering on the border of reality and fiction.

"I guess you could say we don't indulge in any *real* feelings for each other," I laughed and shook my head, looking down at my fingernails that needed to be re-polished. "He asked me to marry him once." I let that settle in the air, gauging her expression. Her wide eyes and stiff shoulders made me feel like I was winning a race.

"Oh, so . . . oh." She stuttered. "I thought you said . . ."

I was a terrible liar and although it felt good to have the upper hand, I just couldn't do it. It wasn't who I was and before long I was giving away more than I intended.

"We were kids—elementary school." I looked down and to the left, a slight smile playing at my lips as I recalled the sweet memory. "He was pretty impressive, even at that age. It must've been Valentine's Day . . . he gave me two bears with magnetic arms. When you hold them close, their arms lock around each other. I still have them." I shook my head. "I didn't even know the *Will you marry* me note was tucked in the pocket of the heart between them." My voice faded, recalling the look on Cooper's face the next few days at school.

"Oh. My. God. How sweet. When did you find out about the note?" She leaned in, ready for the entire story.

"Two or three days later. I remember he acted so weird around me those few days. Kept staring at me like he was waiting for something." I chuckled. "He was waiting for my answer and I hadn't even seen the question. Finally, he stormed up to me after school and said, *'Never mind. Just forget it!'* By the time I found the note, the moment had passed and we never talked about it."

"Wow. And you kept the bears?"

"Of course. I mean, they're in my room at my mother's house."

"You guys are still pretty close, huh?"

"Very." I enunciated the word; a warning, I hoped. "Always have been and always will be." I didn't realize how lame and middle school-ish it sounded until it was already out of my mouth, riding through the air on an uncomfortable silence.

She stood, taking her glass to the sink. "Thanks for the lemonade, Briley. I'm still holding you to your promise of going to the clubs with me."

"Make it happen. I'm so ready to move on and have some fun."

Forty-Two
Briley

A week had sped by since I'd heard from Cooper last, leaving me little time to think about anything other than work. Although the recent trip to Nashville was exciting—especially sitting two tables over from Nicole Kidman—I would liked to have shared it with someone other than my assistant.

Lack of sleep from spending two nights in a hotel with thin walls, meant another day of editing after my article was finished. Fully concentrated on the task at hand, I got started.

Cooper called at eleven thirty and I stared at the phone like it was foreign. On the third ring, I slid the bar over and answered, not knowing what kind of mood would greet me from the other side.

"Hello?"

"Hey, it's me." He paused for a moment and I wasn't sure if it was my turn to say something. I didn't. "Wanna grab some lunch?"

"Um," I lingered a moment, taking time to contemplate my answer. He was acting like nothing happened between us and I wasn't sure how to take it. Then again, it would be fine for me to move on and forget everything. Start fresh. "Sure, okay."

"I'm on my way," he announced and ended the call.

By *on my way,* did he mean he was walking to the car, or driving toward me? I rushed to the closet and rifled through my clothes, choosing a pair of khaki shorts and a blousy coral top. The shirt was too much, so I flung it onto the bed to hang later, and chose a pale pink polo instead. Usually by now I had a summertime glow and chose to forgo makeup, but I needed a little color on my cheeks and a dab of concealer under my eyes.

The doorbell rang, answering my question of whether he had already been on his way over when he called. I grabbed my tan boat shoes, well-worn and comfortable, and grabbed my purse before greeting him at the door.

"Hey, Coop."

"Hi, B." He shoved his hands in his pockets. Hopefully we could sever the tension and get back to the comfortable state I relished.

"Where do you want to eat?"

"I'm dying for a burger, is that good for you?"

"Yes, The Pit? They have the best shakes." I pulled the door closed and locked it behind us.

The Pit was crowded, but we managed a booth by the window. Cooper ordered for both of us, something I wasn't accustomed to, but he was spot on, ordering exactly what I would have chosen for myself.

"I'm sorry I disappeared on you, B. I needed some time and I thought you did too."

"Yep." I nodded, glancing out of the window at a passerby. "Let's just start fresh and move forward, okay? I don't want any more uneasiness between us."

"It's going to take more than that for me. I don't want to lose you, but it's hard being around you right now."

"What?" My eyes widened. A knot formed in my stomach pulling all goodness from my mood. "Why?" I had to blink away the tears forming.

"I want more. You don't. I'm a fighter, B, you know that and once again I have to suppress my feelings. Pretend there's nothing between us so we can save our friendship." He leaned back in the seat, one arm slung over the back.

"It's hard for me, too, Coop. But you're worth it." I tore a tiny piece off the corner of the paper napkin in my lap and rolled it into a ball. I couldn't look into his eyes and read the expression behind them. It was too risky. We needed to get some things out in the open, but it was harder than I thought and causing me to lose my appetite. After straightening my silverware, I reached across and lined up his. I needed a reprieve from the subject—a brief one would do—so I changed it.

"So . . . did you call Madison?" The words left my mouth before I could take them back.

"Not yet." No amount of curiosity was worth the pain that was inflicted with his answer. I tried to hide the shock and disappointment by picking at a tear in the faux leather fabric of my seat. When I looked up, our eyes locked. I was sure mine were unable to hide the pained expression.

"But you're going to?"

He nodded and shrugged.

"Great." Someone's voice cracked. It was mine. "That's so great. She's great. You'll like her, she's really . . . great."

"For chrissakes, B! You're so jealous, it's comical."

Shaking my head, I creased my brows. "I am not." My arms folded across my chest defensively.

"Admit it."

"What? Jealous of *Madison?* That's ridiculous. She's—she's . . ."

"Great?" he interjected.

"What-ev-er." I sounded like a valley girl. "Jealousy's not my thing. I'm glad you found someone to . . . whatever it is you want to do."

The thought of his lips against hers made me queasy. Yeah, I was jealous. So what? That didn't change the fact that *we* couldn't go down that road. She might have his lips, his body, but I had his friendship. *Really? Was that really a prize worthy of cheering?* Suddenly, I wanted to spew a string of curse words, mingling her name between a few of them. The subject needed to be changed and my milkshake was immediately required to cool me down.

The waitress set our shakes in front of us and I sipped mine with a force that made a tornado seem tame.

"Fuck, I won't call her. Happy?"

"I don't care if you call her or not. But it will be awkward, since she's *my friend* and all." I tried to keep my voice steady, but the anger took over.

"Fine." He spooned out the chopped cookies atop his shake and chewed. "You have any other *friends* you don't want me to date?"

My body tensed at his words. He was right. If it was up to me, I'd come up with a reason for him not to date anyone. How freaking selfish of me. I could do this. I loved him enough to put aside my feelings, let him be happy.

"No. Date whoever you want." I poked my straw around, taking the aggression out on the frozen concoction. "I just want you to be happy, Coop. Surely you know that?" My words softened, but my insides raged at the thought of him dating *her*.

"B—" Before he could say anything, our server delivered the food. I was too hungry to hold on to my chaotic emotions, so our conversation melted as easily as the cheese on the hamburger calling to me.

"I didn't realize how hungry I was." I covered my mouth as I chewed and tried to talk.

"You've lost a lot of weight, B. Eat up." He winked and sunk his teeth into his own burger, grease, ketchup, and mayonnaise dripping from the bun.

Only able to finish half of the monster burger, I sipped on my shake, letting the cool coconut and vanilla cleanse my palate.

Cooper's eyes darkened without warning and his forehead creased with anger. I whipped my head around, trying to find the cause of his distress. Blake had seen us through the window and was making his way to the entrance. Cooper flung his napkin onto the seat next to him and stood.

"Cooper, sit back down . . . please!"

He ignored my plea, closing the space between him and Blake near the hostess stand. "Outside," he commanded, pushing the door open.

"I didn't come here to talk to you," Blake said and took a step in my direction.

Cooper grabbed him by the arm, shoving him outside. Knowing it would end badly, I threw two twenties on the table—too much, but there wasn't time to wait for change—and rushed outside to calm the storm. Nothing physical had taken place yet, but words were spat at each other, and if they had been dogs, there would've been raised hackles as they circled each other.

"Stop this!" I demanded, my words either unheard or ignored as neither acknowledged me. "I'm serious. Blake! Cooper!"

Nothing. Not a glance in my direction. They eyed each other and if they'd blinked, I hadn't witnessed it. No matter what I did or said, they carried on, slinging words like swords, both trying to get the deepest cut.

Cooper repeated a lot of the same things I had already said to Blake during our many fights, but he infused an abundance of curse words.

"Why won't you leave her the fuck alone? You had the best and you pissed it all away because you couldn't keep your dick in your pants."

Blake fought back, defending himself and cutting Cooper with accusations that didn't hold any weight.

"Fuck you. You've always been in love with her, you just weren't man enough to do anything about it." He chuckled, revealing a sadistic side that even I hadn't seen before. "Funny thing is, she was desperate to run to your arms, but you weren't here. Where were you . . . in the military? No, no. Now I remember, you were in prison. Fucking loser."

Blake went beyond crossing a line and it was obvious he was provoking Cooper. It would benefit him to have Cooper back in prison and all it would take is one punch. I saw a glint of fear in Blake's eyes, knowing he was getting closer to having his nose shattered, or jaw broken.

Cooper's body tensed, his fists balled at his sides, the veins in his neck protruding. I knew this look, this stance, all too well. He'd been a fighter his entire life. He'd command me to stay out of the way—behind a tree, or on top of the slide at school— many times as he battled. He always won and as much as I would've loved to have seen Blake on his ass, blood dripping from his broken nose, I couldn't let it happen.

I had to do something, but as heated as they both were, I didn't know what would work. They ignored my verbal pleas.

A murderous rage flashed in Cooper's eyes as Blake continued to provoke. "She's lousy in bed any—"

Before I could move to intervene, Cooper gripped Blake by the shirt, jerking him forward before his fist made contact with Blake's face. He must've held back because Blake was able to stumble back to his feet. If Cooper had intended to knock him out, he could easily have done it. Blake brushed himself off, rubbing the soreness from his jaw.

"You insane prick! You've just earned a ticket back to the slammer." Blake began to walk away. I called after him.

"Wait! Please, Blake. What do you want?" The desperation in my voice had a pitch that I hardly recognized. "Leave Cooper out of this and I'll give you whatever you want."

Cooper gripped my arm. "The fuck you will." He gave Blake a warning glance. "Do what you have to do, you little punk. Run and tell. But I swear to God, if you come near her again, I'll kill you with my bare hands."

Blake backed up, getting some distance between him and Cooper before answering, "Good luck reaching me from your cage."

Cooper was on him again, fists and knees knocking relentlessly into Blake. Blake tried to fight back and got a few throws in, but it didn't faze Cooper in the least. Everyone knows that when two dogs are caught up in a fight, there's nothing to be done. Stupidity—laced with an ample amount of desperation—took over, causing me to attempt the dumbest thing I'd ever done to date. I jumped in front of Cooper, trying to get his attention.

His clenched fist, aimed for Blake's face, hit me instead.

Forty-Three

Cooper

It happened so fast, I didn't see her jump in front of me until it was too late. I caught myself as soon as it registered that she was in front of me, but there was still enough force to knock her down. I fell to my knees, beside her crumpled body that lay face down.

"B? Oh, God, B. I'm sorry. Are you all right? Talk to me."

She moaned and tried to move. At least she was conscious, thank God. Scooping her into my arms, I helped her sit up, checking for damage. Her knees were scraped and bloody, along with a layer of flesh lost from her hands as she'd slid against the pavement.

"I'm fine," she grumbled.

Blake spewed off a few obscenities and walked off.

"I'm so sorry, B. You jumped right in front of me. Why would—?"

"Because, asshole . . . you were going to punch him."

She brushed her hands along her shorts, dotting the fabric with blood, and tried to stand. Holding her arm and supporting her back, I helped, holding on until she was steady.

"I couldn't just sit there like a pussy and do nothing. He's a bully and the only way—"

She interrupted again, "I know, but can't you see? He *wants* you to throw a punch. If you're in prison, he has control again. Why wouldn't you listen to me?"

It was my turn to interrupt. "Ah. So I was supposed to stand there like a douche and let *you* handle everything?"

Maybe Briley had changed more than I realized while I was away, her sweetness fading and a bossy bitchiness taking over. Telling me not to fight, who I could and couldn't date . . . what was next? Picking out my clothes? *Don't think so.*

"You can't save me from everything, Cooper. Be someone else's hero if you need to, but I'm not going to be the reason you end up back in prison." Her words spewed like venom, piercing and poisoning. With her purse slung over her shoulder, she turned and stormed down the sidewalk.

"Briley, wait!" I was right behind her, but she wouldn't turn.

"Please, Cooper. Leave me alone. Just this once . . . let me be!"

She rushed around the corner and slipped into a tight alley. I gave her the space she needed, waiting against the brick wall after looking to see that she was alone and safe. She couldn't see me, but I could hear her sobs.

It took all I had not to rush to her side, especially when she began talking to herself. I cupped my hand, trying to hear what she was saying. I couldn't hear everything, but enough to know she was infecting herself with sad lies.

"My body's . . . busted up just like my insides. How could I be so stupid . . . think . . . be worthy . . . anyone's attention? Now . . . Blake . . . prison . . ."

I heard her shuffle to her feet, so I leaned against the wall and pretended to check my phone. She sighed when she saw me, but didn't say a word. We drove to her house in silence, the drive seeming twice as long as usual. Pulling into her driveway, I had to say something before she got out of the truck. We couldn't leave things this way.

"I'm so sorry, B. Please, forgive me?"

She turned, narrowed her eyes, and answered. Her voice was so full of emotion, I had to rub the ache settling in my chest.

"If you cared about me like you say you do, you would never, ever risk leaving me alone again." She was angry, eyes squinted and teeth clenched as she spoke, but I could hear the emotion behind her words. More than angry, she sounded hurt. "I needed you, Cooper. Needed someone to talk to and laugh with when things got so tough I didn't want to live. I needed your stupid jokes to get me through five-hour crying jags, but where were you? Prison." Her hands were up in the air one minute and slamming back down to rest in fists by her sides the next. "I know you didn't deserve prison and that I owe you my life for defending me. I'm grateful. Believe me, I am. I just thought once I got you back . . ." She lowered her head, studying her hands like the answers were written on her palms. "I didn't think you'd risk everything so fast . . . over someone as unworthy as Blake."

She rubbed her swollen cheek, already bruising, and climbed out of the truck. I jumped out and caught her before she could fish her keys from her purse. It took a little force to hold her against me while she tried to wiggle free. She finally settled, letting me hold her, but never moved her arms that dangled at her sides.

"I'm sorry, B. I really am. My crazy can't be tamed when it comes to you."

I pulled back after a moment, gazing into her glassy eyes. She was too stubborn to cry in front of me, letting the anger win over sadness.

"Blake's not going to press charges. He's too scared, knowing what I'd do to him before they locked me up." I smiled, trying to convince her . . . and myself.

"You're wrong, Cooper. Blake got what he wanted, what he'd planned all along. He'll press charges. And there's nothing we can do now, unless you've got a ticket out of the country and a whole lot of money stashed somewhere."

She turned, walking into the house at a snail's pace. I'd fucked up royally and now I had to pay . . . again.

***

Driving home, all I could think about was how to get out of the mess I'd made. All roads led me back to the slammer; there was no getting out of it. My only hope was relying on Blake's cowardice. I pulled into the driveway, shut the engine off, and got out. Before I could shut the door, two police vehicles pulled in behind me.

"Cooper Sterling?" one of the cops asked.

***

Same room, different person. I thought as a petite woman with a badge sat across from me in the interrogation room. Her blond hair was pulled back into a low ponytail with bangs she kept brushing to the side like it was a nervous habit. She had a kind face, unlike the dude who processed me the last time. It didn't matter—kind or not—the outcome would be the same. I knew the drill now and wanted to save her the trouble, but kept my mouth shut for some reason. Maybe it was out of respect for a newbie. She was much too fidgety and nervous to have any time under her belt. I thought since it was a clean, easy case, they were letting her practice on me.

She looked up, her expression one I knew too well. She wasn't nervous, she was flirty. "You like to fight?"

I shrugged.

"Let me guess, boxer?" She smiled. "Nope, MMA fighter, am I right?"

What was this, *Raising Arizona? Did she honestly think a cop and prison rat could have a relationship?* I had to stifle a laugh. Did she think we'd hook up *before* I went away, or would she wait for me to get out?

She looked down at the papers in her folder, studying them again before she spoke. "Felony battery, third degree felony battery . . ." Shaking her head like a parent disappointed over a child's report card, she asked, "Do you have any idea how much trouble you're in, Mr. Sterling?"

Of course I did, but I kept my mouth shut. I knew the drill and wouldn't say anything until my lawyer arrived. A knock on the door interrupted my interrogation and drew her out of the room. She was gone for at least an hour, leaving me alone with my thoughts and a plastic cup of water.

When she returned, she didn't take time to sit as she spoke. "Sorry to keep you waiting, Mr. Sterling." She studied a piece of paper for a moment, a flash of confusion in her eyes before she addressed me again. "You're free to go. All charges have been dropped."

I stood slowly, waiting for her to burst out laughing and yell, *"Got ya!"* before telling me how long I'd be spending in prison. Instead, she opened the door and led me toward the front to sign some papers.

On our way through the halls, I asked the obvious question, "Why were the charges dropped?"

"Are you complaining?" she asked.

"Hell no. Just curious. You seem just as surprised."

"I am," she said, shaking her head. "I don't have answers for you. Only a letter stating your release, signed by the Chief."

I stopped walking and tried to process what she said. Who gave a shit whether or not I went to prison besides Briley and my parents? None of them had any power to change a thing. Hell, even a well-paid lawyer could only bring my sentence down by a few months. Who had that kind of power?

"Who dropped the charges?" I asked. She didn't budge, just stared at me. I decided to play on her affections, leaning against the wall casually, flashing a flirty smile. "Miss," I looked at her badge, intentionally raking my eyes over her body before meeting her eyes again. "Locke. I need answers. Please don't send me away unsatisfied." It was a cheesy, creepy line that I was ashamed of, but she fell hook, line, and sinker.

After looking around to make sure we weren't heard, she leaned in, whispering what she knew. "All I know is, someone called and the Chief obeyed without question."

I shook my head. "Doesn't make sense."

"No, it doesn't, but just like that," she snapped her fingers. "Charges dropped and you're free to go."

She gave me her number before I walked out of the building, a free man. I'd never call her, of course.

***

My phone was dead, so I had to wait to get home and let it charge enough to call Briley.

"Hello?" Her voice was somber.

I couldn't help play the game; I was in a fantastic mood. I shouldn't have done it and knew better as soon as the words were out of mouth . . . too late.

221

"Don't hang up. They gave me one phone call."

"Oh, Cooper." She sounded distraught.

"I'm sorry, B, I shouldn't have done that. Look at your caller ID. I'm calling you from my cell. Not my jail cell, my cell phone. Look." I heard her pull the phone away from her ear to look at the screen.

"How? I know you were arrested, your dad called and told me."

"The charges were dropped." I popped the cap off a bottle of Rolling Rock. I still couldn't believe my luck.

"Why would Blake have you arrested and then drop the charges? Is that even legally possible?"

Pulling the bottle away from my lips, I swallowed hard. "Wasn't Blake."

"Who then, and why?"

"No idea but I'm not going to press my luck and ask questions."

"Yeah . . ." She mumbled. "I wouldn't either. I'm curious though. No one does anything without expecting something in return."

Later that night I couldn't let it go. Someone with enough power to do so had dropped the charges against me. After racking my brain over every possibility, I made a dick move and dialed the number Officer Locke gave me.

"Hello?" she answered with a sleepy voice.

I looked at the clock. Two in the morning, *shit!* "I'm sorry to call so late, I should've looked at the clock. I'll call you another time."

"No, it's fine. I'm awake. Is this—?"

"Cooper Sterling."

"I thought so." Her voice sounded bashful suddenly, more girly than before. I hated being this guy but I needed answers. I'd have to find a way to make it up to her.

"Listen, I was thinking about what happened earlier. I won't be able to sleep until I know who dropped those charges. I don't have many friends so I need to know if it's someone I need to watch out for. You know a favor for a favor kinda thing? Because I don't play like that."

I heard a heavy sigh on the other end of the phone. I was losing her. "When you find something—anything—maybe we could meet up for a coffee or something?" I ran a hand through my hair and grimaced. *Schmuck!*

Forty-Four
Briley

After another restless night of Cooper-filled dreams, I needed to clear my head. Two weeks of barely talking to Cooper was forcing a wedge between us that would be difficult to remove if we didn't do something about it soon. Other than his time away, we'd never gone this long without hanging out. He was busy with a new project and I was traveling with my new job, but I had hoped he would go with me on the last trip. We both enjoyed rides and although I was there to write about Epcot's many fine dining choices, I was looking forward to riding Tower of Terror and Rockin' Rollercoaster with him. But he said he needed space, time away from me to reset.

A morning jog always did the trick of lifting my mood and clearing the cobwebs. Eager to get outside, I put on my tennis shoes, fit the ear buds of my iPod Shuffle into my ears, and clipped the miniature piece onto my tank top. My pace started slow, warming up my muscles and filling my lungs with the early morning air. Running before sun up was always my preference, the air absent of humidity. I loved starting the day before the sun, welcoming the early morning rays as they brought color to the gray scenery around me.

I started running faster when the Foo Fighters sang "My Hero"—one of my favorites. Even through my ear buds, I heard footsteps behind me. I picked up my pace, not fond of letting anyone pass me, and risked a quick glance at the shadow gaining on me. My competitive streak took over as I rounded a corner and I hoped they would back off. I couldn't keep that pace for much longer.

"Briley!" I heard my name being called and glanced back. Slowing my pace to an easy jog, I let Madison catch up.

"Sorry, I didn't know it was you." *Even if I had, I wouldn't have let you pass me!* I thought to myself. Since she'd shared her feelings about Cooper, I'd lost interest in her as a friend. Maybe it was petty of me since I didn't want more than friendship from Cooper, but I couldn't stand the thought of them together. "Are you just starting or finishing up?"

"Just starting."

We jogged alongside each other, one ear bud still in, the other dangling so we could hear each other. She must've had a lot on her mind, too, as we ran mostly in silence. We passed by Madison's house first at the end of the run.

"Good run," she panted.

"You, too." I returned. There was an obvious tension between us. I knew why on my side of things, but didn't understand why she'd feel the same. Maybe I'd been a bad friend. I was terrible with girlfriends, so that shouldn't have surprised me. But it did. Madison and I had been getting along and planned on going out soon. I tried to shake it off. Maybe she was just having a bad day.

"Hey . . ." she called, as I turned to leave. When I looked back, she seemed to be tossing an idea around in her head, like she was unsure if she should say what she was thinking.

"Yeah?" I nudged.

She waited a few clicks before spitting out what she wanted to say.

"You going to watch them play Friday night?" She kept her eyes on me, waiting for my answer as she swallowed half of her water bottle.

"Who?"

"Cooper and the guys. They're playing Maxims."

"Oh, right. Sorry, I thought you were talking sports," I lied. I had no idea Cooper and the guys were playing Friday night. He hadn't played in two, maybe three years. When did he have time to pick it back up, let alone get a gig? I tried to hide the surprise—or was it jealousy?—that he'd told her about it and not me. I wanted to ask her when he'd talked to her and how. Had they run into each other at a coffee shop? No way had he called her. No . . . way. At least that's what I tried to convince myself. He hadn't told me because we hadn't talked. Still, this was huge and normally he'd want me there. The hurt from my tone bled through when I answered her. "I'm not sure if I can make it. I've got a lot on my plate."

She seemed pleased that I wouldn't be there. It wasn't obvious, but there was a glint in her eyes that gave her away. That sealed the deal on my decision of supporting Cooper the first time he was back on stage. I'd be there. It was selfish to want Cooper to wait for me, but I couldn't let Madison near him. Anyone else, just not *her*.

Forty-Five

Briley

Maxim's wasn't a large club, but on a Friday night it would be packed. Since I didn't leave in time to get a spot in front, I decided to be fashionably late and stand in the back. I was torn between wanting to surprise Cooper before the show and waiting until it was over. He never got stage fright in the past, but this was his first gig in a while. It made sense that he might be a little jittery. Plus, he hadn't had the decency to tell his best friend about the gig, so I was a little miffed. Either way, I wanted to look good. Unless hell froze over and I hadn't been notified, Madison would be dressed to kill.

I chose a pair of black shorts—dressy enough for eveningwear, short enough for the club—and a plum off-the-shoulder top. Taking my time with makeup, I created a smoky eye and lined it, pulling the eyeliner to the edge and finishing with a cat tail. After staining my lips with a color similar to my top, I added gloss for shine and slipped into a pair of black stilettos. Looking myself over in the full length mirror gave me a confidence that would carry me through the night.

As suspected, the club was packed. I ordered a shot of tequila, needing the liquid courage as fast as I could get it, and took a lemon drop martini with me to stand at the back of the room. Looking around, I couldn't find a single familiar face. A continuous roar came from the crowd. Nothing specific, no words that I could make out, just a rolling noise that let me know everyone was having a good time.

When the lights dimmed, a spotlight focused on Danny, the drummer, and the crowd settled into a silence that had my heart racing—partly from anticipation, mostly from nerves. I missed him walking out onto the stage, he was just magically there when the stage lit up. It was a good effect, exciting the crowd before the rest of the band appeared. Danny was a total hipster with thick, black framed glasses and spiked hair. Although I couldn't see, I knew he had on skinny jeans. I didn't know him well, but enough to know he was the shyest of the group. He played a few beats, getting the crowd pumped until the rest of the members found their place on stage.

I spotted Cooper immediately, to the left of the lead singer from my point of view. I knew all the guys except one and let my eyes rake over the stranger briefly before getting back to Cooper and studying every detail of his exquisite body. Shredded jeans sat low on his hips while a black T-shirt hugged his muscular arms and chest. He looked out of place on stage amongst the others. He and Ryan were the only ones not rocking the hipster look, but at least Ryan had longer bangs that swooped over one eye. Cooper looked like someone they drug out of an UFC arena. He looked nervous, which made me tense. *Please, God, let him do well. He needs this.* I knew he was good, but without practice, he was most likely feeling insecure.

I kicked myself for not calling him, giving him a pep talk. But we hadn't spoken and I wasn't sure he wanted me there. After telling me he needed space, I caved to my cowardice, standing against the back wall so I could watch in secret. He readied his guitar, adjusting it to hang comfortably and checking the amp cord to make sure it was plugged in properly. My heart pounded, worrying for him, with him. Cooper strummed the guitar, bringing the first notes to the room. His fingers danced along the strings with expertise and my nerves melted away. He was in his element, the crowd going wild. I knew the song immediately and my flesh pebbled with goose bumps. It was one of our favorites, although I couldn't tell you the name right then. At that moment I could only concentrate on his hands working that guitar, eliciting cheers from the crowd.

When the drummer eased in on the cymbals, pulling the swell into an intensity that had the crowd going wild before he even began on the toms, I realized they were covering "Everlong" by the Foo Fighters.

Our song. I smiled, the memory of sitting next to Cooper day after day while he learned to play it by ear. Another memory flooded my mind, squeezing my heart muscle until it ached—Cooper serenading me with this song on my back porch. My gaze finally unlocked from his hands, moving up to his face. His grin was wide, flashing white teeth and dimples that I'm sure had every woman in the place salivating. Music flowed through the room like a wave of energy, the crowd pulsing with rhythm as they danced to the beat. The lead singer, Ryan, encouraged them to clap along and the room obeyed. Everyone sang along, knowing every lyric, as I did, but I couldn't sing or clap. My eyes were focused on Cooper and how his body moved as he handled the guitar. The muscles in his forearms bulged with each stroke, his eyes focusing on the strings when he had a more difficult riff to play. I shook my head in awe as I watched him, working the crowd into a frenzy with his skills and cocky attitude.

For the first time I felt like a teenager with a massive crush. Sweaty palms, flushed cheeks, accelerated heart rate, and a smile that wouldn't go away, no matter how I tried. The combination threatened to make a fool of me if anyone had taken their eyes off of Cooper for even a moment to glance my way. But they didn't and I couldn't blame them.

By the time the song ended, I was a mess. I hadn't looked at Cooper as my play-in-the-mud buddy in a long time, but looking at him now, you couldn't have convinced me he was *ever* just a friend. I was silly, head-over-heels crushing on him.

After two more songs, Cooper took a swig of water and stepped into Ryan's spot, smack center of the spotlight. He set his electric guitar down and picked up an acoustic, tucking his head under the strap so it hung across his body. He spoke into the microphone, his voice low and laced with a tension I didn't understand. He seemed so comfortable on stage, but now melancholy radiated off of him so richly, a liquid silence rushed over the room.

"This song . . ." He cleared his throat and paused, an uncomfortable silence wafting through the crowd as they stood and stared. I wanted to save him, yell at everyone for watching his misery. More than anything, I wanted to understand his pain, erase it. What was going on with him? He continued, strumming a few chords as he spoke. "Let's slow things down a bit and then we'll get the party started again." He closed his eyes, strumming the strings until he coaxed out a melody so alluring the crowd swayed under his spell.

He kept his eyes shut as he began to sing, his voice rich and sultry but laced with heartache. Danny beat on the drums softly, enhancing Cooper's lyrics. I focused on the words, the story he was relaying. He sang of trying to hold his head up and not being able to call. His fingers swept across the strings, a spine tingling sound that had me shutting my eyes with the pleasure. He continued the song, my imagination convincing me he was singing those words to me. The intensity in his voice pierced through my soul as he sang about how he'd fucked things up as always and how it didn't seem to matter when he was with me.

I chuckled and shook my head for letting myself believe for a moment he was singing to me. Opening my eyes, I watched him, his focus now on the strings he manipulated. He lifted his head and sang into the microphone again, not looking at any one person.

I'd heard him sing before, watched him play. He was amazing. But I'd never heard this much passion in his voice. It was loaded with heartbreak and angst. I didn't feel the tears streaming down my cheeks until it was too late. My makeup was ruined, black mascara covering the backs of my hands as I wiped away the wetness, but I couldn't stop the flow. It was the closest thing to an out of body experience I'd ever had. Looking at myself from a distance, shaking my head at the stupid girl standing there without a clue. Why didn't she see it before? How could her feelings have been hidden so deeply that she was unaware? I wanted to walk right up to myself and give her an abrupt movie slap.

I loved Cooper, I'd always known that. I would do anything for him, of course. I thought living without him was best for him, even though I was dying inside. It dawned on me then that maybe I *could* make him happy. I'd do anything to make it work, learn how to meet his needs and fill his life with joy. It was the most obvious light bulb moment; in fact I think there were flashing billboards. I wanted Cooper. More than I'd ever wanted anything in my life, I wanted him. I loved him.

He ended the song with lyrics that twisted my stomach in knots of pain. The sexiness of his voice struggling with the sadness of the words.

"Why must I feel this way? Just make this go away."

I couldn't wait to make my way to him, tell him how I felt. For so long we'd been playing a game. Tonight it would end with me wrapped in his arms where I belonged. My eyes finally open, my heart replete at last.

Since I had to wait until the set was over, I made my way to the restroom and fixed my makeup, washing the streaked mascara off my face as well as I could with water and a paper towel. The band covered a few more songs. Kings Of Leon, Seether, Pearl Jam, and another by Foo Fighters. They were rocking the place and the crowd was wild, singing along and dancing. My hips swayed to the music, enjoying the show in my newfound happiness.

After the final song, during an encore to appease the crowd, I started to make my way through the thick sea of bodies. It was a challenge getting through as I was bumped and pushed, but I made progress moving toward the prize. Cooper was flashing that cocky smile that made you weak in the knees as I inched closer to the front, eager to get my hands on him. I knew I wouldn't be able to wait for privacy, I was desperate to kiss him.

Madison and I made eye contact and I started to smile until I saw the look on her face. It was an *eat-shit* face if I'd ever seen one. She looked me up and down like a jealous girlfriend before gracing me with the phoniest smile. Before I could decide whether to smile back or return the look, I was bumped so roughly I lost my balance. It was difficult enough balancing on such high heels and I hit the ground fast and hard. Shaken, it took me a moment to realize that a stranger was apologizing and trying to help me up. I took the offered hand and got to my feet, brushing myself off and leaning on the dark-headed stranger until I was steady.

"I'm sorry, you okay?" he asked.

"Yeah, I'm fine. Thanks." I offered a quick smile and glanced at the empty stage. Cooper was already gone.

The crowd began to dissipate and I found him. He was walking with Ryan, talking and laughing as they made their way toward the bar. I began to move again, saying excuse me as I pushed my way through. My heart stopped at the same time my feet refused to go a step further. With a mix of emotions the equivalent of poison, I watched Madison wrap her arms around Cooper's neck and her lips invade his with the familiarity of a lover.

A stun gun wouldn't have been as shocking. At first I couldn't move, I just stared at the floor, begging my feet to take me out of there. When they finally obeyed, I ran out of the place, the polite side of me absent as I pushed and shoved through the crowd until I reached my car.

Within the safety of my car, I hit the steering wheel, imagining Madison's face. "Bitch!" I screamed out, wishing I had the guts to punch her in the throat. It was my fault, I knew that. I'd pushed Cooper away too many times. But in my despair it was easier to blame Madison. She went after him and got him.

Driving home was a dangerous task as I sobbed, blinking rapidly so I could at least glimpse the blurry road enough to make it home. All I could think about was his hands roaming over her slutty outfit, peeling her tight dress off of her body. His tongue exploring her mouth while he whispered in her ear about wanting her. I pulled into my driveway, thankful I hadn't crashed in the state I was in, made my way to the bedroom, and threw myself onto the bed. I cried for what seemed like hours, realizing the weight of my loss. It's amazing, really, the clarity that comes with wild jealousy.

At one point my phone rang, but I shut it off. I couldn't talk to anyone, not for a while. In fact, I needed to get out of town, but my next business trip wasn't scheduled for another three months. That reminded me that I still hadn't applied for my passport and needed to get it done before time ran out. Not knowing where I would go, I started packing, adding the envelope with my birth certificate in case I felt like checking that task of my list. Anywhere would do. I just had to get out of there, away from Madison. One glance at Cooper and her together, or even his truck parked in her driveway, and I'd go bat shit crazy.

Forty-Six

Cooper

"I keep getting her voice mail. Are you sure she was here?" I asked, dialing again. The bartender poured a round of Crown and Coke and slid them in front of us.

"I'm sure," Ryan began, swiping the back of his hand across his mouth after he swallowed his drink. "I saw her. She was on the back wall." His arm was wrapped around his newest girlfriend, Joselyn. "Did you see her?" She shook her head, an apologetic look on her face.

"Fuck! I should've told her we were playing tonight. She's probably pissed as hell."

"I told you." Ryan scolded. "She *should* be pissed at you."

"I thought we'd suck. I didn't want her to see that."

"We didn't suck. We rocked, right babe?" He gave the brunette a squeeze.

"You guys were amazing." Joselyn pulled Ryan closer, kissing and biting his neck.

My envy churned, watching the desire between them. I needed to find Briley, straighten this out. She didn't want me the way I wanted her and I'd thought being away from her would be best. Instead, it was hell. I needed her, anyway I could have her. Even if it was just friendship, I needed to be near her.

"You're sure she was here?" I asked once again.

"Dude, she was wearing a purplish shirt that hung off of one shoulder. I'm telling you, she was here. I didn't see her leave though."

"I know that shirt," I murmured. "Shit, she *was* here." I started to type a text as Madison walked up.

"You were amazing tonight," she purred. Her actions were so forceful, I nearly dropped my phone and had to brace myself against the wooden countertop. With an arm wrapped around the back of my neck, she pulled me in, her sticky, bubblegum flavored lips covering my mouth. When I felt her fingers roam down my stomach, my body reacted. It was flattering and felt good to affect someone so fiercely. Her body clung to mine, one of her legs wrapping around my thigh, pulling me as close as two people could get with only a pair of jeans as a barrier. Madison was an aggressive woman, her hands finding my crotch and stroking right there for everyone to witness. In a matter of seconds I went from turned on to annoyed. She felt clingy and desperate. I peeled her away, an audible, whiny groan preceding a pouty-lipped expression.

"Have you seen Briley? Did you know she was here tonight?"

"Nope," she answered, a flash of annoyance in her features.

"I'm out," I called over my shoulder, walking toward the door. The guys and I always celebrated with a few drinks at the bar after we played but tonight I wasn't in the mood. Again I tried to text Briley but was interrupted by an incoming call.

"Hello?" I answered with annoyance.

"It's me." I recognized the voice of the female officer. Had I ever asked for her first name? I must've paused too long so she continued, "Kelly."

"I know who you are." I tried to lighten the tone of my voice so I'd sound more interested than pissed that she interrupted my task at hand.

"I've got some information for you. I know it's late but since you're nocturnal, I thought we could meet for a drink?"

"Perfect." I thought about asking her to come here but thought better of it. The last thing I needed was for her to meet my buddies, find out I was in a band, and start hanging out at future gigs. "I'm out now and it's pretty crowded for a Saturday night. Why don't we meet at Beckett's Brew? Do you know where that is?" Double points for suggesting coffee instead of alcohol.

"I do. Give me thirty minutes."

***

Kelly Locke cleaned up nicely for a cop. I'd hoped—and succeeded—to get the information from her without having to lead her on too much.

"The warden dropped your charges." She smiled proudly and took a sip of her sugar-spiked coffee, never taking her eyes off me.

"Poluski? Why the hell . . . he hates the fact that I breathe the same air he does."

Her expression faded. "I don't know? I can keep digging?"

Flashing an appreciative smile, I offered, "You've gone out of your way already. Thank you."

After some research on the computer and a little help from an old prison buddy, Rowland, I learned that Poluski wasn't only the warden but also the father of the guard I'd defended in the laundry room.

Forty-Seven

Briley

Pulsing jets of hot water massaged my tense muscles and attempted to wash away my blue mood. I'd convinced myself it was too late to take off, driving with blurred vision as I sobbed. I didn't even know where to go. I'd think on it and leave in the morning, driving around the block in the opposite direction to avoid the vision of Cooper's truck in Madison's driveway. Just when I thought my heart couldn't stand another infraction—not even a microscopic tear—it shattered into a million pieces as I thought of losing Cooper to a snake.

When the water finally ran cold, I sat crumpled on the tiled floor of the shower, my tear ducts completely emptied. After drying off, I pulled on my favorite "sick" pajamas. The cotton pants and long-sleeved top, covered in pink daisies, always made me feel better. That, paired with a cup of hot cocoa and a comedy, would surely get me through the night.

The absurdity of my situation washed over me and I let the puzzle pieces fall into place. I was so blind, not seeing Cooper's feelings for me until it was too late. Now that my eyes were open, I was too late.

After mixing the packet of cocoa with hot milk, I picked up the steaming cup, added a handful of marshmallows, and took a sip. The too-hot liquid scalded my tongue, eliciting a string of curse words from my burnt mouth.

The movie was light-hearted and funny, but couldn't hold my attention. I was consumed with jealousy and riddled with sadness over losing Cooper. It seemed like a perfect time to work on my manuscript and let the emotion bleed through the keys.

It was my habit to read over the last chapter written before continuing, putting me in the story, and knowing what path I was on. My protagonist was vacationing in Greece and had just been mugged. With no passport or money, she sat on the curb and wept. Of course, it was a romance, so the next few chapters would be about the tall, perfectly-built Greek with dark hair, intense blue eyes, and an accent to make any woman weak in the knees.

I rolled my eyes as I read over my notes and mumbled to myself, "He'll save her, they'll fall in love, and have at least three beautiful Greek babies." *Or, she'll fall in love with him and he'll run off with a blonde gutter slut!*

Watching my cursor blink continuously drove me insane. Words weren't flowing or bleeding like I thought they would. I was about to shut it off and give up when I decided to research Greece. It would occupy my mind, letting me escape into the beautiful pictures for a while and I could get some great stuff to use in the book. Google pulled up the last page I visited, displaying pictures of my favorite place in the world, Sanibel Island, FL. My parents owned a condo and we vacationed there often. Some of the best times my mom and I had were on that island. We made sure at least two weekends a year were set aside for a girls' trip. I hadn't been back since I met Blake. He always had an excuse for why it wasn't a good week, or had something else planned.

Instinctively, I glanced around the room, wondering if I could make a long trip work. My job could travel with me and it was easily justified. Most good writing happened in a relaxed atmosphere lacking distractions. Living like this—marinating in misery over Cooper and Madison, worried about Blake's next move—wasn't for me.

***

Early the next morning I packed the trunk—trusting that my spontaneous packing job from last night was sufficient—rearranging each piece of luggage until I was satisfied, and made myself keep my head down. One glance down the street and I might be able to see Cooper's truck in Madison's driveway. It was killing me not to know, but the confirmation would destroy me.

After a short drive to my mother's house, I pulled in the driveway and got my nerves together before going inside. Cinnamon, apples, and melted butter permeated the house. I followed the scent—my mouth watering for a sample of my mother's famous fried apple pies—into the kitchen. She was in her element over the large iron skillet *her* mother had passed down. The smell, along with the view of her in the black-and-white polka dot apron she'd worn all my life, made me feel like a child.

A strong desire to wrap my arms around her waist came over me as I leaned against the door frame, watching her. It would've been so easy to let her wipe away my tears, convince me everything would be all right, and sip a cup of milk as I nibbled one of her pies. But long gone were the days of letting my mother erase my troubles. Grownups—old enough to choose the wrong path and make irreparable mistakes—had to face their own problems. *Or, if you were strong, bold, and confident like* moi . . . *run and hide.* I rolled my eyes, wondering if they would eventually stick that way as I seemed to be doing it a lot lately.

"Smells heavenly," I said, inhaling deeply.

My mother jumped and slung her spatula across the kitchen. "Great gloriosky, Zero! You scared me to death!"

"What on earth, Mom? You come up with the weirdest sayings!"

"My mother used to say it. Zero was the name of Little Claire Rooney's dog, a comic strip character."

"Okaaaay," I scrunched my brows and shook my head."

"I didn't know you were coming over. Everything all right?"

"Yup," I began, shoving my hands into my pockets. For some reason, I searched for my voice in the deep recesses of denim. "I'm taking a trip."

"Oh? Where to?"

"Sanibel."

"Sanibel?" she repeated before shutting off the stove and taking a seat at the round oak kitchen table. "Explain." She motioned for me to take a seat and I obeyed.

"I thought it would be nice . . . beneficial even, to get away. Let Blake cool off . . . move on, hopefully." I held up a hand. "Don't try to talk me out of it, Mom. I'm really looking forward to it."

"It sounds like a fine idea. I'll pack a bag." She untied her apron and hung it on the hook.

"I'm sorry, Mom. I love spending time with you and a girls' trip sounds fabulous but . . . I need to do this by myself." I grimaced, hoping not to hurt her feelings. "Please understand?"

"What are you trying to prove, Bee? What's happened is not your fault. How could you have known Blake would turn out to be such an—?"

"Ass? It's just a word, Mom. Too mild a word for someone like Blake, in fact." My mother could stand up to anyone and spout a slew of insults that would make anyone blush, but curse words weren't in her vocabulary. "You tried to warn me about him," I whispered. "So did Cooper. I guess I got Dad's stubborn streak." This trip wasn't about Blake at all and I thought my mom would've seen right through me. She didn't so I kept it going. It was a lot easier to blame Blake than tell her about my feelings for Cooper and explain how my stupidity ruined everything and I'd lost him before I had him. My mistake was mentioning his name. Anyone could've seen the pain in my eyes when his name rolled off my tongue.

"Speaking of Cooper, I thought you were happy to reconnect?" She eyed me curiously.

My body tensed, trying to find a way to get around the subject. "It's been wonderful."

"Then why are you running from him?" She laced her fingers together and rested her chin on the knuckles of her pastry-laden hands. The stance conveyed her knowing answer to the question.

"I'm not running from *him.*" I huffed. "I'm running from Blake!"

"All right, Bee. Keep telling yourself that. Maybe some alone time will be good for you after all . . . give you some time to get real with yourself." If she only knew how real I *had* gotten with myself. How real Madison was getting. I blinked back tears, turning my head so she wouldn't see.

"I don't know what's happening, Mom." I sank down in a chair, cradled my head in my hands.

"I'm a pretty wise gal, sweetheart. Maybe I can help?"

"I'm losing it." I dragged my hands through my hair and held them there. "I've got to get away before . . ."

"Before what?"

"Ugh, I don't know." I wanted to get on the road. I'd done a fine job of blocking Cooper from my mind for the last few hours and I liked that control. Telling my mother the whole story would not only delay my trip, but have me doing the ugly cry in her kitchen. "I just need to go, Mom. I don't want to miss the sunset."

"Oh, no, you don't. What's going on, young lady?"

"I . . . Cooper . . . he has a right to be happy, right?"

"Yes and so do you. Now, can we speak in complete sentences so I understand what's going on?"

"We kissed."

"What?" Her pitch was high, a mix of surprise and question. "Okay, and—?"

"What was I thinking?" I stood, shaking my head. If I could make her think it was a mistake, we could drop it and I'd be on the beach by lunch time.

"What were you thinking?" She moved beside me, clasped her hands around mine, and gave them a squeeze. "Let me ask you something, and indulge me until the end, okay?"

I nodded.

"When you and Blake kissed for the first time," She narrowed her eyebrows, refusing my interruption. "What were you thinking about? Concentrate, think back."

"I don't know?" I twisted my face in frustration, remembering the cold evening outside of his car after a movie.

"I'm pretty sure I was hoping my mouth didn't taste like popcorn and hoping I didn't screw up the kiss." I shook my head, not seeing the importance of sharing that ridiculous information. Wasn't that what went through everyone's mind?

"Now, what were you thinking when you kissed Cooper? What went through your mind?"

"I don't know? Nothing?" A shiver danced along my spine remembering his green eyes devouring me before his lips touched mine, igniting me. "Jeez, Mom, my brain was turned off. All I could concentrate on was . . ." I sighed, a tear escaping down my cheek before I could gain control again. "I have to go."

"You're still leaving? Bee, why do you need to run? Embrace it."

"I did, Mom." The tears flowed freely, just as I suspected they would when the truth came out. "But I blew it."

"No, baby girl, you didn't blow it. I know how he feels. You can do no wrong where Cooper's concerned."

"I pushed him away and he's with . . . someone else." I couldn't make myself say her name; it was like cursing in my mother's home.

It was the first time in a while I'd rendered my mother speechless. We stood there for a few awkward moments before she found words. "I don't believe that, can't believe it. You must've misunderstood. Have you talked to him about it?"

"I haven't talked to him, but I saw him kissing her." I wiped the tears from my cheeks but more fell. "This is too big for me, Mom. Too much right now." I raised a hand, halting any further discussion. "Please," I whispered with the last bit of energy left in me. Wrapping my arms around my mother, I lingered, wondering whether or not I needed to state the obvious. Just to be sure, I did. "Please keep my location just between us. I'm begging you, Mom. I need this time alone."

"Of course. Be safe and call when you get there."

"I will." I hugged her once more and smiled, trying to make her feel better about me driving. "Let's go for a weekend soon."

"That sounds wonderful."

Answering my mother's overabundance of waves with my own while trying to back out of her narrow driveway was nearly impossible. Concentrating on not hitting the small stone walls erected on either side, I crept out with one foot on the gas and one on the brake until I was in the clear. Two honks and another wave sealed the goodbye and I was on my way.

Peacefulness was among the many emotions swirling through me as I thought of the waves rolling onto the sandy beach. I imagined myself with a frilly cocktail served in a coconut and accessorized with the clichéd umbrella. Bliss was only two and half hours away and I could already smell the salty sea air.

Flipping through the radio stations, I settled on a hip-hop song to keep my heavy lids from clamping shut. I was never good at functioning on such little sleep. Add an emotional night of crying to the mix and I was toast. The cold temperatures that teachers often used to keep students awake had the opposite effect on me, so I rolled down the windows, letting the warm, early summer air bring me to life.

An espresso was the only thing that could get me through the next hour and half, so I pulled into the drive-through and placed my order for a venti non-fat caramel latte.

I paid for my latte, pulled into a parking spot, and retrieved my phone from my purse. It was a mistake to turn it on, I knew that, but my curiosity won in the end. I'd missed several calls and texts. All were from Cooper, as expected.

Where R U? Need 2 talk

Hello?

I know U were at the club

CALL ME

After shutting off my phone, I threw it inside my purse and started for the highway again. The island was calling to me and I couldn't wait to find rest in its sanctuary. I turned the radio up and bobbed my head to the beat of "Dog Days Are Over" by Florence and the Machine. Letting the lyrics wash over me, I started to believe them. Leaving everything behind—past mistakes, pain, loss—I'd still have to work on my confidence and feelings of self-worth, but I felt like the dog days would soon be over.

They say salt water heals all wounds. I was counting on it to heal my broken heart.

***

Gabby, the name I'd given the chatty GPS that came standard with my white Maxima, alerted me to the close proximity of my final destination. My heart leapt as I lowered the windows again, letting the sweet, salty air waft through the car.

As I approached the Sanibel Causeway that would take me from the mainland to the island, I fished for my credit card and handed it to the lady at the toll booth.

"Sorry, we only take cash."

"Oh," I said, fumbling through my purse to find my wallet again. I found a ten dollar bill and handed it to her. "What do you do if someone doesn't have cash? I don't see a place to turn around."

"We'd let you go on through. A camera takes a picture of your license plate and sends you a bill." She handed me four dollar bills. "Here's your change. I suggest always using cash if you can. It's six dollars every time you come on island, but if we bill you, they charge a fee."

"Thanks for the heads up." I flashed a smile of thanks and drove through the open lever. Making a mental note, I decided to keep a ten in the glove box at all times. I couldn't risk having them send a bill to the house, alerting Blake of my whereabouts.

I couldn't wait to get to the condo and hit the beach, but the view from the Causeway was so inviting. Windsurfers riding the waves, jet skis trying to outrun the dolphins that played alongside, and boats anchored while sunbathers soaked up the warm rays of the sun. Pulling over, I got out of the car and stretched, feeling each tight muscle loosen and relax. I took in my surroundings, unable to stifle the smile that played at my lips. I was here. Finally.

Forty-Eight
Briley

Kicking off my flip flops, I walked down to the shoreline and stuck my feet in the ocean. The water was perfect, matching my body temperature and easing over my feet like silk. My attention was pulled toward the lighthouse, usually a brown metal, but now wrapped in white.

"What's going on with the lighthouse?" I asked a guy preparing his windsurfing board for the water.

"Renovations," he answered, keeping his attention on the board. "Should be done by the end of this week."

"And they'll take the paper off? It's still brown, right?"

He looked up then, only for a moment, and smiled. "Yep, still brown."

I turned before he felt obligated to entertain me any longer. Climbing into my car, all I could concentrate on was the hunger pangs attacking my stomach as it growled in protest of the emptiness. A sandwich from Bailey's would tide me over until dinner, so I ate it in the car as I drove to the condo.

Finally inside, I dropped my bags near the entrance, walked to the master bedroom, and fell back onto the bed, arms overhead. A mix of elation and peace washed over me as I lay there. I'd never traveled anywhere alone, but it didn't frighten me or make me feel lonely. It was a chance to relax, regroup, and take all the healing the island and salty sea water had to offer. Being alone gave me the chance to walk the beach during sunrise, have a cocktail during sunset . . . I jumped off the bed at that thought and unzipped my suitcase. *Who says I have to wait for sunset?*

I pulled out my coral bikini with turquoise and brown beading. No magician could have matched my stealth speed as I flung my clothes into the hamper and slipped into my bathing suit. Bikini and flip flops on, sunscreen slathered all over, and condo key in hand, I practically pranced down to the poolside bar. Walking through the lush tropical landscape, sweet floral mixed with salty air, intoxicating my senses. An irrepressible smile played at the corner of my mouth.

Only a few people sat at the bar. I planned on taking my drink toward the beach. In a few short moments, the bartender greeted me. She seemed to be in a good mood, her chocolate brown curls bouncing as she walked. *Who wouldn't be in a good mood working in this atmosphere?* I thought. "What can I get for you?"

Crap! I never know what to order. I should've thought this through before I came down. The only drink I could think of was Sex on the Beach. What kind of girl orders something like that? Think! "Um . . . I'm sorry, I have no idea." I smirked, embarrassed that I wasn't a connoisseur of beach drinks.

"How about a Bay Breeze? It has vodka, pineapple, and cranberry juice. Or a Sea Breeze—vodka, cranberry, and grapefruit."

"Oh, that last one sounds good, with the grapefruit. I'd like to take it on the beach, please."

"Sure."

I watched her mix my drink, pour it into a plastic cup, and add an umbrella straw for fun. "Here you go." She slid the drink in front of me.

"Thanks." She took my credit card and scanned it. When she returned, I looked at her name tag. *Anna. I think Anna and I will be good friends before this week is up.* I grinned and took a sip of the delicious concoction before turning toward the ocean.

Several empty chaise lounges faced the sea, so I took a seat and watched the clear, celery green water roll in, pause, and then roll back out. Sand castle works of art were being constructed on either side of me by tanned children, while teens played on boogie boards in the waves. I was perfectly content sipping my drink and feeling the tension slowly release from my muscles. After my second Sea Breeze, it was time to flip onto my stomach and let the sun kiss my back.

Dozing in and out from the warmth of the sun and the sound of the waves rolling onto the beach, my thoughts drifted into the danger zone . . . Cooper Sterling. His unique scent, fresh and intoxicating, his voice, telling me not to run away, his strong arms—fantastic with new muscles—pulling me in for comfort as I cried, and those eyes . . . green as . . . *the water behind me. Pull it together, Briley. You came here to heal and get away from these thoughts. You can't have him. He's just a friend! Just a friend . . .* I repeated, drifting off to sleep.

"Excuse me?" I heard someone say, waking me from a doze that must have turned into an afternoon nap. Slowly I lifted my head and realized my neck had seized and wasn't happy about moving.

"Yes?" I asked, looking up at an older woman with a large, floppy hat.

"You're starting to burn, sweetie. I think you fell asleep."

"Oh," I sat up, flashing her a sleepy smile as my eyes tried to focus. "Thank you. Yes, I think I did fall asleep."

Gathering my two plastic cups, I walked to the bar and deposited my trash. Anna was busy with the late afternoon crowd, but took time to wave as I passed by. After rinsing the sand off my feet in the outdoor foot shower, I slipped my flip flops on and walked to the condo elevator, taking it to the second floor. Loneliness crept up on me before I could get my key in the door. I'd need to find something to eat for dinner, a way to spend the hours before I could indulge in sleep and it was against everything in me to miss a Sanibel sunset.

Feelings of regret over coming to Sanibel alone washed down the shower drain along with the soap suds. After blowing my hair dry and slipping into a pair of white shorts and navy top, I felt a lot better. I never liked sitting at a table by myself, so I went over the list of restaurants with bars and chose to eat at the Lazy Flamingo. Between sips of Rolling Rock and taking notes for my book, I devoured a platter of mussels. A couple next to me, obviously on their first date, provided tons of dialogue ideas for my characters.

The poor guy began to bomb on his end of things, talking about his new iPhone and all the features it had. I wanted to turn to him and whisper some hints, but kept to myself and shook my head ever-so-slightly. The girl, sporting a dark blond pixie cut, picked up the conversation. She was clever, acknowledging his magnificent technology, but turning the discussion to something she was more comfortable conversing about. *"Have you tried paddle boarding?"* I smirked. *They might be okay after all.*

My sunset view was from the Causeway—the only spot that had parking spots still available at the last minute—on the hood of my car. A scattering of thin clouds intensified the deep shades of red, purple, and orange, hiding the bright ball of fire as it slipped beneath the sea line. Everyone clapped and drove away as soon as the show was over, but I stayed behind, enjoying the peaceful waters and light breeze blowing through the palm fronds. I had no one to go back to, no plans to rush to or get ready for. It was funny, but something I'd always craved—taking time simply to myself—in reality only seemed overwhelming. At twenty-five years old, I still wanted my mother.

Maybe it was mother's intuition or perhaps her ears were ringing as I thought of her. For whatever reason, my phone rang. I hurried off the hood and stretched across the driver's seat to reach my purse. Rummaging through the too-large bag, I finally reached the device and answered, breathless. "Hello?"

"Bee, you all right?" My mother's concern radiated through her voice.

"Yeah, I'm fine. I couldn't get to my phone." I leaned against the side of the car, trying to calm myself.

"I wanted to make sure you were settled." I could hear water running and imagined her cleaning up dishes from dinner. She was in the habit of making enough for a family of four. After taking out a small portion for herself, she would take the rest to her next door neighbors, Martha and Robert.

"I am. It's beautiful here. I just witnessed a magnificent sunset—ouch!" When the sun went to bed, the no-see-ums came out to play. "Dang, I'm getting eaten alive!" I complained, scooting into the driver's seat and shutting the door.

"Didn't you bring spray?"

"Yes, I did. But I didn't bother to put it on." I could actually visualize my mother shaking her head. Both hands would be planted on the edge of the sink, head down, shaking back and forth. If I wanted to be very detailed, she'd have her dish towel thrown across her right shoulder. It was confirmed to me in that moment, coming alone was a good idea. I loved my mother, she and I were closer than most mother-daughter relationships and I was grateful for that. However, I needed to prove my independence to myself. Briley Sheffield was a strong girl. Scratch that, a strong woman! "I won't forget it next time, that's for sure." I giggled, trying to lighten the mood and erase any worry from my mother's mind.

"Tell me about the beach. Has anything changed? How's the water, the sand, the . . ."

I recounted every step toward the beach, describing each smell and sound, the way the sand felt beneath my feet, and what I'd eaten for dinner. Once I felt she was satisfied, we disconnected the call. Between words, my subconscious screamed out *"I'm so lonely . . . I wish you were here, mom."* My thoughts never came through in our conversation though, I needed this time alone, to rediscover who Briley Sheffield really was.

A glass of Chianti, along with my well-worn copy of *Wuthering Heights,* took me into a deep sleep. Compared to Cathy and Heathcliff, my problems were nothing. My dreams, however, convinced me otherwise.

Walking along the beach at sunrise, I was distracted by a family of dolphins playing a few hundred yards from where I stood at the edge of the water. Strong arms wrapped around me from behind. After jolting from the surprise, I relaxed into his embrace, knowing from his scent that it was Cooper.

We were comfortable, as always, in each other's presence. I'd always loved his arms around me, comforting, protecting, even when we were young. It was always friendly—the embrace of a big brother hugging his little sister—never anything more.

But this embrace held something deeper, something that had already been tried on for size and accepted as new truth. Cooper and I were a couple.

I turned at the new realization, wanting to see confirmation in his eyes. It was there, the love and desire every woman longs to see from the one she gave her heart to. Before I knew what was happening, his mouth was on my neck, nibbling my earlobe as his hot breath tickled and singed my flesh at the same time. I closed my eyes, feeling a rush of heat course through my veins. Unsteady legs barely held me as I tilted my head to the side, allowing him better access.

His hands cupped my face as he looked at my lips. My body ignited, knowing we were about to share our first kiss. Instinctively I licked my lips, the anticipation nearly too much. My eyes closed as he neared and time stopped. The ocean stilled, along with all sound, and his lips touched mine. Before I could memorize his taste, he was gone.

Opening my eyes, I looked around. We were back in the present, all sound returned, the violent waves back to their duty of crashing noisily onto the shore. Cooper was walking down the beach, away from me, holding someone's hand. "Cooper!" I called, causing him to turn. He didn't say a word, but the woman did.

It was Madison, her long blond hair flowing in the wind. She was prettier than I remembered. Shiny red lips curled into a possessive smile. "He's mine, Briley. You pushed him right into my arms and now he's mine."

My knees hit the sand first and then my hands. On all fours, I wept over the loss. With her words she proclaimed my defeat and loss . . . not only the man I loved, but my friend, too. The hardest part was the contentment on Cooper's face. He was willing to let our years of friendship go, just like that, for her.

The sensation of warm liquid running down my face into my hair woke me. I sat up, looking around to get my bearings. Using the back of my hand, I wiped the tears from my cheeks. The bedside clock silently announced the time: three forty-five in the morning. Too early to get up, too late for any good shows, and I'd suffer the next day for lack of a good rest. A cup of hot tea and the sound of the waves kept me company for the next few hours. I hugged my knees to my chest as I sipped the warm brew, watching the ocean beneath the light of a half moon. Imagining being stranded out there alone in the dark, on nothing but a raft. I shivered and went inside.

Not able to fall back asleep, I pulled on a pair of shorts, a T-shirt, and tennis shoes and went for a run. I loved watching the sunrise and this morning I'd do it on the beach. I took off at a slow pace, the darkness haunting but liberating. No one else was on the beach so I pretended for a moment that it was all mine. As the sky transformed from navy blue to lavender, birds began to wake and fish for their breakfast. I picked up my speed when a few more joggers joined me on the sand, each of us nodding a good morning as we passed.

All sadness was erased from the night as the sun began to rise, creating an artist's pallet of pastel watercolors. Marking my spot ahead, I decided to run to a set of condos with brown roofs before I turned back. The morning jog proved to be better than my mother's shower remedy, leaving me refreshed and ready to embrace the glorious day on Sanibel.

After a breakfast of grapefruit and yogurt, I called my mom. I didn't want to take my phone with me and knew she'd worry if I didn't check in with her.

Before dressing, I sat down at the kitchen table and opened my laptop, pulling up my work in progress. I needed to get a couple thousand words down to feel good about saying this was a business trip. My main character, Clarissa Jameson, was in Greece. Her surroundings were beautiful and I easily described the scenery, smells, and tastes of local foods. When I got to the place where I'd left off—her being rescued by the dangerously handsome Stefanos Palimaris—my mind quit working. I tried to type the dialogue between characters.

"Hello, I'm Stefanos." His tone was rich and sultry as he spoke, offering a hand to help her up.

"Hi," she said, looking down at her torn stockings stained with dried blood from her fall. *"Thank you."*

Ugh! This sucks! I shut down the computer and stood, stretching my arms overhead. *How can I write a romance novel if I don't feel it? Hell, I don't know anything about it! I just want to write my character back to her room and make her sleep! Guess I'm doomed to more eavesdropping at the bar tonight. Surely someone will know how to romance a woman. I'll just have to land a spot close enough to listen in on the lucky couple's flirty banter.*

Stuffing a bag with necessities such as sunscreen and a towel, I wrapped a black sarong around my bikini and headed down to the beach. After plopping my bag onto a chaise, I walked back to the bar. It was busier today, maybe because it was Friday, so I waited for Anna to pour and deliver drinks before addressing me at the other end of the bar. "Hi, again. Another Sea Breeze?"

"Great memory. Let me try something different today. Something frozen maybe."

"You like mangos?"

I nodded. "Love them."

She whirled my concoction in the blender and poured it into a large plastic cup, adding the necessary umbrella straw before sliding it to me. "Frozen Mango Margarita." She waited for me to take a sip and report my opinion.

"Delicious, thanks!" I turned to leave and then decided at the last minute to introduce myself. I'd never been good at making friends or talking to other women, but if this trip was going to have an impact on my life—change me in any way—I needed to take charge. Putting on a friendly face, I said, "I'm Briley by the way."

"Nice to meet you, I'm Anna." She pointed to her nametag as she said her name. "How long you here for?"

"I'm not sure. At least a week."

"Nice. You here with family?" She talked over her shoulder, pouring another mixed drink and retrieving two longnecks from the glass cooler.

"Nope. Just me. I'm trying to meet a deadline, but so far I'm stuck."

"Really?" She leaned across the bar, facing me, elbows resting on the wooden counter. "What do you do?"

I wished I could say something more interesting, to match the excitement in her curious gaze. "I'm a writer."

"Oh? For the paper?"

"I write for a travel and food magazine, but I also write romance."

"Ohmigod! Like Nora Roberts?" Her excitement increased over the possibility of having someone famous at her bar. I hated to disappoint her, but it was out of my hands.

"I guess, but at least a billion copies behind her."

I satisfied her curiosity about my newest book's premise, telling her enough to whet her appetite and hoping maybe she'd remember to buy it when it was finished.

"Sounds intriguing. So what are you stuck on?"

"The romance part." I laughed. It was ironic that I was a romantically broken romance writer. "I stink at it."

"You're not serious. If you're a romance writer, you've got more experience than most of us."

"No," I shook my head and took another sip of the margarita. "Really, I'm like a repellent for romance."

"Whatever." She rolled her eyes. "I don't believe you." She excused herself to take care of drink orders and returned to me afterwards. "How long did your last relationship last?"

We'd crossed over the friendly conversation zone into deep, dark water, reserved for close friends and family only. I didn't know how to answer, so I sat there in silence.

"Sorry, you don't have to answer that." Reaching under the bar, she pulled out a bowl of mixed nuts. "Eat some of these, the way you're going after that margarita, I'll have to drag you back to your room."

Maybe I had finished my drink too quickly. Before I could stop to think about what I was telling my new acquaintance, I had spilled my guts. ". . . and I finally left him."

"Wow," she said. It seemed to be her answer for every one of my pauses. Listening intently when she didn't have to serve a customer, she folded her hands together and rested her chin on them.

I sipped the third mango margarita she fixed, a little slower this time and continued to tell her about Cooper. "See what I mean? Repellent!"

"I don't think so. You give up too easily. Didn't even give the poor guy a chance." She collected an empty glass and set it in the sink behind her before getting comfortable in her stance again. "Why did you push him away in the first place? Sounds like you were into each other."

"Because—" I started to say, leaning forward to exude the confidence of my response. It was such an easy answer, obvious to anyone who knew the entire situation. Now, suddenly, I was at a loss. Why *did* I push him away? Wasn't I tired of everyone telling me what to do, trying to help me make life decisions that should be solely mine? A flood of emotions embraced me, reminding me of the why. "I'm not good at relationships. Cooper's a great guy. He's always been so good to me and *for* me. I couldn't risk losing him. At the same time, he deserves to be happy. I didn't think *I* could make him happy."

"Wow, it must be exhausting playing God." I gave her a questioning look. "You're a control freak. I can see it now." She wiped down the counter after the guest to my right left.

I continued as if I hadn't heard her, my hands holding my focus while I talked. "My friend was crazy about him . . . at least I thought we were friends . . ." My shoulders slumped at the thought of him falling for Madison. It was a feeling I'd never felt before. More than an ache, but not a stabbing pain either. It was as if my muscles were suffocating after being deprived of oxygen. It was as though I knew what the slow pull of death felt like and every time I thought of losing Cooper, the blackness started taking over.

"She went after him, knowing how you felt?" She slapped her hands down on the bar in front of me, her eyes wide.

"She didn't know how I felt. I hid it from everyone, including myself."

"Gawd!" She rolled her eyes.

We talked at length about my dilemma and how she disagreed with every single way I had handled things. No surprise there, but every step seemed like one that couldn't be backtracked, couldn't be changed in another direction. I was on a path that led me in one direction . . . farther away from Cooper.

A commotion on the beach piqued my curiosity. I shimmied off the bar stool, my legs now moist with sweat, sticking to the seat. A young girl with a brown French braid and polka dotted tankini had found a junonia. Anyone who had ever traveled to Sanibel knew it was the rarest and most coveted of shells to find. She jumped with joy, waving her treasure in the air. Spectators gathered around, photographing the event and congratulating her. I joined the crowd and clapped my hands in celebration. "Good for you! I hope someone sends a picture to the Island paper . . . that's news worthy."

"Can we, mom?" the little treasure hunter asked.

***

After ordering a Cajun-spiced chicken wrap with tomatoes, lettuce, and guacamole, Anna and I continued our conversation. Skillfully, I turned the discussion, focusing on her love life. Which, surprisingly, was as empty as mine.

"Do you have any idea how hard it is to find a decent single guy? Then add the fact that I work at a bar, in a tourist area. The only good guys that cross my path live halfway around the world."

I bit my lip, contemplating her situation. Dating seemed impossible in her shoes. "What do you do on your off days? Don't you have friends with *friends*?"

"I have the best idea!" Her thinly plucked eyebrows shot up. "Let's do a girls' night. We can drive into Fort Myers. I know a hopping little club. I'll call a couple of friends to join us. It'll be a blast."

"I don't know." It sounded intimidating going out with people I didn't know.

"C'mon, you'll have a great time and my friends are really cool. You'll fit right in."

"I don't want to be fixed up."

She laughed. "They're all girls. We're just going out to have fun . . . celebrate being single and miserable."

Forty-Nine
Briley

Five-O was packed. A live band covering Arctic Monkeys was in the back corner, their music assaulting my ears with the provocative dynamics of their talented guitarist and drummer. As we passed by the stage, I slowed to let my eyes roam over the lead singer. His faded jeans sported tiny tears in all the right places. He was thin, rocking the hipster-meets-bad-boy look. By the time I made my way up to his dark eyes, they were locked on mine, a cocky grin across his lips. He kind of looked like Colin Farrell, but much thinner.

"Seriously?" Anna popped a hip into my side. "We haven't been here two minutes and you've gotten the attention of Jude?"

"Who's Jude?" I asked, dropping my head to hide the flush creeping up my neck.

"The lead singer. He's hot as hell, but a total player."

"He's got a great voice," I yelled over the thunderous roar of the crowd. "But not my type."

"So your type isn't crazy good-looking?" She giggled. "Seriously, if you're looking for a hookup that will rock your world and change your life, go for it." Her eyes lingered on him for a long moment and I wondered how much of him she'd experienced. "Just take your heart out of it. In fact, lock it up tight."

I'd talked about wanting to live a little but I was nervous. One night stands weren't my thing. Maybe if I drank enough to get Cooper out of my head, I could go through with it but it was doubtful.

We slid into a booth, my tight jeans restricting my waist as I bent. I felt sexy and confident, until I parked myself. *C'mon, stretch jeans, do your thing.*

"He's every girl's type after a few drinks, Briley." Her eyes were glued to the stage, one elbow propped on the table so her hand could easily cradle her chin.

"So you've been with him?" I asked. It surprised me how much I sounded like a dude, passing around a girl.

"No, but a friend of mine was with him off and on. He shattered her heart and stepped over it on his way out."

Before I could mentally list all the germs he must have acquired over his singing career, a waitress walked up, asking for our drink order. "What can I get ya?" she asked, her eyes covering everything in the room but us.

Anna spoke first, ordering a pear martini that sounded refreshing and delicious, so I ordered the same. We listened to the band while we waited. They were good, a totally different genre than Cooper's band. It made me realize that Cooper didn't have a name for their band, or if they did, I wasn't aware of it. Surely, they must've chosen something before they played. I'd have to remember to ask him about it . . . if we spoke again.

Two women walked up to the table, pausing for introductions. Anna wagged her finger back and forth between me and the others, casually spitting out names. "Briley—Liz—Sarah."

After exchanging polite greetings, they sat.

"We ordered drinks at the bar," Sarah informed. "Didn't see you sitting here until it was done. They'll bring them over."

Stealing glances at the two, I tried to sum them up. Sarah was slim with strawberry blond hair dipping down just below her shoulders. She had severe bangs that accented light brown eyes and a sprinkling of freckles across her nose. It was too soon for a personality assessment, but my first impression was snooty.

Liz, on the other hand, bubbled with personality. Short dark hair, parted to one side, needed a repetitive tucking to stay behind her ear. She sprayed me with questions, her chocolate eyes smiling as she asked about my vacation plans, job status, and love life.

"Whatever shall four, smokin' hot women do on a Friday night?" Her eyebrows popped up along with her tone.

"I can tell you what smoking hot woman *he* wants to do." Anna bobbed her head in the direction of the lead singer, drawing the attention of the table toward him. He smiled, the way a cocky band member grins when he's enjoying being ogled by women. The fact that he thought we were easy irritated me and made him less desirable suddenly.

"Wanting isn't getting, Anna." Sarah opined. Her comment helped me decide two things: I hated her and I was on a mission to prove to her that he at least wanted me. Whether or not I'd let him in would be determined by my level of drunkenness, I'm sure, but she wouldn't question the fact that I could have him if I wanted him. It was on.

Our drinks arrived and I guzzled half of mine, eager to take the edge off of the uncomfortable night. I was ready to relax and not overthink why Sarah was looking at me like she was offended by me breathing the same air. And what would I say, exactly, if the singer made a move? I took another drink.

"Whoa, slow down there. We're not dragging your ass back because you drank too much, too fast." Anna complained.

"Just needed to take the edge off. I'm good."

After two rounds, the band announced a short break while top forty hits played through the speakers. Liz and Anna were on the dance floor, showing off their moves among the crowd while Sarah and I sipped another round of drinks. I'd learned my lesson about accepting drinks from strangers but not the one about drinking too much *with* strangers. Not that Anna was a total stranger but I really didn't know that much about her and I sure as hell didn't trust her snooty friend sharing the table with me.

From across the room, I saw him staring. As inexperienced as I was with the club scene, I knew the look. According to the movies, he'd be walking my way soon.

I lingered on his gaze, a few seconds longer than my instinct to turn away. You could tell just by looking at him that he'd manipulated and broken more than a few hearts. I sucked down the last of my martini—my cheeks numb from the alcohol—was that three?—and looked up to find the spot he occupied empty. *So much for that.*

"Oh, I love this song," I said, scooting out of the booth to join the others on the dance floor. Sarah ignored me, doing something on her phone.

Mr. Hot Stuff, the lead singer, stepped up to the table and held out a hand. Not a word was spoken, that's how confident he was that I wanted his invitation. It was true, I did. Wobbling to my feet, I paused to steady myself. He pulled me onto the dance floor, pressed our bodies together, and swayed us across the hardwood floor. I stifled a giggle listening to Miguel's lyrics, *". . . how many drinks would it take you to leave with me?"*

"What's your name, luv?" He leaned in, speaking into my ear so I could hear him over the crowd.

Help me, Lord, he had a British accent. My name eluded me and when it did finally come, I debated which version to give him. Since I'd never see the guy again, I made something up for fun.

"Henley. Yours?" *Henley? Where did that come from?*

"Name's Jude. In town on holiday?"

God, you're killing me. Holiday. How can I make you say that again? "No, business. How long have you been singing? You're very talented."

"I'm sorry, luv, I can't hear you over the noise." He cupped his ear with one hand and motioned for the door. "Come, let's talk outside."

I knew I shouldn't go with him, but it really was impossible to hold a conversation over the noise. We'd be right outside and I'd come back in after a few minutes. I shrugged and let him lead me through the doors. The warm air, carried by a light breeze, cleansed my lungs of the stifling club air. Before I could repeat my question from earlier, I was being pressed against the brick wall and kissed. Leaving all formalities for the normal people, he went straight for intimate after only learning my first name minutes earlier.

As hot as I found him, the kiss was greedy and selfish, his tongue forcing its way inside my mouth, tasting me without my permission. My brain, partly numb from the alcohol, tried to process what was happening, but there were too many things at once: his tongue darting around like it was searching for something, a hand gripping my ass and squeezing so hard I knew I'd be bruised, and another hand tugging at my shirt, finding its way to my breast. Trying to relax, I kissed him back, pretending it was all I wanted and more. It didn't work. I could have made out a grocery list while it was happening. I felt nothing.

Pulling away, I put my hands on his chest, giving us enough separation to talk. "I'm sorry, this isn't going to work."

"What's wrong, luv? The wall scraping you?" He spun me around, his back to the wall, and pulled me in. He tasted of beer and cigarettes. His hands moved over my body, gripping, kneading. It was a good thing my jeans were painted on, not allowing access. He was moving fast and my reactions were too slow with all the booze swirling through me.

"No," I tugged out of his grip. "It's not the wall. I'm sorry but I can't do this." I turned to leave but he grabbed my arm and pulled me back. His mouth was on mine again before I could protest.

"Dude!" I mumbled into his mouth, trying to loose myself from his grip. "Seriously. I'm not interested."

"You seemed quite interested earlier. What are you, a cock tease? Or do you prefer the chase?"

I didn't know where the bitch cape came from, or how it got tied around my nape, but there it was and I embraced it. "Maybe you should spend a little less time practicing on the mic and use your time studying up on how to properly kiss a woman! You're much too hot to kiss that badly." With that I strode away, hoping I was fast enough to get inside before he punched me in the throat. I sure as hell deserved it.

"Where did you go?" Anna's eyes were wide with worry. "Please tell me you didn't—"

I dropped my head. "Almost. He's an ass."

"I told you! Are you all right?"

"Oh, yeah. I'm fine." I smiled. It was sweet of her to care what happened to me. We hadn't known each other long enough for her to feel obligated about my safety.

"We're ready to leave. Nothing for us here. You good to go?"

"Yes." I heaved out a long breath. "So ready to go."

Fifty

Briley

Sleep eluded me for most of the night. My theory had been tested and I was right. A one night stand—or rebound since that sounded better—wasn't going to work in getting my mind off of Cooper. My feelings were much too deep. They'd gone beyond lust, beyond friendship, and grew into something I'd never felt before. Even if the guy at the bar had proven himself a perfect gentleman instead of the ass he'd been, it wouldn't have changed anything. There wasn't even the slightest spark. But when Cooper kissed me—hell, when Cooper looked at me—my insides soared.

By four in the morning, I still hadn't figured out what to do besides take one day at a time trying to forget about him. There was so much to think about, worry about. What if he fell for Madison? What if they married, had kids? Could Cooper and I still be friends? I could easily picture myself as the old maid, pining away for someone I could never have.

It was all too much for my stomach. My insides shook with the threat of someone else having the man I loved. The more I thought of Madison's hands on him, her head snuggled in the crook of his neck—*my* spot—his arms wrapped around her, the more it ate at me. For all I knew they hadn't even slept together, but the more my mind wandered down that dark path, knowing how she was, the more I was convinced they had . . . and the more I hated her.

I could threaten her and tell her to back off. *Yeah, because that always worked.* I could get my mom involved. Have her kidnap him and hold him hostage until I could get home. *All brilliant ideas, Briley, really.* I rolled my eyes in the empty, dark room.

***

Pale, buttery sunlight filtered in through a crack in the curtains shortly after I woke up. I had dozed on and off through the night, unable to settle into anything worthy of calling a rest. Snuggling deeper under the covers, I opted for a little more time in bed. As the minutes ticked by, the rays crept up the side of the bed, eventually landing on my face.

Instead of spending the day in bed, marinating in self pity, I threw back the covers and sat up. I was on a mission to erase my mistake of letting Cooper go. I needed to tell him how I felt about him, see if there was a chance of getting him back. Even if he *had* slept with her . . . No, I couldn't think about that. He was twenty-six years old, had been with plenty of women, and I'd never cared. But *Madison?* I shivered. I was sure I could move forward from it, as much as it gutted me. I wanted his heart and I had to get to him before he shared that part of himself.

Seven-thirty was too early to call anyone, but this was an emergency. If one more vision danced through my head of Madison's pink lipstick rubbing off on Cooper, I'd be physically ill.

Grimacing, I dialed and waited for the line to ring. I hated waking up to the sound of a phone ringing, so I was sure everyone else did, too. But Cooper was a gentleman and would never bark at me like *I* did when woken up. On the second ring,

I cringed with the thought of Madison picking up or moaning in the background. My fist clenched around the phone so hard it bit into my flesh. The third ring passed, still no answer. After the forth ring, I heard his voice. Goosebumps ran along my arms and legs, prickling the back of my neck as my heart rate elevated to an almost dangerous level.

"You've reached Cooper Sterling. Sorry I missed your call. Leave a message and I'll get back to you as soon as I can."

Voicemail. I struggled with the decision of leaving a message or hanging up. Either way, my number was on caller ID, so he knew I called. What would I say? Scream a warning into the phone: *Don't sleep with her! Don't do anything with her! I want you! I love you!* I ended the call before I was tempted to say something asinine. *Oh, God!* Slapping my hand across my mouth, a little too forcefully, I tasted the sulfuric tinge of blood. Maybe he didn't answer because he's in *her* bed. Leave it to Coop to be the perfect guy and turn off his phone.

My next call was to my mother. Desperate measures, right? She answered on the third ring. *Thank God!*

"Mom! I'm so glad you answered."

"Are you okay?" Her voice shook as she spoke. My fault for sounding so needy and childlike. But I did need. I needed my mom to reassure me that things would be all right. I needed her to deliver Cooper, untouched, to me.

"I'm fine. I just wanted to hear your voice."

"What's happened, Bee? Something's wrong."

"Really, Mom, I'm okay. I just needed to talk to you. I've been doing a lot of thinking. You know, that's the reason I came here . . . to think."

"Mmm hmm."

"Well, I've discovered something. Don't laugh and I'll totally be able to tell if you're rolling your eyes!"

"I wouldn't laugh at you, sweetheart. Just tell me what's got you so jittery."

"Sorry, I didn't get much sleep last night. I need to find Cooper. Have you seen him?"

"Uh-uh," she answered, seeming distracted. I could hear her busying around, shuffling through papers.

"You haven't seen or talked to him?" I asked again.

"Okay, he called the day you left," she sighed. "Bee, I don't understand why you're running from him. He knows something is wrong and I hate lying."

"Mom, what did you tell him?"

"Just that you were taking off for a few days." Her voice faded, as if she were caught by another thought. "I'm still not sure I understand *why,* Bee. Now, settle down and tell me what's going on."

"I love him." It felt good saying the words, feeling them roll of my tongue. "I love Cooper. I don't know, maybe I always have? I mean, I've always loved him as a best friend, but this is different. It's the strangest and most wonderfully confusing feeling." I rambled on, not sure any of it made sense. But it made sense to me and the more I talked it out, the better I felt. The knots in my stomach loosened and tension released from my shoulders. I inhaled and continued the excessive banter. "But I saw him with my neighbor, Madison, after I pushed him away. She's a snake, Mom. She'll get her fangs in him and he'll never be the same. I'm afraid I've wrecked everything."

She was silent. "Mom? Are you still there?"

"Yeah, I'm here. What are you going to do, Bee?"

"I don't know. That's why I called you. Tell me what to do. How do I fix this?"

"Have you called him?"

"Yes, this morning, but he didn't answer. It might be too early. I'll try again later. How could I have been so blind?"

"At least you see the light now, honey." She giggled, rolling into a long, hearty laughter. "Finally!"

"Yeah, yeah. Get your laughs out, while I'm hours away dying because the man I love is most likely in the arms of another woman."

"Oh, come on, you don't really think he'd jump into a relationship with a stranger so quickly?"

"Sure I do. He's a man. A lonely, rejected man." The tension returned to my shoulders and my stomach suddenly felt like it was full of cats playing with balls of yarn.

***

A cup of coffee always brought me to life and today the added bonus was common sense. *Ding, ding, ding! Get in your car and drive home, B.* Wishing I'd thought if it last night, I shoved my clothes in the suitcase, not taking time to fold anything, and took the elevator down to my car. There was no time to waste. Getting to Cooper and telling him how I felt was suddenly the most important thing in my life.

After shoving the suitcase in the trunk, I climbed in the driver's side and turned the key. A clicking sound let me know the engine was trying to turn over. *C'mon, c'mon.* I tried again, giving it gas and offering promises if she'd only start up for me.

"Damn it!" I shouted. Tapping my fingers on the steering wheel, I thought about what to do. There wasn't any one around to offer a jump so I looked up the number for the local garage on the island, talked to a man named Bill, and convinced him I was in a hurry. I'd only have to wait about thirty minutes for him. Of course we were on island time so that could easily turn into an hour.

Bill showed up in fifteen and gave me a jump.

"Looks like a new battery?" he asked.

"It is. I just had it replaced about a month ago." I watched him look around my engine, using a cloth to poke and prod different instruments.

"It's a good battery, should hold a charge. You didn't leave interior lights on?"

I shook my head.

"We'll leave her hooked up a few more minutes and test the charge. Might be the starter or alternator."

I hoped that wasn't too bad and could be fixed quickly.

After letting the battery charge, he had me turn off the engine and restart it immediately. The same damn clicking sound was the only reaction.

"I need to get it to the shop," he drawled. "Let's jump her off again so you can follow me in."

All the air left my lungs and my eyes closed, wishing he would add, *"Just kidding."* He didn't. "Okay. Think you can get it fixed today?" I asked, hopeful.

"Depends on what's wrong, ma'am. Let me have a look and I'll get back to you as soon as we know what's wrong."

"Thanks. Let me just grab my suitcase out of the trunk."

***

My entire morning was spent calling Cooper. He never answered, but I listened to his voice message and hung up before the beep every time. After a cup of coffee and a granola bar to settle my stomach, I showered, tied my hair in a low ponytail, and went for a bike ride to get my mind off things for a while.

With the wind in my face, the thrill of experiencing new sights and smells, and not being on a schedule, the bike ride did the trick, erasing my worries for a time. Time passing always brought good news and I couldn't wait to get back and check my phone.

As soon as I got back to the condo, I ran to my phone, still attached to the wall charger. Nothing. No calls, no texts. I typed a text to Cooper:

Call me. It's urgent. I deleted it and tried again.

CALL ME. ASAP! No, that sounded too alarming.

Finally, I typed in a version I was happy with:

call me. need to talk to U.

I hit send and waited. Maybe he'd answer a text, even if he wasn't answering my calls. It didn't dawn on me until then that he could be pissed. I hadn't answered his calls or texts and then I disappeared out of town without telling him. After twenty minutes, I got desperate and did something I wished I could take back. I texted Madison.

is cooper with u?

Shit! Crap! Why did I do that? Too late, it was sent and irretrievable. I waited, scrunching my forehead, for her response. It never came. What the hell? Did the apocalypse occur and I was the only one left? Not able to stand another moment of the guessing game, I slipped on a bikini, loaded a bag with necessities, and hit the beach.

After slathering on sun block, I set my bag by a lounge chair, and began walking down the beach. The water rolled in on my right, its white caps calling me to wade in ankle deep, letting the refreshing liquid spill over my feet and splash in front of me as I walked. Starting off with a peaceful stroll, I watched pelicans ski across the water and settle in a group of five, floating effortlessly in deeper water where the waves were calm.

A family of three built a sandcastle on my left, a little girl in a pink polka dot tankini finding shells to decorate the walkway leading to an entrance her daddy had perfected. I walked further, watching my step as shells rolled in under and around my feet. One of my favorite shells—a banded tulip—washed up in front of me and I swooped down to scoop it in my hands before the tide took it back to sea. After making sure it was empty and I wasn't robbing a creature of his home, I turned it over in my hands, admiring the lightly striped, pastel beauty.

The shell fit just inside my palm and proved to be a perfect stress reliever as I gripped it, occasionally stroking my thumb across the smooth surface. It was the only thing that kept me from going insane as I passed two young lovers holding hands. My chest and thighs started to feel warm, which usually meant the sun was winning over my layer of sun block. It was my cue to turn and walk back toward the condo, let my backside have a turn against the rays.

Certain that Cooper had returned my call by now, I picked up the pace, walking with purpose. I was still pissed that I made the mistake of texting Madison. *Stupid!*

Passing the pool bar, I noticed Anna wasn't working. A tall, masculine guy with sandy hair and a smile that had girls gathered around, was pouring drinks. I smirked at the scene and hummed a few lines of Bob Marley's "One Love" as it played through the speakers. Taking a seat on the lounge chair, I fished through the bag for my phone. I needed to see if Cooper called, talk to him, and explain how wrong I was to push him away.

I slid the bar across, waiting for it to come to life. No missed calls. No missed texts. It was only mid-afternoon. Maybe he was working and couldn't get to the phone. Maybe he was pissed and wanted to punish me for not returning his calls. I wouldn't let it get me down yet.

The sound of the waves along with the warmth of sun beating down on my backside had me dozing in no time. I'd only been out a few minutes when the shop called to give me the news about my car. The alternator needed to be replaced. *Damn.* A part had been ordered that would arrive tomorrow and they'd try their best to get it fixed before closing time. It wasn't the news I wanted but surely I'd get a hold of Cooper before then and another day wouldn't kill me.

After a quick rinse in the shower, removing sand and sun screen, I dressed in a pair of khaki shorts and white tank top. My stomach growled in protest of not feeding it more than a granola bar all day. I rode my bike to Doc Fords and sat in a booth with my leather-bound journal.

I hadn't been asked to do an article on Doc Fords, but I'd do it anyway and who knew, maybe it would be good enough to replace one of the establishments I didn't care to visit. I took notes, describing in great detail the flavors and presentation of my Yucatan Shrimp dish. I gave it five stars after I sopped up the last of the spicy, citrus-infused garlic butter with a piece of crusty French bread. While sipping the last of my mojitos—one pineapple and one classic for comparison, I jotted a few more notes into my notebook, and paid the bill.

Desperate to talk to Cooper, I checked my phone again. Still nothing. It wasn't my personality to chase, but I couldn't resist sending another text. My next step would be to call Mrs. Sterling. She'd shoot straight with me, tell me everything I needed to know.

Coop, u ok?

The night was still young, so I drove to Bailey's General Store and picked up a movie. I'd seen it, but it was hilarious, and promised to keep my mind off Cooper for the night.

***

Waking up with a crick in my neck and my phone still hugged to my chest, I lolled my head to one side and then the next, trying to work out the kink. Scrolling through my phone all night, checking for texts, and stalking Facebook pages, the battery had died. I plugged it into the charger, slid into running clothes, and laced my tennis shoes.

The sun hadn't waited for my lazy bones, and rose without me, warming the moisture in the air and making each breath difficult, like I was trying to inhale pudding. Despite the humidity, I prodded along, keeping a steady, faster pace than usual. During the run, I concentrated on keeping my arms loose and unwinding the knots that had formed in my stomach. Several times my mind wanted to focus on Cooper, but I'd change its course and plan my day. After a shower, I'd grab a coffee at The Bean, maybe a bagel with cream cheese, too. Would I read the paper and sip my brew at one of the tables inside, or take it to the beach and watch the waves? *Inside The Bean! It was too hot outside to enjoy coffee.*

Other important things needed to be decided, every detail planned. Where would I have lunch? Maybe I'd focus on getting some work done. There was so much to do and see, I wouldn't even have time to think about why Cooper wasn't returning my calls. The man I loved. Most likely had loved my entire life. What was he doing right now? Was he thinking of me? Or . . . her?

Drenched from a three mile run, I kicked off my shoes, pulled a water bottle out of the fridge, and emptied the entire contents in one swig. Picking up my phone, I saw a missed call. My heart stopped, then picked up a chaotic rhythm as I hoped it was Cooper but feared it was Madison. The caller ID was blocked, so I assumed it was Madison with a nasty message.

It was Bill, from the garage. *"Miss Sheffield, they sent the wrong part, I apologize. I sent one of my guys off island to get the right one. We should have it fixed by morning."*

I sat down and exhaled a frustrated breath. Normally I'd be grateful to be on Sanibel—my favorite place in the world—but I needed to get home and share my revelation with Cooper. Apologize and tell him how much I wanted him in my life.

The room was cool, too cold for my sweat-soaked clothing causing me to shiver. In the bathroom, I turned the faucet and started a hot shower. Steam billowed from the shower stall as I thought about my morning. Sanibel was my happy place, full of wonderful memories with my parents, and more recently just Mom and me. But I couldn't shake the sadness, the overwhelming feeling that I'd lost the only person I'd ever fully given my heart to.

It was obvious Cooper didn't want to talk to me. For some reason, neither did Madison. There was only one explanation. They were together and afraid to face me. *Or they're too busy.* I shook my head, trying to erase those images but it was too late.

It made sense, really. I'd pushed Cooper away so many times, insisting we remain friends and never cross that line. He knew me better than anyone, even my own mother. Knew that I couldn't give him what he needed, even now. Especially now. I was tainted by cynicism.

Drying my hair was a monotonous routine, one that I especially loathed today, while drowning in gloom. My mom always said, getting fully dressed and 'put together' would make a person feel better. She was wrong.

The Island Sun newspaper provided company as I sipped my Tropical Delight coffee inside The Bean and nibbled a soft, fresh bagel slathered in cream cheese. I was reading about a teenager catching his first Red Snapper on a deep sea fishing trip, his picture in the upper left corner of the article. A mouth full of metal braces grinned wildly as he held up the monstrous catch. My phone rang, sending my heart skidding inside of my chest. *Cooper!*

"Hello?" The smile across my face was evident in my voice.

"Hey, Briley. It's Anna. Whatcha doing?"

"Oh, hi, Anna." I blew out a breath of disappointment. "I'm having a coffee at The Bean."

"You got plans today?"

"I, um, I was . . . not really. Just the vacation-y kind of stuff. Why?" I was not in the mood to club hop again, taking a chance of seeing Mr. Asshole, or his plethora of clones that roamed bars, looking for one night hook ups. Tried that . . . hated it.

"Come to the bar for lunch, on me. It's going to be super slow today. We can talk about Saturday night."

"I have to leave tomorrow morning but what's happening Saturday night?"

"I'll tell you at lunch. Give you a reason to show up. I really don't want to work today, so—"

"No need to explain how you're using me for your entertainment." I smiled into the phone. "I'll be there."

Fifty-One
Briley

Ding Darling, a natural habitat perfect for sighting the rare Roseate Spoonbill or a flock of pink flamingos, got me through the next few hours. It was a successful trip, getting shots with my camera of Egrets, flamingos resting on one leg, and a close up of a raccoon climbing a tree while pausing to look at me. The highlight was a tour group gathered around, looking into a canal. I walked up, asked what they saw. "It's a manatee and her baby. See 'em?"

Squealing with delight, I focused my camera, getting several shots of mom and baby, swimming, poking their noses out of the water. I followed them as far as I could down a grassy pathway, until they were out of sight.

For lunch with Anna, I slipped on a turquoise sundress that tied around the neck in halter-top fashion. Brown slides were the only thing that matched, a little on the dressy side with a small heel, but they'd have to do. The salty, humid air gave my hair a slight wave, so I left it down for a nice beach look. At home, I'd tried for hours to get my hair to do this. There were products, curling wands . . . and what do you know? All it took was a walk in the salty air.

Anna was behind the bar when I arrived, leaning over the countertop, watching a guy swim laps in the pool. She was the vision of boredom and I giggled upon approaching. "Calm down, Anna, your excitement is contagious."

"Good, you're here!" She pushed off the counter, smiled at me like I was the best friend she hadn't seen in months. "I've got a new drink for you to try. You'll love it."

Turning around in my seat, I watched the man in the pool. No telling how many laps he'd finished before getting out of the pool, his sculpted abs rising and falling with each labored intake of air.

"Wow, he's nice looking for his age." He must have been in his fifties, hair an even mixture of dark brown and gray.

"Yeah and he's got the endurance of Michael Phelps. I'm surprised the women aren't flocking to him. But like I said, it's a slow day." She set a drink in front of me, atop a white cocktail napkin. It was creamy white and frothy with a hint of pink in the bottom. A lime twist garnished the sugared rim.

"It's beautiful, what is it?" Twirling the stem, I studied the drink, begging me to take a sip.

"It's called a frost bite. Perfect for this heat wave that came through. Rum, triple sec, sour mix, and raspberry liquor." She waited for my reaction as I took a sip. The flavors mingled against my tongue, enrapturing me in a tantalizing flavor fest.

"Oh. That's . . . really good." Taking another sip, I slid my eyes closed. "Potent, but really great."

"Yeah, slow down and enjoy it."

For lunch Anna and I shared a grilled chicken sandwich and sweet potato fries with a sweet cinnamon dip. Conversation was easy, natural with her. Dipping a fry into the amazing sauce, I moved my hips to "Wonderwall" by Oasis. "I love this song!"

"Me too. It's old though."

Nursing my second frost bite, we talked about movies, music, and past loves. "Hey, what do you make of this?" Retrieving my phone, I laid it on the bar. "I've called and texted my friend, Cooper, but he hasn't returned any of them. Neither has my neighbor, Madison. It looks like they went through, but I don't know how to tell on this new phone. Maybe they didn't? Cooper always calls me back and Madison wouldn't miss an opportunity to tell me every detail about her dates with him." That must be it. My calls and texts weren't going through.

"Madison . . . she's the one you handed your guy to on a silver platter?" She rolled her eyes and shook her head at my stupidity. *Yeah, that's what I needed . . . a reminder.*

"I didn't realize I had feelings for him before." Taking another sip of my drink, I let the warmth of the alcohol travel through my veins.

Not making eye contact with me, she talked matter-of-factly as if listing the ingredients of my new favorite cocktail. "And now you have. Too little, too late."

"Uh, yeah. But you don't have to be a bitch about it."

"Sorry. I'm not trying to be," she answered, her eyes still on my phone as she scrolled through. "I was just looking . . . yep." She looked up, bad news dulling her hazel irises. "This isn't good."

"What? Is it broken? That's good news, actually! I can get it fixed. It means—"

"No, friend. I'm sorry, it's not broken." She laid my phone down, held her finger down beside the text. "See, right here. Cooper has his read receipts turned on. It shows under each of your texts that not only has he received them, he's read them."

I grabbed the phone, held it closer to my face. Flipping through my sent messages, my heart sank. There were read receipts on each text, including the one sent to Madison. What the hell was happening?

As if on cue, our song played in the background, tears already forming in my eyes from the rejection. They spilled over and down my cheeks as I listened to words that meant nothing to us as kids, but everything now.

"I'm so sorry, Briley. Are you okay?" She squeezed my hands in hers.

"I will be. I can't believe this song is playing. What are the chances?"

"It means something to you?"

"Yeah." I looked down at my hands, twisting in my lap. "Cooper learned how to play this his junior year of high school. He serenaded me on my back porch."

"It's a great song." She leaned on the bar, arms folded as we listened to the words.

"You've got a thing for guys in bands, huh?" she asked with a smirk, trying to lighten the mood.

"Sure, I guess. Cooper just plays for fun. He's in construction." I paused, knowing that made it sound like he wasn't good. "I mean, he's good. Really good, but it's not all he does."

The sultry sound of guitar strings and the uncanny resemblance of Cooper and Dave Grohl's voice had my eyes glassed over with tears. I tried to blink them away, but it was too late. Once they started, they wouldn't stop. All I could think about was the night Cooper sang that song on my back porch. Me giggling as he pulled out a guitar and started playing while fully decked out in his tux.

The song must have affected Anna the same way. As "Everlong" came to an end, she gave my hand another squeeze. I looked up to see tears in her eyes. She was grinning, looking over my shoulder and encouraging me to turn and look at the man in the pool. I started to tell her how little I cared about Mr. Olympics, expressing my distaste in her timing, but she was adamant I look. Maybe he was naked and we both needed a good laugh?

Slowly, I turned, unable to think of anything that could lift my spirits. I heard my mother's voice, *"Not even an ant pushing a jellybean through a pile of hay?"* Where did she come up with such lines? *No, Mom, not even that.* A guitar strummed in the background, too close, too real, and distinguished from the radio tunes we'd been listening to. My eyes landed on someone standing behind me. Sandy flip flops held a man's feet. Scanning up his legs, my eyes roamed over khaki board shorts to an acoustic guitar being played by skilled hands. Moving up to a white T-shirt that hugged the most perfect body I'd ever laid eyes on, my chest heaved, trying to calm a heart that thudded frantically, vibrating against my collarbone. His jaw was smooth, freshly shaved, tormenting my senses with the anticipation of his aftershave scent. When I finally made it to his blazing green eyes, as clear and bright as rain-kissed leaves in spring, my heart stopped. Long enough to realize it, but not long enough to kill me, it actually ceased.

Not a word was spoken as Cooper coaxed the haunting tune of "Wait For Me" by Kings Of Leon from his guitar. He played an acoustic version, slowing the song down and giving it his own spin. I hung on every word he sang, the sound of his tone rich and deep. The emotion in his voice matched the lyrics, flooring me as I clung to the promise of his words. He sang about opening his heart right where the scars were. After glancing down at his hands briefly, his eyes locked on mine again as he asked me to wait for him, telling me it was all better now.

My eyes remained glued on his, letting the tears fall and splatter wherever they wanted. I was frozen, caught up in a moment I'd remember my entire life. My mind struggled to take it all in, trying to convince me it was only a dream. None of it made sense in reality, but it felt so good I didn't want to move for fear I'd wake up.

Cooper flashed a cocky grin when he came to the part of the song that talked about seeing the surprise in my eyes. My insides had already been filled with lava, burning me up, but his smile undid me. Desperate for his touch, I longed for the song to end. I needed to feel his strong arms around me. I watched the muscles in his forearms flex as he strummed the guitar, bringing the song to a close.

After lifting the strap over his shoulder, he set the instrument down, leaning it against a chair. He reached out a hand and I took it, allowing him to pull me to his body. *Please don't wake up.* I held on to the dream as long as I could, enjoying the feel of his arms around me, his large, rough hands rubbing down my arms trying to erase the goose bumps, the way his firm chest made me feel safe and sheltered from the world. I quietly gasped at the sudden peacefulness that came over me.

The sound of Anna sniffling behind me caused me to pull back and look into Cooper's eyes. He dipped down toward my face, his eyes focused on my lips. The world around us disappeared, all background noise muted. A warm breeze blew across my shoulders just as his lips met mine, as soft and light as the tickle of a live sand dollar resting against your hand. Instinctively, my hands slid up the nape of his neck, one hand fingering its way through his hair, the other pulling him closer. I deepened the kiss, desperate to keep the dream alive for as long as possible.

The dream didn't end. He was real and here with me. Questions flooded my mind, pulling me back to reality. "How?"

"I love you, B."

"What about—"

"I said I love you, B."

My head was spinning. I had too much to say, so many apologies, an overwhelming amount of fear. Was I good enough for him? Could we make it, or would we end up like me and Blake? My heart couldn't take that much pain from Cooper. But the only words I could form were the most important ones. "I love you, too, Cooper. So much."

He pulled me into him, hard and fast, his mouth crashing into mine. My body ignited with a passion that was almost too much. My knees weakened against his exploration, my own mouth memorizing the feel and taste of him. A soft moan escaped my lips, vibrating across our tongues, and sending a jolt of electricity dancing along my spine.

Gently gripping my shoulders, he pulled back, rested his forehead on mine, and exhaled, "finally."

"I've been such a fool, Coop. It was always you. All along it was you."

"Shh," He cupped my face in his hands. "I'm just glad you finally realize that you belong with me."

"Me too." I couldn't keep my hands off him, lacing my fingers through his.

He took my hand, led me toward the bar. Anna swiped her hand across her tear-soaked cheeks. "Oh my God, that was the most romantic thing I've ever seen."

Two fresh Frost Bites were waiting on the bar, but my hands were too shaky to grip the glass. I narrowed my eyes at Anna. "You knew, didn't you? That's why you were so desperate to get me here for lunch?"

"I swear I didn't know what was going on." She raised her hands in surrender. "Some lady called and told me to have you down here at a certain time. Seemed sweet. I was sold when she begged me to help her, said you deserved some happiness after all you've been through." She chuckled, shaking her head. "Honestly, I thought it had something to do with Jude from the other night. I was ready to pop a beer and enjoy a showdown."

"Who the hell's Jude-from-the-other-night?" Cooper asked, his fists clenched by his side.

I'd never cared for the jealous type, but when it came from Cooper, it made me feel wanted, protected. I took his fist in my hand, rubbing a thumb over his knuckles until his hand relaxed, opening to take mine in his large palm.

"Just a loser looking for someone to dance with."

"Is that code for hookup?" he asked.

Anna and I both giggled. It sounded condescending and I wished I could've taken it back. She and I answered at the same time.

"No."

"Yes."

"Anna!" I scolded before turning to Cooper. "It was a failed attempt."

Cooper pulled me in for a kiss. Each time he touched me, the world melted away and I forgot where we were. The sound of Anna clearing her throat finally pulled us out of it. If she hadn't, no telling what she may have witnessed.

She ogled Cooper and let out a breathy giggle. "Damn, Briley, you guys are a perfect fit."

I looked at Cooper, hoping it was true. I was comfortable with him, around him. Too comfortable, maybe. He knew my deepest secrets and I knew his. For an introvert, that was hard to swallow. I trusted him completely as a friend. Whether or not that would work as lovers would soon be tested.

"I'm curious, who was the mystery woman?" My eyes narrowed at Cooper, but the answer was obvious—my mother, the traitor—God bless her.

"You know your mom can't keep a secret," he answered, brushing a knuckle across my cheek. "But she sure can carry out a plan." Cooper's hand slid across my bare knee, leaving a trail of fresh goose bumps behind. I turned to face him, resisting the urge to climb in his lap and risk propriety with a public make out session.

"You didn't answer my calls or texts."

"Nope."

My eyebrows creased, trying to process his simple answer. I thought about asking him details of his relationship with Madison, but this moment was too wonderful to be poisoned. Thoughts of her weren't welcome.

Finally, my hands calmed enough for me to grip the glass in front of me. Condensation dripped down the sides, making it slippery, but I held it to my lips and took a long drink. Cooper followed suit, grimacing afterward.

"Girly drink. Too sweet. What's your friend's name?"

"Anna," I called, getting her attention. "Can Coop get a beer?"

She slid a Rolling Rock in front of him and smiled. "So, what now?" Settling in for a story, she leaned against the counter, resting her chin in hands propped up by her elbows.

I looked to Cooper for answers. Hell if I knew what was next. All I cared about was now, in the moment.

"I've got the weekend, but then I've got to get back." He shot a glance of disappointment my way, but it didn't stay long. "One of the biggest jobs yet, I've got to make sure it's on schedule and done right." He took both my hands in his, circling his thumbs across my knuckles. "But knowing you're mine, that I've got you to look forward to each night—even if only over the phone—makes it easier."

"Why over the phone?" Now that he was mine, I wanted everything. His breath in my ear whispering goodnight, my body draped over his every morning. "Where is this job?"

"Cape Coral. About two and half hours away. For the next few weeks, I'll only have the weekends."

"Then we'll make the most of those weekends." I flashed him a wink and dropped my head, studying my hands that looked childlike in his. My hands had rested in his hundreds of times, but now they were clammy. I knew him inside and out, but this feeling was new and made me feel unsteady, unsure of myself.

"Yes, we will." He grinned, lifting my chin to meet his gaze. "Would you be up for staying here this weekend? We can play in the waves, walk the beach each night as the sun sets. I booked a room. It's on the other side, but we can still get up early and watch the sun rise. You still enjoy that, right?"

"I do." My cheeks flushed, something I wasn't accustomed to. I could feel the warmth traveling down my neck. He'd booked a room. Didn't he want to stay with me? Was he taking things slow for my sake? Every pore of my skin tingled with desire, wanting to take everything all at once. Now that my feelings for him were out in the open, knowing he felt the same about me, it was hard to control myself. A cold shower was desperately needed.

Questions invaded my mind, nearly squelching my desire. Why hadn't he answered my texts? What really happened with Madison and why wouldn't she answer me either? Had he been with her, but dumped her when he listened to my messages? Those questions would have to wait. Right now, all I wanted to concentrate on was the fact this glorious man with a body to drool over and eyes that melted me to the core was mine. Finally mine.

Fifty-Two
Briley

After trying on every ensemble I'd packed, I finally settled on a sheer white blouse and mint dress shorts. Dressing it up, I added a chunky mint green necklace and slipped on nude heels. Since Cooper was tall, I could get away with wearing them. In fact, the only shoes I'd packed that weren't heels were running shoes and a pair of flip flops. Dabbing a little fragrance behind each ear and finishing with some lip gloss, I was ready. There was just enough time for a quick call home. Give my mom a friendly chewing out for putting me through what she did.

"Hello?" Her voice cracked, trying to stifle her giddiness. I thought about telling her that the plan backfired, but I was in too good a mood to play a game with her.

"You should be ashamed of yourself, putting me through that."

"Wha—?"

I couldn't wait for the politeness of small talk, so I invaded her evening with all fourteen thousand words in what probably sounded like the world's record for longest run-on sentence. My mother was silent, except for the sound of her hand slapping across her chest and a long sigh. "I love him so much, Mom. And he loves me."

"I—I know he does, Bee. You're the only one who didn't know. I can't wait to—"

"I've gotta go. He's here. I think we're going to dinner. Love you."

Opening the door, the most stunning creature stood before me in a black dress shirt and khaki slacks. Man, did he know how to pull out all his weaponry. His eyes against the shadow of early evening stubble across his jawline left me itching to feel its burn across my neck. Part of me wanted to pull him inside, skipping dinner and going straight for dessert, but the other side of me—the weaker one—knew it was best to play along with the courting. This was new territory and we needed to experience it the right way.

Cooper greeted me with a chaste kiss on the cheek. "You're beautiful."

"Thank you. Where are we headed?"

"Dinner and sunset." He didn't ask what I wanted to do, he took charge. Holding out his arm, I took it, letting the door shut and lock behind me. He could've packed peanut butter sandwiches and led me to watch the sunset from the bed of his truck. In fact, that didn't sound bad at all. Instead, we pulled into Traders.

We were seated beside a window in the spacious restaurant, wooden beams spaced evenly across the vaulted ceiling. Once we settled in, got used to the idea that we were actually on a date, the conversation was easier. Cooper ate while I picked at my food, curiosity wrecking my appetite.

"What happened with Madison?" *Way to kill a moment, Briley.* But I had to know.

"I don't want to talk about her." The way he said her name, without even a hint of kindness, made my heart feel lighter.

"Please, Coop. I need to know."

"It didn't work out. She wasn't for me." I saw the sadness and regret in my expression reflected in his eyes.

"She knew how I felt about you, yet she went after you anyway. This is why I don't get along with other woman. They're snakes."

"No she didn't, B. You told her we were only friends and you never wanted more than that. You said you were excited to finally live and get a few one night stands in," He jabbed his fork in my direction. "Which, by the way—"

"Are you serious?" I interrupted, smacking my hand on the table. It made more noise than I'd anticipated, drawing a few glances our way. I lowered my voice, my words hissing through clenched teeth. "That filthy bitch! She twisted my words. I can't believe she would share something like that with you in the first place, but then to flat out lie . . ." A disgruntled noise vibrated in my throat. "You're right, I don't want to talk about her. That dirty, rotten, gutter slut."

He laughed, his eyes wide from my rant. "Get it out, Briley. Don't hold back. I'd like to know how you really feel about her."

I narrowed my eyes, stuffing a spinach-topped oyster into my mouth before things started rolling off my tongue freely, my thoughts growing uglier by the second.

Cooper finished chewing a bite of grouper and looked up. "She knew my heart belonged to you. If it makes you feel any better, that really pissed her off."

His eyes locked on mine, not embarrassed or shy to admit something so personal. Warmth filled my chest, healing the ache inside. Tears flooded into the crevices, threatening to spill over.

"No, baby, don't cry." He was out of his seat and next to me in an instant. "This is why I didn't want to talk about her. This is our weekend, I don't want anyone or anything tainting it."

His arms wrapped around me, pulling me in to soak the front of his shirt with my tears.

"These are happy tears, you fool." I smacked him on the arm teasingly.

He kissed the top of my head before speaking into my hair. "Good. I prefer you happy. Pissed Briley is scary."

I pulled away, swiped at the tears with the back of my hand. "Damn straight! You better fear me."

We shared a healing laugh before realizing how public our discussion had gotten. Now I was in his lap, giggling into his chest in the middle of a crowded restaurant.

"That's my girl." He stroked a hand down the length of my hair.

"Hey, Coop?"

"Yeah, babe?"

"Thanks for waiting for me."

***

We drove to Captiva Island, turned down Andy Rosse Lane, and found a parking spot at the Mucky Duck. The air was warm, a soft breeze blowing as I stepped out of the car. Tropical music played in the background and I racked my brain trying to figure out the name of the familiar tune. We walked around the restaurant to witness the vast stretch of ocean behind the patio area. It was gorgeous with rich green palm fronds swaying against the light blue sky.

Cooper walked to the restroom while I looked around and listened to the musician cover Van Morrison on the guitar. A few people were lined up playing a game so I walked over to watch.

"You have to swing the ring dangling on that string over the hook," said a man in a Hawaiian shirt. He looked to be in his thirties with short dark hair, a cleft chin, and aviator sunglasses.

"Oh, okay."

"Give it a try." He nodded for me to take a turn, handing me the ring.

I tried several times to swing it onto the hook, but it was tougher than it looked. On my fifth swing I heard the triumphant clink of metal on metal and the ring settled over the hook.

"You did it!" Mr. Hawaiian shirt patted me on the back. "So, where are you from?"

"Tampa," I answered. I didn't really want to have a conversation with him, but didn't know how to walk away without being rude, so I tried my luck with the ring game again.

"What's your name?"

"Briley."

"Briley." My name rolled off his tongue like a fine wine. "I'm Trent. Can I buy you a drink?"

"Oh, no thank you, I'm here with—" Before I could answer, Cooper walked up and put his arm around me. He towered over Trent, giving him an eyeful of pure male testosterone that wanted to be tested, provoked. It was obvious and awkward, and I felt bad for Trent as he flashed an apologetic smile and walked off.

"That was rude." I lightly smacked him in the gut with the back of my hand.

"Sorry, would you like me to call him back? I can see where that Hawaiian shirt would do it for you."

He was seething with jealousy and I found it flattering and unattractive at the same time. "Cooper, you're awful." I tried to lighten the mood by kissing him on the cheek. My lips lingered there a moment longer than I intended, inhaling his intoxicating scent.

He pulled me in, kissing me until I was putty in his arms. It didn't matter that we were in public, the crowd disappeared easily when his lips met mine. My hands linked around the back of his neck, pinning my body to what it craved. He pulled away, breathless as he spoke.

"And apparently, very jealous. I left our drinks at the bar."

"Hurry back to me. Hawaiian shirts might not do it for me, but I did see one with flamingos. I'm a sucker for a man in pink," I teased. My eyes were glued to him as he walked back to the outside bar, retrieving our drinks. His body was outstanding and I couldn't wait for this damn sun to set so I could get my hands on him. This taking it slow bit was not for me. Cooper and I had waited long enough to be together and I was ready to throw propriety into the salty sea.

We found two Adirondack chairs facing the ocean and sat there until the sun began to set. It felt like a scene from a movie when everyone started walking to the beach in unison to witness the big orange ball of fire, showing off as it displayed vivid colors of orange and purple. I wouldn't normally put orange with purple, but the sky was breathtaking and the colors seemed to flow together like a masterpiece painting. The only word I could think of to describe it was *transcendent*.

Fifty-Three
Briley

Cooper drove back to the condo and walked me to the door. "Where's your car?" he asked.

"In the shop. They had to replace the alternator. Maybe you could drive me over to pick it up tomorrow?"

"Sure." He pushed a strand of hair away from my face with his thumb. My body registered the trail of sparks left beneath his touch. "Thank you for joining me tonight, B."

"It was perfect. Well, almost." The questioning look on his face almost made me giggle. "Kiss me." My voice was breathy, not my own.

Aware that his mouth was only a whisper away from mine, my breath hitched. Wetting my lips in anticipation, I leaned against the door, unable to hold myself up beneath his powerful gaze. He had the patience of a monk, letting his knuckles run down my cheek to the base of my throat. A heavy dose of desire surged through me when he leaned into my neck, inhaling. I tilted my head to the side, giving him the access he required, groaning when his lips found my earlobe. He traced my jaw, kissing and nibbling until he found the corner of my mouth.

I gasped, his mouth absorbing the sound as he claimed my lips. My heart pulsed against my chest so violently I felt it shaking me. The way he kissed me, gentle yet hungry had me gripping his shirt to steady myself. Trying to deny my desire wasn't an option. I wanted him, needed him. There was no doubt in my mind that we belonged together. I'd been his since we were kids and I knew he would guard my heart better than anyone, even better than I could.

I managed to push him back a fraction. "Hold on a second." My key was at the bottom of my purse, making me crazy as I fished around for it. Breathing a sigh of relief, I pulled it out, unlocked the door, and stepped inside. Cooper remained outside, trying to catch his breath.

His eyes looked weary as he took a step back. "Good night, B. I'll pick you up early for sunrise?"

Without saying a word, I gripped his shirt, pulling him inside. "B," he exhaled. His hands resting on my waist, his forehead pressed against mine. "If I come in, kiss you like I want, I won't be able to stop." He tried to back away, giving me an out.

I clung to him with all my might, panting with need. "I'm counting on it."

The room was dark, but enough light from the full moon filtered in through the open curtains for me to see his body tense. Desire swooped in, sending a current through my limbs, and resting in my belly. I'd never wanted anyone, anything, as much as I wanted him. It was an overwhelming feeling that overtook me, controlling my every thought, every move.

A lascivious smile curled the corners of his mouth before it crashed into mine, causing my knees to buckle. A delicious current electrified my senses and the world melted away. My lips parted, allowing him in. A slow, seductive ballet of our tongues gliding, probing, tasting, took place. His hands remained at my waist, gripping me tightly as we stood, making out like teenagers for what seemed like an eternity. It was natural with him, filled with desire. I had craved him for so long, I couldn't have stopped kissing him. Even if I had wanted to, I couldn't. It was a force that couldn't be tamed.

With my back against the wall, I arched, trying to get closer to him.

"There's no rush, baby. I want to savor every taste, every feeling."

I slid my hands up over his broad chest, rounding his massive shoulders, and up the base of his neck. I couldn't resist nibbling, licking, and kissing his neck, his cologne so enticing. I heard the air *whoosh* out of his lungs. I loved that I was capable of doing that to him. He pulled me back and it was an effort to open my heavy lids. When I finally focused on him, he had a look in his eyes that sent a thrill up my spine.

He gripped the hem of his shirt and pulled it over his head, popping buttons as he did. He must've forgotten he wasn't wearing his usual T-shirt. I drank him in, letting the wooziness overtake me. His shoulders were beautifully inked, but the one I loved most was scripted from underarm down to his waist. I closed the space between us, tracing a finger over the words, *"Not all who wander are lost."* He trembled beneath my touch, his abs contracting when I touched him.

With gentle fingers, he tried to slip my blouse off. It was a tricky one, so I lifted my arms and literally wiggled myself out of it. He wanted to savor each moment, but I was already primed and panting, and we'd only gotten to first base. Eager to get my hands on him, I worked his pants, getting the button undone and fumbling with the zipper while he tormented my neck with his lips. I moaned loudly when he found my ear. It was the invitation he needed, losing the control he had wanted to maintain. He pulled away, stripping out of his pants in one swift motion. My eyes, along with my breath, caught at the bulge imprisoned beneath tight white boxer briefs.

He eased me back against the wall and covered my mouth with his while his hands slid up my waist. Gently but firmly he cupped my left breast, kneading it through the lace material of my bra. While he lavished my breast, he moved his other hand behind me, his fingers unclasping my bra within seconds. I sighed in relief when they were freed momentarily and whimpered when he took a nipple, sucking like it was candy. My hand went to him in a flash, taking my sweet time stroking his broad length in my palm.

Every single muscle in my body tightened in anticipation and a delicious torture spread throughout.

He whispered praises between kisses, fondling every part of my body except the one place I needed it most. He traced over my arms, legs, stomach, and breasts as he licked and kissed along my jaw and neck. His kiss was enough to entertain me for hours, lost in the drunkenness of him. But I wanted more, craved it, needed it.

"Wrap your legs around me," he commanded, lifting me up. My legs and arms hugged around him. The sensation of our stomachs sliding against each other as he walked was heavenly. He never stopped kissing me as he walked through the condo, no light to lead his way. Somehow he knew which way to go, making a right and carrying me into the bedroom I'd been sleeping in. He set me down, my body never losing contact as I slid down his form, feeling his erection twitch against my stomach.

He cupped my face in his hands, kissing each corner of my mouth with a delicate kiss.

"So beautiful," he breathed. "So fucking perfect."

We stepped backward until the backs of my legs felt the mattress. I sat down on the edge of the bed, not taking my eyes off him as he pulled the fabric of his boxers down. He stood before me, bared and hard and I gripped him, stroking once, twice.

His breath shuddered, a low groan in the back of his throat escaping before he moved my hand. "Whoa, my control is shot to shit as it is."

Pushing me back on the unmade bed, I scooted back across the white sheets until my legs were no longer dangling off the edge. He crawled with me, looming over me, devouring me with those eyes of his. I couldn't keep from focusing on the muscles in his arms, flexing and tightening as he moved.

For a moment, and only a tiny moment, I wondered if this was a mistake. I wanted him desperately, no doubt, but this was the fault line that could ruin everything. Not a skilled lover, to say the least, I worried I would disappoint him. Any hint of frustration in his eyes would ruin what little confidence I had.

I shook the thought completely as his hand snaked up my thigh, inching closer and closer to where I needed to feel him. My body ached for his touch. When he reached my panties, my back arched, pushing myself into his palm. I felt so out of control, all of the worries that invaded me earlier rushed out on a breath.

He exhaled a ragged breath as his fingers moved the tiny triangle of lace material to the side, slipping a large finger in to stroke across my already slick entrance before dipping into me deeply. The intensity was almost more than I could handle. I was beside myself, ready to combust as he worked me, stroking gently, plunging with purpose. He had me on the edge, ready to release all the sexual tension that had been building for much too long. Before I tumbled over into the abyss of pleasure, he stopped and peeled my panties off.

I was quivering by the time he rolled a condom on and positioned himself at my entrance. His lips were on mine, careful strokes of his tongue taming and calming me as he pushed in. Moving my legs a little wider and lifting my right one the slightest bit, he was able to ease in further. I was more turned on than I could ever remember, but I still felt an almost painful stretch as I accepted him. A string of curse words hissed through his clenched teeth as he pushed the last few inches inside.

I gasped as he pulled out and drove back in, a low groan vibrating in the back of his throat. He felt good, too. Perfect. All of the lust and affection that had been pushed away far too long was almost too much all at once. The lonely desperation that had left a hole in my core was filled, healing and making me whole again. His hands were everywhere at once, stroking, rubbing, driving me closer and closer to the edge. He moved slow and heavy. My hands gripped at his shoulders and then clutched the sheets. He worked my mouth, his kiss equally as sensual as his lovemaking. A slow, rolling pressure built inside of me. I wrapped my legs around him, lifting my hips to push him deeper. He hit a spot, causing me to squirm and cry out. He seemed determined to hit the same spot again and again until it was too much and my core clenched around him in spasms. Panting, whimpering, and finally calling out his name, my head pushed back into the pillow as my body shook with the most intense orgasm I'd ever experienced. He followed seconds after, his face buried in my neck and his breath escaping in gasps.

With his head still buried in the side of my neck, he whispered, "I knew it would be good with us."

"I . . . it was, right?" The uncertainty in my voice was meant for his end of things, not my own. It was the most incredible sex of my life. Several reasons crossed my mind. He was the hottest guy I'd ever slept with; he took care to get me ready, almost to the brink of orgasm, instead of ramming into me like there was a race to the finish line; and finally, most importantly, I loved him. There was no doubt in my mind about it. I loved him as a best friend, someone who had my back no matter what. I loved him as a person, each perfect fault and the depth of his strength. And to complete the circle, I loved him as a lover, as skilled and unselfish as someone who studied the craft for a living. My doubt came in the insecurity of our lovemaking on my end. If I was any good, Blake never would have cheated.

Cooper lifted his head, his worrisome eyes boring into mine. "Are you okay?" He pushed up on his elbows, studying my face. "Don't overthink this, Briley. Don't do it. We fit. We—"
I cut him off, placing a finger over his lips, shaking my head. "It was the most incredible . . ." I couldn't finish the words. So overcome with emotion, it was all I could do not to weep. When I found my voice again, I continued, "I don't regret it and I'm not overthinking anything . . ." I sighed, closing my eyes to hide from the humiliation. "I know you've had way more lovers than me. I just—"

It was his turn to cover my mouth, hushing me before I could finish. Except, he did it with his lips instead of a finger. He kissed me deeply, taking my breath away, along with my insecurities.

"I've never felt anything so perfect, so good in my entire life," he said, before he ground into me again, still hard enough for me to feel his movement. "So fucking good."

My eyes closed, a small moan escaping me. His words washed over me, melting me into the sheets. He left me for a moment to clean up. When he returned, he opened the glass sliders leading to the balcony. Our condo was the closest unit to the water, so the sounds of the waves filtered into the room.

I took a turn in the bathroom and when I returned, I stood in the darkness where he couldn't see me. He was on his back, arms folded behind his head, the sheet, hugging his form, pulled up to his waist. It stumped me, no matter how hard I tried to work it out in my head, why this perfect creature chose me. I climbed in beside him, resting my head on his chest, breathing him in, listening to the life force pulsing in his chest.

The sound of the waves crashing onto the shoreline and the summer breeze whistling through the palm fronds all faded into the background as we made love again.

Fifty-Four
Briley

Waking up from a beautiful dream was hard to do. As the sun filtered in through the open sliders, I kept my eyes closed, listening to the waves, focusing on their rhythm and trying to go back to sleep. Warm knuckles grazed my back, between my shoulders and down my spine. With my eyes closed, I smiled, squirming beneath his touch.

"Pinch me," I asked on a giggle.

"No," he answered, continuing south.

"Yeah, never mind. I don't want to wake from this dream, anyway." My head remained buried in the pillow.

Cooper pulled the sheet down, gaining the access he needed to move down my back and over my ass. His lips felt divine across my flesh, turning my body into a limp host of white hot desire. Traveling lower, he spread my legs and lifted my hips slightly. As many rounds as we'd had the night before, I was surprised he wanted more. I was also surprised by the way my body was ready and screaming for him, as sore and exhausted it was.

Instead of fingers readying me for a wakeup call, I felt his tongue stroke across my sex. My body tensed, partly from the exquisite feeling, mostly from shock. Slamming my legs together, I rolled over in protest.

"What's the matter, B?"

"I'm going to have to say no to that." I cringed. *What a stupid line.*

He laughed. An all-out belly gut laugh. "Why?"

"I don't know, because . . . because it . . . I . . ." How the hell was I supposed to give him a reason? *No one's ever done that before. I don't know what to expect, how to feel about it. What do I do with my hands?*

"You're nervous." He studied my face before I could slap my hands over my eyes. "You don't like it? Just say so."

"I don't know if I do or not," I admitted, my face still hidden beneath my hands.

"What the ever living fuck? Are you telling me no one has ever . . . ? Shit, now I'm speechless." I felt the bed move, his absence making me uncover my eyes. He looked pissed. How did I always manage to mess things up?

"Are you mad?" I asked. A medley of emotions invaded me. I hated being the cause of his strife, but if it was so easy to piss him off because of my inexperience, well, frankly, that pissed *me* off.

"Not at you, baby. I'm pissed at every guy you've ever been with that didn't worship you like you deserve."

"You make me sound like a street walker, Coop. I've only been with two people. That prick from college and—"

"Blake?" he interrupted, wrath poisoning the word. I could only nod as he fisted his hair, a string of curses tossed violently at my ex.

His facial features relaxed as he walked toward me and sat on the edge of the bed. He cupped my face in his big hands, kissing the corner of my mouth with a feather light touch.

"I'm going to taste you. I'll wait until you're relaxed and ready to give me every ounce of your trust." His eyes flashed with desire before he kissed the opposite corner of my mouth in the same manner. "When I'm finished with you, you'll never remember you were ever with anyone else. The only name you'll ever exhale from this day forward is mine."

He had the ability to make my entire body dissolve into a thick puddle of fervor. Like a snake charmer, he coaxed me into wanting things he thought I should have. I would've followed him straight into the pit of hell if he'd wanted it. I was completely lost to him.

"I'm starving," he smirked. "I'll whip us up some breakfast while you shower. When you're finished, get that fine ass in a bikini so we can hit the beach."

All I could focus on were the words *fine* and *ass*. With a Cheshire grin, I threw off the sheet and strode to the bathroom with the confidence of the sexiest woman alive. That's how Cooper made me feel. He deserved the most beautiful woman in the world, but he wanted me.

After adjusting the water temperature, I stepped into the shower and relished the feeling of the hot water on my skin. Standing under the spray, I let it ease my sore muscles for a moment before washing my body. I heard the shower door open and turned to see Cooper stepping in to share the space.

"I thought you were making breakfast?"

"It can wait." He made a sound in the back of his throat, a grunt maybe, as he watched the soap trail down my body.

I grinned and then tilted my head back to get it wet.

"Your turn," I told him, switching places so he could get under the water. I poured shampoo into my hand and began to lather as he ran the bar of soap over his chest and arms. My arms stopped mid-lather and watched him, wishing my hands were on him. After I shampooed, I waited for my turn under the water.

When we switched places again, he held my waist and brushed against me. A wicked grin played on his lips. He was teasing and I decided to play along.

I leaned my head back, letting the water rinse the shampoo from my hair, taking in deep breaths so my chest would rise and fall seductively. He traced a bead of water between my breasts and down my stomach. Fire coursed through my veins when he touched me, but I kept my eyes closed and rinsed the last bit of shampoo.

He swapped places with me again, our eyes meeting during the exchange with matched heat. I needed to feel him beneath my hands so I grabbed the bar of soap and worked up a lather. I slid my hands over his strong chest and arms, letting my fingers trace the words written along his side.

I felt him tense beneath my hand as I traveled down his stomach, tracing a finger down the path of coarse hair leading to his arousal. My hands were still slippery with soap when I took him with both of my hands, feeling him jump in my fisted palm. His form was mesmerizing as it glided easily in my slippery hands, growing even harder with every stroke. Glancing up, I was robbed of breath when I saw the intensity in his eyes. It was obvious he was trying to control an animalistic hunger. I'd experienced his gentleness and control all night and didn't mind encouraging him to take what he wanted, how he wanted it.

"Take me," I persuaded. With those two words and the look in my eyes, he'd gotten my meaning and the animal was unleashed.

Turning me to face the wall, he placed my hands against the tile and bent me at the waist. He ran his hands possessively over my legs and ass, reaching around to take my breasts in his palms, kneading until I whimpered in pleasure. He took my nipples between his fingers, rolling and pinching with enough pressure to make me squirm, but not enough to hurt. Encouraging him, I ground my ass into his erection, circling my hips until his hands were on my hips, fingers digging into my flesh. Without warning he sank himself deep inside of me. My knuckles whitened as I gripped the slick tile and cried out in undulated pleasure. Each time he thrust into me, I searched for something to hold onto. He wasn't gentle like he was last night but he wasn't rough either. He was incredible. The heat of his breath washed over my ear as he sang praises and curses. His words were a heady elixir that sent my body into another stratosphere. I'd never felt anything like it in my life. It was as if his body was created specifically for my pleasure. He had only started to quicken his pace, finding a rhythm that played our bodies like an expensive, well-tuned instrument, bringing forth the most beautiful melody.

"God, Cooper," I moaned. I didn't want the feeling to end. It was too soon. "Wait."

"Let go, baby."

I could barely hold myself up as my body contracted around him and penetrated the stratosphere. I thought that was the end, but he kept moving and the sensation started all over again. It started slow, brewing deep within my core, spreading throughout my muscles, and along my spine. It was all I could do not to crumble into a heap at the bottom of the shower after a second orgasm ripped through me.

When he found his own release, he gripped me tightly around the waist with one arm and laced his fingers through mine with the other, holding my hand against the wall. He grunted with the last thrust and held still, resting his head on my back.

After a moment he released me and I was overwhelmed with an emotion I didn't recognize.

"Baby? You all right?" he asked, nuzzling my shoulder.

I held still, unable to move or think.

"Fuck," he whispered. "I'm sorry." Cooper turned me around, panic in his eyes. "I didn't even think to use anything."

I waved him off. "I'm on the pill." A flutter of fear flashed through my chest. "Do I have anything to worry about?"

"No." His hands were up like I was about to shoot him. "I'm clean, I promise."

"I didn't even think . . . to worry about it." *What the hell just happened?* My heart felt like it would burst from fullness and when Cooper pulled me into his arms, the water washing over us, my skin was so sensitive it was almost painful.

He pulled me into his arms, the water washing over us as my body shook. "What are you upset about, B?"

I felt ridiculous, my body in overdrive, super sensitive to a single touch or caress. I realized at that moment that sex had never been intimate for me. It was something I did because that's what lovers were supposed to do. Blake never hurt me or asked me to do anything I didn't want to do, but compared to what I'd experienced with Cooper, it was shit. With Cooper, the feelings he put my body through were shocking. He was a skilled lover, no doubt, but it was more. I trusted him completely and I truly loved him. The realization hit like a wrecking ball, opening my eyes. I never loved Blake. I didn't even know what love was until I experienced it with Cooper.

My arms were wrapped around Cooper's waist in a death grip, face pressed against his chest when I finally answered. "I'm not upset. I think my body's in shock." I tried to giggle but my voice cracked.

Cooper brought his mouth to mine and kissed away all my rambling thoughts. "Mine, too. It's a good shock though, right? One that I plan on experiencing again right after breakfast."

I nodded and looked into the eyes of the man who'd unleashed a side of me I wasn't aware of. Although I didn't think my body would survive another escapade, I also knew I'd never be able to get enough of Cooper Sterling.

Fifty-Five

Cooper

Cooking together wasn't new for us. However, I owned the chef hat in the breakfast department. Briley sat on the counter, wearing a braless tank and the tiniest cotton shorts I'd ever seen, sipping coffee while I flipped pancakes. Her hair was still wet, tied up in a messy bun that reminded me of Pebbles from *The Flintstones*. Knowing the pancakes had a few minutes to cook, I moved between her legs and offered her a bite of bacon.

"Mmm," she moaned as she chewed. "You're the best bacon maker."

"I'll cook everything in your fridge if it means having the most beautiful woman sitting on the counter keeping me company."

She scrunched her nose, brushing a few strands of hair from her face. "You need glasses."

"Listen up," I gripped her thighs, pushing my hips between her legs. "I'm a connoisseur of women. I know beauty when I see it."

"A connoisseur of women?" She giggled, taking another bite of the strip of bacon in her hand. "And bacon."

I pulled her closer to me and she emitted the tiniest sigh, giving in to me. "Don't forget it."

We feasted on pancakes and bacon, talking about the most random things. It was always easy with Briley, our conversation shifting from my workout regimen to zombie's and then shifting back to exercise again.

"You're not going to the gym *this* weekend." She stabbed her fork in the air to emphasize her point. "This weekend is all play and relaxation." I had a bossy one on my hands, but I hadn't planned on finding a gym anyway. I wanted to spend every minute of the weekend with her. Besides, if I had my way, we'd both be burning enough calories to feel justified skipping the gym.

"What would you like to do today, Bossy Pants?" That induced a sly grin from her.

"Outside of this condo?"

"Yes, outside of the condo. We could lay out, play in the waves, rent scooters or bikes . . ."

"All of it!" She clapped her hands together. I want to do it all with you. But, first things first . . ." She moved to sit on my lap, her arms slung around my neck. "We need to cancel your room at the Inn, get your bags, and get *your* fine ass in a bathing suit."

With her so close, I couldn't resist kissing her lips, still sticky with syrup.

***

Briley was stunning in a white cover up and flip flops. Her hair still piled on top of her head, she looked like she was raised an island girl. We decided to hit the beach and relax first, finding a spot away from the crowd, and settled there. Two beach chairs, an umbrella, a bag of "necessities" as Briley called it, holding our towels, water, and sunscreen, and two boogie boards came with us on a rolling cart.

I set up the chairs and umbrella while Briley grabbed the sunscreen out of the bag and removed her cover up. It was like a scene from a movie, where the man stops what he's doing to watch the beautiful woman lift her dress up and over her head in slow motion. Her body was perfect. Curves in all the right places, a flat, toned stomach, tapered runner's legs . . . and damn, the way her breasts were lifted as she removed the dress—not too much, just enough. Her bikini covered the necessities, but it was way too skimpy. The halter-type top pulled her chest together, offering a voluptuous amount of cleavage.

"Shit, B, it's a public beach. Don't you have anything more modest?"

"Are you serious? This suit covers more than any of the others you've seen me in. I didn't even pack my sexy suits." She looked at me like I was an idiot, like I'd completely lost my mind. Maybe I had. Now that she was mine, I wanted to protect her, hide the goods from the perverted males who were ogling her. She was a prize—a stunning beauty, yes—but she was much more on the inside. Smart, funny, and . . . *mine.*

Looking around, I tried to find someone looking at her. If one single dude looked at her body in the way any sane man would look at a woman like her, I'd punch him in the throat. Luckily, we'd found a secluded spot and the only passersby were a couple of teen girls and an older couple holding hands.

Briley walked over and began spreading sunscreen over my chest and arms.

"What's going on in there?" she asked, nodding toward my head. "You've never said anything about my bikinis before, and like I said, this one covers way more than the others."

I pulled her in, planting a kiss to her forehead. "I don't know, B. My crazy peeks out when it comes to you. I can't stand the thought of some random stranger lusting after your body."

"I can handle myself, Coop. You don't have to worry about me."

"False. I do and I will." I could feel the tension in my shoulders relaxing as she dug her fingers in, spreading the lotion. Her hands were magical, working the sides of my neck, calming me. "You're sweet and vulnerable, B." Her eyes narrowed. She didn't like that. I took her hands down, held them in mine. "I love your sweetness and vulnerability. I love that you trust me with it."

"I do trust you, Cooper. You and my mother are the only people left in my life that I will ever feel that perfect trust with."

"Good," I whispered, pulling her in for a deep kiss. "But you shouldn't trust me around water." Tossing her over my shoulder, I ran full speed into the celery green water until it was deep enough to toss her in.

She came up laughing, the sweet, vulnerable Briley hidden away and replaced with retaliation Briley, splashing water furiously in my direction as she strode toward me.

"Okay, okay, I give!" I yelled until she ceased fire.

"So not cool, Cooper. You're much too big to manhandle fragile little ladies."

"Fragile, my ass. You're the meanest girl I know."

With hands fisted on her hips, she narrowed her eyebrows in a pout. "Meanest? I've never been mean to you."

"Fine, toughest. I *throw* you in, you try to *drown* me." I reached my arm around her tiny waist, my hand covering her back. "Actually, I take it back and default to the earlier adjective. You're mean."

"Why would you say that?" She asked, wiping away a few beads of saltwater from her forehead before it trickled down into her eyes.

"All the years you made me suffer, drawing the line at friendship."

"Yeah, right." She rolled her eyes. "You really suffered. How many girlfriends have you had? Wait! Let me rephrase that. How many *girls* have you had?"

"Not many. Besides, what's a guy to do when he's got the vision of you in his head and he's been 'friend' zoned?"

"Not many? So, 'not many' by your standards is what, fifty, a hundred? Never mind, don't answer that." She lolled her head to the left then right. It was something she did when she was stressed. Sometimes you could hear little pops and cracks, but the sound of the waves rolling in made it difficult to hear the little things.

"None of them were you, Briley. As much as I wanted them to be. The imagination is a powerful thing, but not the real thing." I pulled her closer, lifting her chin. "Although I won't be needing it anymore. Now that I've got you in my arms, I'm never letting you go, baby."

She stood on her tiptoes, laced her hands around the back of my neck, and kissed me. Neither of us considered the families that dotted the sandy beach. Briley snaked a leg between mine, wrapping around my thigh seductively. It was a high I could've enjoyed all day, feeling her lose herself to desire.

She pulled back, whispering in my ear, "Do you know what I want? What I really, desperately want?"

God, she had to be kidding. Here? Now? In front of everyone? I didn't realize she was that brazen. But who was I not to give her what she wanted . . . what we both wanted. I leaned in, my lips protesting her absence.

"For you to go under!" She pulled with all her might. Her leg, the one snaked around mine, trying so hard to trip me up. I braced myself, her strength no match for me. The frustration on her face was enough to make me laugh.

"Oh no, you're so sneaky!" I chuckled, over exaggerating my fall. "No, not the water . . ." When I came up, I shook my hair, watching her cover her face with her hands.

"You're too much, Coop. I so would've had you, if you hadn't seen it coming."

"Oh, yeah, for sure. Small but mighty."

"I'm not small, you're too big. Besides, God only lets things grow until they're perfect. I guess I was finished way before you."

"Smart ass, it's on!" I tickled her ribs until she begged for mercy. I could've lived on her laugh alone, innocent and free.

We played in the water for hours, splashing, jumping waves, and riding boogie boards until we were exhausted and starved.

"How about a shower, early dinner, and sunset?" I asked, packing up our things.

"Exactly what I had in mind," she answered, pecking me on the cheek.

***

Letting Briley shower alone was a hard choice, but I knew her body needed a rest and I didn't want to wear her out. We had the whole weekend. I mixed a couple of vodka and cranberry juices for us, setting hers on the kitchen table as I took a drink of mine. When I heard the shower turn off, I picked up her drink to bring it to her, but knocked her purse off the table. After setting the glasses down, I scooped everything up, putting it back in the bag. The last thing to go in was a sheet of paper folded in half. Curiosity got the best of me so I unfolded and read it.

"What's this, baby?" I asked as she stepped out of the bathroom.

"Where did you get that?" Her hair was in a towel turban on top of her head, with a matching white towel around her body.

"I knocked your purse over and it fell out." I handed her the drink and took another sip of mine.

"Notes. It's the strangest thing, Coop." She took a seat on the arm of one of the sofas and crossed her arms. "I paid for that ancestry company to find information about my mother's side of the family—I'm doing a special for the magazine—but they can't find anything. My mom swears she gave me accurate information but . . ." She shrugged. "I guess it could be user error. Highly doubtful though since I'm gifted in every area."

"I agree ninety-nine percent but there is that one percent that's technologically challenged. Let me take a look."

She pulled up the site on her laptop, typed in her username and password, and stood behind me as I tried to find the answers she was looking for. "Let's start with something simple like your mom and see where that takes us, and then we can dig deeper."

"Sure."

She hovered over my shoulder while I entered her mother's first name, maiden name, birth date, and the city where she was born.

"No results," I repeated what showed up on the screen. "Okay, let's take out the city and go with name and birthday." Again there were no results.

"I told you it's not me. Let's try another site and I'll get my money back."

"Hold on. This is the number one ancestry site. Let me look for my mom." I typed in my mother's information and it pulled up pages of information. No matter how much or little I typed, it had no trouble finding my mother, father, grand and great parents.

"What the hell?" She huffed. "Why won't it do mine? *I* paid for the damn thing!"

"I don't know? Let me try your father." I typed in Gerald Sheffield's information and got several results. "See, it's working."

We scrolled through the names, trying to find one that matched. They either had the right name but wrong birth date or the right birth date but wrong middle name.

"Maybe he lied about his age? A lot of people do it." I finally settled on clicking the six closest choices.

"What's going on? None of them match. It's like my family doesn't even exist."

"I don't know, baby." I turned around and pulled her into my lap. "We'll figure it out. I'm sure it's nothing your mom can't clear up when we get back home."

"I don't know? I have a bad feeling about this, Coop." She rested her forehead on my shoulder. "Something's not right at all."

Without warning, she popped up and walked across the room to retrieve her purse. "Maybe this will shed some light." Her fingers carefully worked the seal of the envelope before pulling out the birth certificate. After scanning the document, a hand covered her mouth.

I closed the space between us. "What is it?"

She handed the paper to me and whispered. "It's not mine."

"Who's is it?" I searched the page, not really knowing what I was looking for.

"I don't know? Isabella Catherine Paciello. Never heard of her, but apparently we share the same birth day."

"Must've been a mix up, babe. I'm sure your mom has another copy. If not, it's not a big deal to order one."

"I told you something was off." She perched on the arm of the sofa and massaged the sides of her head with her fingers. "I think we should go home."

"We will." Lifting her chin in my hand, I brought her gaze up to mine. "If that's what you need, I'll take you home tonight."

She shook her head. "No." Her body language changed—a complete one-eighty. "I'll worry about it when I get home tomorrow. You're most important to me. Let's enjoy the rest of our time here and I'll deal with this when I get back." She took the certificate from my hand, folded it once, and set it on the coffee table. "Let me get dressed." Her right hand came up to rest on my cheek. "You. Me. Nothing else. Deal?"

"Deal." I hoped she put her concerns aside. I wasn't ready to let anything taint our world when it had just been perfected.

Fifty-Six

Briley

I chose a strapless white sundress with a coral ribbon that wrapped around the waist to wear for dinner. Listening to my stomach growl, I searched the pantry and fridge for something to tide us over until dinner. I hadn't planned on guests, so it was slim pickings. I'd have to remember to stop by the grocery on the way home to get a few more things for Cooper. In the meantime, I pulled a bag of almonds out and popped a few into my mouth.

While Cooper was shaving, I took my cocktail to the screened in porch and listened to the waves, letting the summer air dry my hair in beach-style waves. Deep in thought, I nursed the drink, wondering about the mystery of my family. Now that I was aware of some inconsistencies, several things didn't add up. There was no resemblance to either of my parents and my mother sheltered me more than was normal. I had always thought it was her way, but thinking back, she was over the top, not letting me do things other kids my age did. Ignorance is bliss they say, but there was no going back. I wanted answers. Needed them.

"Hi, beautiful. Ready to go?"

"Yes, I'm hungry and I'll bet you're ravenous." His heat-filled eyes responded better than words ever could. Before he could make a move, I popped a few almonds in his mouth and flashed a mischievous grin. "These should hold you off."

"If you think a mouthful of almonds can hold me off, you've seriously misjudged me." He nuzzled in from behind, biting the tendon between my neck and shoulder.

I tried to giggle, but he hit something that nearly brought me to my knees, eliciting a low groan instead. "What was that?" I panted.

"You liked it?" he asked.

"Mmm," I nodded.

"I've got a few more tricks you're sure to enjoy." Cooper offered a hand, helping me out of the chair. "But first things first . . . I need sustenance." He winked, flashing that cocky smile that ruined me for all other smiles. He was dressed in jeans and a white button down, the sleeves rolled half way up his forearms.

We dined on the patio of a cute bistro, enjoying the music from a live band covering Jimmy Buffet and reggae tunes from Bob Marley. After dinner, we decided to walk from the restaurant toward the beach for sunset. It wasn't far, but I was more than tipsy from two lemon drop martinis, so Cooper laced my arm through his and held my waist as we walked.

It felt so good, being on my favorite island with my favorite person. All worries washed away with the tide as we waited for the sun to put on a show. He stood behind me, arms around my shoulders as I leaned against his large frame. All I could concentrate on was the warmth of his body against mine. Everything felt warm and wonderful.

When streaks of tangerine and fire engine red graced the purple sky, the sun took its final bow, dipping into the dark ocean. Everyone clapped and then scattered. Cooper and I lingered in the sand, enjoying the feeling, not wanting the night to end. I could still hear the music from the Bistro, just barely, but enough to make out the song.

"Do you know this song?" I asked, swaying my hips to the muted tune.

"I do." He turned me around, holding me tight to his body as we swayed together, all alone on the dark beach. He sang along on a whisper, in my ear, "I know no one feels the way I do . . . I'm sure you're gonna be the one that saves me."

"That's not how it goes, Coop." I giggled.

"It's exactly how it goes, baby." He was making up his own words and they fit perfectly.

***

My buzz was gone by the time we reached the condo. Cooper wasn't pleased and started to pull the vodka from the freezer.

"None for me, thanks." I held up my hand before plopping myself into a bar stool. "But you go ahead."

He poured a three count of vodka over a glass of ice, added a splash of cranberry juice, and sat beside me, taking a sip. Without thinking, I reached for it and took a sip. He didn't mind of course and in a matter of minutes, we'd drained the glass. A hint of a buzz swirled through me again, but every sensation was present as Cooper trailed his fingers across my thigh, resting his hand at the knee.

Scooting off my barstool, I pushed myself between his thighs, taking his face in my hands. His jaw was smooth beneath my fingers, contradicting his chiseled, masculine features. The way his eyes darkened when he looked at me caused a delicious stirring deep in my belly.

"Cooper," My timing was always impeccable but I was unable to wait for answers. "Why did you come here? I mean, why now? When you didn't answer my calls or texts, I assumed our relationship was in an unsalvageable pit."

"It was all about timing, B. I knew we belonged to each other. I also knew that deep in here—" he placed his hand over my heart—"You knew it too. You just needed to find your way to me." With his hands resting on my waist, he kissed the top of my head, breathing me in. "Ryan said he saw you at Maxim's the night we played. I put two and two together. Figured you must've seen me and Madison together. If that had you upset enough to run, it meant you felt something. I took a chance on believing in that timing and I was right."

He knew me so well, better than I knew myself it seemed, and I was better for it. But I still didn't understand why he'd ignored my calls and texts. Was he trying to decide who he'd rather be with, me or Madison? If he had to think about it, even for a moment, maybe we were fooling ourselves. The excitement would eventually wear off, leaving us both—mainly me—heartbroken and uncertain of whether or not our friendship could survive something like this. The trouble with a broken heart of this depth, it never broke in half or evenly. It shattered into a million pieces, leaving the brokenhearted wandering with a hole in her chest, barely able to breathe from the hurt.

"Why didn't you answer my calls or respond to one single text, Cooper?" I asked, incredibly afraid of his answer, but needing it.

He winked, like there wasn't a care in the world. As if his heart were made of steel and nothing or no one could bust it.

"I know how you like surprises." He tipped my chin up with his finger, grinning like he'd pulled off the surprise of a lifetime. "And it was a good one, right?"

All of my worries melted away right then. I'd never tell him how concerned I was or how I doubted his feelings. No, this weekend was one of self-discovery for me, not him. He was sure . . . he was always sure of everything.

"One I'll never forget," I admitted. Our lips met and the world melted away once again. I couldn't seem to get enough of him. My hands intertwined in his hair, then roamed over each bulging muscle in his shoulders, arms, and back. I managed to unbutton his shirt with my eyes closed, concentrating on the way he kissed. Soft, urgent, sultry. He was an amazing kisser, the best I'd ever experienced, worshipping my mouth with his tongue, leaving me woozy and intoxicated from his spell. He shrugged out of his shirt and my hands went straight to his chest, moving over firm pecs, traveling south over each ripple of his abdomen.

We were in the bedroom, though I'm not sure when or how we got there. With skilled hands, Cooper unzipped my dress and had it piling around my feet on the floor. He scooped me into his arms and laid me on the bed. Pushing up on his elbows, he hovered over me, the heat in his eyes enough to melt me on the spot. He pressed his lips to the right corner of my mouth, so tenderly I barely felt it. Lifting only a fraction, he moved to the other side, brushing his nose against mine as lightly as a down feather falling. When he reached the left corner, he kissed me there, just as tenderly as before. By the time he reached my lips, his kiss as light as a whisper, I had melted into the sheets, my sanity consumed and replaced with desperate need.

Leaning up, I claimed his lips, biting on the lower one as he tried to pull away.

"Really? I didn't see that coming. We'll save that rough side of you for later." He tugged on my bottom lip in retaliation, a flash of playfulness in his eyes before returning to the fireballs of heat again. "But tonight, I'm in charge. All I ask is that you relax."

Reluctantly, I obeyed.

His mouth moved to my neck, kissing, licking, teasing for what seemed like an eternity. My patience faltered when he got to my breasts, giving each one equal attention and eliciting a loud moan each time he pulled a nipple into his mouth. My body ached to be filled by him, it was too much, my need almost painful.

"Cooper, please. I want you."

"Patience, baby," he smiled, dipping down to lick and kiss every inch of my stomach.

He moved further south, his breath alerting my thigh before his lips met the flesh. My body tensed and I lifted my head.

"Cooper," I warned. My head shook defiantly. No one had ever gone there, done that. I didn't want to experience it for the first time now, when I was so eager to be joined together. More research needed to be done, like what I was supposed to do with my hands.

"You trust me, B?"

I nodded, shyness overtaking me all of a sudden. "I do, but—"

"But nothing. Relax. I'm in charge tonight, remember? Trust me." A gentle push on my shoulder had me lying back against the pillow again, my eyebrows squished together in apprehension.

Before he continued, he asked, "Do you need another drink? Would that help?"

I shook my head against the pillow, unable to speak. He must've gotten my message, as I felt his hands slide down my waist and under my hips. He pulled me down toward him, his breath tickling the flesh on my inner thigh before his lips continued the exquisite torture. He bestowed soft, worshipful kisses along my legs, across my stomach, stopping at the band of my white lace thong. Succumbing to his authority, I trusted him with my vulnerability and tried to let my insecurities fall away.

Instinctively, I lifted my hips when his fingers trailed over the place I craved him, needed him. He peeled my panties off, sliding them down my legs, followed by sweet kisses and massaging hands. He was my kryptonite, relaxing me to the point of no return, my muscles pliable beneath his gifted hands. I felt a puff of breath on my inner thigh, so close to my sex, sending a shiver through me. Before I could react, his tongue slid along my slick entrance, causing us both to groan.

I squirmed beneath him, the contact new, frightening, but unbearably delicious. His tongue invaded me again and again, soft, languid strokes from bottom to top. My question about what to do with my hands was answered as I gripped at his dark locks, wishing they were longer. My whimpers and moans were out of control as I dug my fingers into his shoulders, crying out his name as he devoured me like a treat he'd been deprived of for too long.

All I could do was grip the sheets and grind my hips into him as he brought me close to the edge. He stayed with me, like he didn't have a care in the world, pulling a powerful sensation from my depths. It was a slow build, the kind that starts in your toes, works its way into your belly, spreading through the muscles of your limbs, and finally settling in your spine causing your toes to curl.

I said his name over and over, in a whimper, a groan, and finally a whisper of gratitude. With my world fully rocked, I kept my eyes closed, my body reeling from what it had just experienced.

Cooper trailed kisses up my thigh, over my stomach, making his way to my mouth as he sang praises about how good that was, how intoxicating my taste was. By the time his lips met mine, I was ready, trembling with need to be filled by him.

"Please, Cooper. Don't make me wait any longer. I need you inside of me, now."

Without hesitation, he positioned himself at my opening and pushed in, sinking himself to the hilt. That first movement sent a thrill along my spine, my body shivering in response. Our bodies rocked together, his stomach sliding against mine in a rhythm that no one else could play. Love was too weak a word to describe our connection. It was heavenly; rich with an otherworldly aura, working together perfectly like the intricate gears of a mechanical clock.

We came together so forcefully in the end, neither of us said a word or moved for a very long time. With Cooper's head resting on my pillow, his neck buried in mine, I stroked my fingers over his back, massaging his muscles, claiming every inch of him as mine. I wanted to tell him how much I loved him, but hesitated. Not wanting him to think it was an after-sex reaction, I thought about waiting until morning.

After taking turns in the bathroom, I snuggled into his side, my head resting in the pocket of his chest that seemed to be made just for me. He had opened the sliders again, letting the soothing sounds of the ocean permeate the room and lull us to sleep. Just before I drifted off, I whispered into his chest at the same time he whispered into the top of my head, so we spoke in hushed unison.

"I love you."

~The End~

Keep flipping for a sneak peek of *Stay with Me,* book two and the final in the series.

Be the first to know when *Stay with Me* is released by signing up for my newsletter.

Newsletter signup

I take your privacy seriously and will only contact you will important news like release dates, cover reveals, and exclusive giveaways for subscribers.

ABOUT THE AUTHOR

Eleanor Green writes New Adult and Contemporary Romance swirled with mystery.

She currently lives just outside of Nashville, Tennessee with her husband and two children.

CONTACT ELEANOR

Email: contact@authoreleanorgreen.com

Website: http://authoreleanorgreen.com

Goodreads   Facebook   Twitter   The Green Room

Stay with Me (Book 2)

RELEASING SOON!

One

Cooper

Love—such a small word for a feeling that took over my entire being.

Briley had fallen asleep easily in the master bed of her family's vacation home, while I lay awake watching her breathe. The moon was full and lit up the condo bedroom as if a lamp was on. With the sliders open, it was too warm for covers, but she insisted on having the white sheet pulled up over her body. Still, I could make out every curve of her figure as she lay on her stomach, her back rising and falling with each breath.

I'd loved Briley my entire life—that wasn't news. But the closest she'd ever come to telling me she loved me was our silly one-four-three code. Deep down I knew she'd tell me she loved me one day, and I had been willing to wait forever to hear it.

When she finally whispered the words—three stupid words that somehow brought a man to his knees—my heart was healed, made whole. I swear I could actually feel it pumping stronger with more life than it ever had before. You know the saying, so good it hurts? Truth. My heart pumped so furiously, it was uncomfortable, but a pain you'd pay money to feel over and over again.

I knew at that moment I'd do anything for her. It was my job to protect her, keep her safe, and I knew without a doubt that I would lay down my life for her.

I let my eyes take in the marvelous making of Briley. Her hot pink panties visible through the silky sheet caught my eye. Unable to move my gaze from her delectable body, I let it roam over her firm ass to the dip of her lower back. The sheet hugged the curves of her waist and stopped, her back and arms bare. Finally, I couldn't stand it. I had to touch her. My hand instinctively stroked her arm, causing her to stir and wiggle to my side.

I fell asleep with her in my arms, snuggled up to me like I was her lifeline. She was mine, no doubt. Then Mother Nature sang us to sleep, using the sound of the waves crashing onto the shoreline, just outside the sliders. Nothing and no one could intrude on us here in our own little slice of heaven.

Sometime in the middle of the night, I felt her body jerk and she let out a muffled cry. She was still asleep, but her body was shaking and tears rolled down her cheeks into her hair.

Nudging her shoulder, I woke her up. "It's okay. Just a nightmare." Pulling her closer to me, I rubbed her arms, trying to calm her. She swiped at her tears, but they kept falling, her body still shaking. "You're safe. I've got you," I whispered over and over again, until she began to settle. "Want to talk about it?"

She sat up, crossing her legs Indian style, and swiped more tears away with the back of her hand. Reaching for the sheet, she pulled it up to her chin. I couldn't tell if she needed it for security, or if she was trying to hide her bare breasts from me in her vulnerable state.

Short bursts of arrested breaths made me worry she might hyperventilate. Drawing in a deep breath, she began retelling the dream in short, choppy sentences. "It was awful, Coop. Just awful." She chewed on her bottom lip, eyebrows drawn together as she tried to shake the images from her mind.

I didn't know what to say or what else to do besides pull her into my lap and hold her until she cried it out.

"I'm sorry, baby. It was just a bad dream." I pressed my lips to the side of her head.

"It has something to do with that birth certificate. My parents . . . they're not who they say they are, or I'm not who I think I am. Whatever it is, something is wrong . . . very wrong."

Stroking her back, I made promises I didn't know anything about. "No, no. It was just a dream, baby. I promise."

"But the look on everyone's faces . . . like I didn't belong," she cried. "Even you. You were there, standing next to my dad. He was alive, and you knew it all along, it was all a game . . . a freaking game."

I stroked her hair some more, trying to bring her comfort while a chill walked up my spine. "It was your mind playing tricks, baby. None of it was real."

"I know," she finally sighed, resting her head against my chest, her breath becoming steadier. "But it seemed real. And the worst part was the hate in your eyes. I ran . . . I kept running, but I wasn't going anywhere. You were right on my heels, laughing and taunting me."

"Oh, baby, I'm sorry. Look at me." I lifted her chin and stroked her cheek with a thumb. "I'm right here, as serious as I've ever been, and I'm not going anywhere." Not when I just got her. No fucking way. I kissed the top of her head, her tear soaked cheeks, and eyes. "I'll always love you, baby. Even when you don't want me anymore, I'll still be there for you, watching over and protecting what I love most in this world, my girl."

She sniffed, took in a cleansing breath, and looked at me for a long time. Her eyes, glassy with tears, studied mine, searching for the assurance she needed, and I desperately needed her to believe. She was mine, for as long as she'd have me, and I was hers until the day I died. Most likely even after.

"I'll always want you." Her fragile hands, still shaking, cupped my face. "You've always been my rock, Cooper Sterling. I trust you and I love you, so much. I know that I'm safe in your arms. It's where I belong; it's where I always want to be." She kissed me, seeming to savor every slow second. Despite the careful pace, a growing passion quickened and pulsed within me.

Torn between wanting to comfort her and the raw lust developing, I pulled away. "Baby—"

"Please, Coop . . . please." Her lips crashed back into mine, ravenous and impatient.

Peeling the sheet from her body, I cupped her breast, manipulating a nipple between my fingers until it was stiff. She groaned and moved to straddle my lap, my arousal twitching beneath her in anticipation. Before I had the chance to get her ready, my erection was in her hand. Fuck, she did things to me. I groaned, enjoying the feel of her soft hand. Moving her panties to the side, she centered my tip at her entrance and worked her way down my length, moving slowly. The only sound in the room was our heavy breathing mingled with the collision of waves against the shoreline.

I gripped her hips to hasten her movements, but she needed the control and took it. Head buried in my shoulder and fingers gripping my back, we rocked to a leisurely tempo. And breathing through it, trying to hold off, only intensified the sensations. *You're killing me, baby.* Trusting her with control provided a powerful moment, and we both reaped the rewards. Fuck, I loved this girl. She rested her head on my chest, her breath coming out in puffs against my chest as we rode the aftershocks together.

With bodies tangled together, I knew this would be a special place for us. I'd bring her back here someday. Maybe an anniversary. Not our honeymoon, that would be special and I'd love to take her somewhere more secluded where I could watch her splash around for days in crystal blue waters and a tiny bikini. Maybe for a weekend when the stress of everyday life proved to be too much. I envisioned our children one day playing on that beach out there, while we sat on the lanai, watching.

On second thought, we'd be out there with them, jumping waves and making sand sculptures. It was too soon to think about kids, but indulging in a few internal thoughts about the future couldn't hurt. Right now I had exactly what I'd always wanted, nestled into my side.

Yes, love was too weak a word. But knowing Briley, she'd come up with something stronger.

◆ Add *Stay with Me* to your Goodreads TBR:
http://bit.ly/1y5rWUu

OTHER BOOKS BY ELEANOR GREEN

<u>Torn</u>

Stay with Me **(coming soon)**

Eleanor Green

www.ingramcontent.com/pod-product-compliance
Lightning Source LLC
Chambersburg PA
CBHW030638260626
47157CB00007B/2380